Wishes

Three Wishes

Janice Sims

ARABESQUE®

THREE WISHES

ISBN-13: 978-0-373-83011-4
ISBN-10:   0-373-83011-4

www.kimanipress.com

Printed in U.S.A.

Dedication

This novel is dedicated to several longtime couples whom I admire: James and Debbie Jones; Chuck and Candace Nattiel; Jerry and Vivian Simpson; William and Yvonne Sims; Manuel and Lisa Martinez; and Dean and Gerda Koontz.

Acknowledgment

I would like to thank my editor Evette Porter for being the kind of person who is willing to stand behind her writers. It's a pleasure working with her.

I'd also like to thank my agent Sha-Shana Crichton for not only working hard to supply me with writing opportunities but for all her little gestures of kindness. I'm lucky to have found her.

Hear that? The seductive whispered hush
of love recognized at first blush.
Listen now for the exquisite sound
of love rediscovered the second time around.

—*The Book of Counted Joys*

Chapter 1

Beverly Hills, California

As she'd done every morning for years whenever she was in town, Audra Kane drove to her supermarket in Beverly Hills to pick up fresh fruit, bagels and lox.

She leisurely strolled down the aisles, feeling light and free because no one ever bothered her here. She wore jeans and sneakers and a long-sleeve denim shirt open at the collar. Her short, wavy, black hair was finger-combed, and she hadn't even taken the time to apply any makeup this morning.

Julie, the woman behind the deli counter, called out to her. "Good morning, Miss Kane. We got in some of that Russian lox you prefer. Would you like your usual half pound?"

Audra bit her bottom lip as she bent closer to the delicatessen case. Would half a pound be enough? She was expecting a guest: her stepson, Jonas. He'd phoned last night to say he was in town at his father's house. Unfortunately he and his father, Audra's ex-husband, Norman Blake, a film director, didn't get along.

Audra had clearly heard the misery in his voice last night. "Why don't you come stay with me a few days?" she'd asked him. "Momma would love to see you. You're the closest to a grandchild she's ever gotten out of me!"

They'd laughed and he'd agreed that he'd see her the next day at around lunchtime.

"You'd better make that a pound," Audra told Julie. "And I'll also take a pound of smoked turkey and smoked ham. Oh, and some Swiss cheese and sharp cheddar."

Julie, a tall blonde in her early twenties with brown eyes and a lovely smile, quickly went to work preparing Audra's order. "Sounds like you're having friends over for lunch today."

"My stepson," Audra answered easily. "All the way from South Africa. I haven't seen him in nearly a year."

"Then it's time for a family reunion," Julie said as she sliced ham. She glanced up to smile at Audra but scowled, instead, and cried, "We don't allow that in here!"

At first Audra thought she was speaking to her, then out of the corner of her eye she saw that a small crowd of people had formed behind three men with cameras.

Turning around, the flash from the cameras blinded her.

"Security!" Julie yelled. "Security!"

"Audra," said a woman reporter, stepping forward. "How does it feel to have been chosen by Deana Davis to be the subject of her next scathing biography?"

Audra felt like a cornered rat on a burning ship. With the press of the crowd, the reporter and the photographers, she was nearly shoved against the deli case. This was the first she'd heard of the notorious, celebrity biographer's plans to write her life story. Up until a few days ago, she'd been on location in Morocco shooting a comedy.

Her strict southern upbringing gave her the presence of mind to politely turn to Julie and say, "Please have my order delivered." Then she regarded the reporter who had asked the question and said, "You'll have to forgive me but, as you probably know, I've only recently gotten back to the States. Deana Davis hasn't contacted me or any of my people. I haven't had *time* to determine how I feel about her decision to write my bio."

She flashed a million-dollar smile. "Besides, my life isn't over yet. Her book would be only half the story!"

"We love you, Miss Kane!" a woman in the crowd called out to her.

"I love you, too, darling," Audra called back.

She regarded the reporter once again. "Now, if you don't mind, I'll be going."

"Just one more question, Audra," said the reporter.

Audra held back a weary sigh. She supposed since she was constantly in the public eye reporters felt they could dispense with social niceties such as addressing someone with Miss or Mrs. out of respect.

The reporter smirked when she asked, "Is it true that Jonathan Hawkins dropped you for Marisa Freethy?"

Audra's gut clenched painfully at the mention of Jonathan, that snake. Yes, he'd broken up with her for a younger actress. But Audra made it a rule never to discuss her private life with the media. After more than twenty years in the business those in the media were well aware of this.

"Why don't you ask Jonathan," Audra sweetly suggested.

She turned her back on the reporter, and the crowd parted, letting her pass. Walking swiftly through the store, she kept telling herself to slow down. To carry herself with dignity, when all she wanted to do was sprint out of there as fast as she could.

By the time Audra arrived at the Beverly Hills estate she'd

been awarded in the divorce settlement, she'd calmed down considerably. It wouldn't do for her to walk into the house a mass of nerves. Her mother would immediately sense her distress.

She slowly drove the Mercedes through the gates, along the tree-shaded lane, around the back to the garage. She parked and got out. Her legs felt a little rubbery when she stood. Emotional meltdowns were not a part of her normal repertoire. Even though she was an actress and, as such, was expected to be somewhat theatrical.

Feeling better, she hurried to the back door.

Estrella Mendoza, her housekeeper and longtime friend, met her at the door.

Estrella glanced at her empty arms and asked, "Should I get the bags out of the car?"

"No, thanks, Estrella. I asked them to deliver my order," Audra said with a wan smile.

Estrella peered into her face. "What's the matter? You look sick."

Audra laughed shortly as she walked over to the refrigerator to get a bottle of water.

"I just heard that Deana Davis is writing a book about me."

Estrella frowned deeply. "That's enough to make anybody sick."

She went and gently took Audra by the arm, led her to the kitchen table and made her sit down. "You sit there. I'll go get Miss Nette."

Vernette was Audra's mother's name. Estrella and the rest of the staff called her Miss Nette out of fondness and respect. Audra looked up at Estrella with a grateful smile and nodded her agreement.

She drank half the pint of water, closed it and set it on the table. She wasn't upset at the thought of her life being invaded by that barracuda, Deana Davis. She was used to reporters trying to dig up dirt on her. When it came down to it, there was nothing to be ashamed of in her past. She hadn't stabbed anyone in the back on her way up in Hollywood. She hadn't slept on any casting couches nor had affairs with married men.

Her only marriage had lasted ten years and she hadn't been the one to stray, he had.

In a lot of ways, Audra Kane was still a country girl from Georgia. She sincerely believed her fellow man was innately good. Even the ones who lived and worked in Hollywood.

As an actor, she believed in professionalism. No tantrums on the set or diva-ish behavior. She showed up on the set on time, put in an honest day's work and treated her fellow cast and the crew with respect. She was a joy to direct and to work with.

That was her reputation. She had worked long and hard to earn it.

In the course of twenty-six years in this business she'd earned two Tony Awards, several Golden Globes, People's Choice Awards, Screen Actors Guild Awards and an Oscar. The Oscar had come late in her career. Long after she stopped being offered leading lady roles that depended heavily on her sex appeal.

It was funny how actresses who were willing to forgo the glamour and get down and dirty were somehow considered better actors. She'd won the Oscar playing a drug addict who turned to prostitution to support her habit, but somehow found the strength to pull herself out of the gutter for the benefit of her child. She'd looked like a crack hag throughout her performance. The critics and average moviegoers alike had loved it.

An Oscar at forty-five. Finally. After that it almost appeared as if she'd never get another meaty role. She thought she'd been earmarked for the Oscar Syndrome in which actors who'd won the award suddenly found themselves in utter obscurity.

However, that wasn't to be. She turned her attention to television and landed a juicy role on one of the most critically acclaimed series on HBO, *The Cul-de-Sac*.

The series was about close-knit neighbors on a dead-end street in Baltimore. They were connected by lust, murder and various other passions. She portrayed the wife of a serial cheater, who ended up leaving him and making a life for herself. Women wrote in by the thousands saying they identified with her character and applauded her bravery.

That job had ended last year. Lately, she was keeping quite busy working in the movies again, and her schedule was full well into 2010.

As she sat there at the kitchen table, she wondered how she'd gotten on Deana Davis's radar. Davis usually targeted celebrities who were notorious as well as famous.

Actors with drug problems or multiple sexual affairs. Billionaires with proclivities for young flesh and debauchery. Davis had been sued numerous times, to no avail. If you were in the public domain you were considered fair game. Anyone could write about you and get rich for their efforts.

Estrella returned to the kitchen with Vernette on her heels, still in her bathrobe.

Vernette went straight to Audra, pulled up a chair and sat down. Her silver hair was wrapped around pink sponge rollers that she wore to bed every night. No matter how hard Audra tried to get her mother to give up the rollers and allow a hairdresser to do her hair each week, it didn't faze Vernette. "Child, please, you might have money now, but if you start wasting it on foolishness like that, you'll be broke before you know it!"

Audra rose and started removing the rollers. "Momma, you know Jonas is expected any minute. You can't flirt outrageously with him looking like Big Bird." The fluffy yellow bathrobe and fuzzy slippers did make Vernette resemble the famous *Sesame Street* character. Her mother loved *Sesame Street*, saying that anybody who's anyone had guest-starred on the show. Audra had appeared on it a couple times herself.

Knowing her daughter liked to stay busy and removing her rollers was just a way to help calm her nerves, Vernette didn't protest. She closed her eyes and went with the flow. "Okay, honey, let it out—the real reason you're upset about that Davis dame's plans to snoop in your life."

Audra sighed. "You're the only person I ever told about her."

"Then won't she be safe from her?"

"No, Momma, I don't think so. Deana Davis will go to the ends of the earth to find something incriminating or, at the very least, embarrassing about her subjects. If she's chosen me, then she knows there's something there to sink her teeth into."

Across the room Estrella was peeling shrimp at the sink but listening intently. She loved her employer. She'd been with her since her marriage to Norman Blake, that dog. She usually spat when she thought, or said, his name, but that wouldn't be very sanitary during food preparation, so she rolled her eyes in disgust instead.

After the divorce, he'd wanted her to be his head house-keeper. He was moving to an even more palatial estate. But she'd remained with Audra. The divorce had been hard on Audra. She'd actually loved Norman Blake. However, Norman had simply exchanged one beautiful woman for another. Estrella had predicted his new marriage wouldn't last six months. She'd been wrong. It had lasted nine.

Audra had been wife number two. Today he was married to wife number four.

"I can't let her destroy an innocent person's life," Audra was saying. Out of concern, Estrella strained to hear more clearly. She would do anything to help Audra because Audra had always been good to her and her family.

There had been mean years when she'd been married to Juan. He'd had a hard time hanging on to a job whereas she'd found a wonderful position with Audra and Norman Blake. Juan often physically abused Estrella when he got home drunk.

In the end she'd had to take their three children and run away in the middle of the night. That was soon after Audra and Norman's divorce became final. Audra had welcomed all of them into her guesthouse. Estrella had turned the guesthouse into a real home for her and Juan, Jr., Maria and Miguel.

The four of them had been happy there for years. Today all three of her children were college graduates. Juan had remarried while she had remained single. She was happy now, and in another year Audra told her she was going to retire her with a nice pension.

She could buy her own house and live out the rest of her life in peace. Somehow, living in peace did not include having a man in her life. She was only fifty-four, but Juan had turned her off men and marriage.

Which was another thing she had in common with Audra, it seemed. Audra had no desire to remarry, either, and considered life to be perfectly wonderful without a man always underfoot. She dated, though, and was even in long-term relationships.

Her relationship with Jonathan Hawkins had lasted over two years. But Estrella hadn't once thought Audra would consider marrying the younger actor.

She was saddened when she'd learned Jonathan had left Audra for a starlet. It had been a pleasure having him around the house. He was always charming to a fault and there was no denying he was eye candy. The man was a beautiful specimen.

Men like Jonathan were rarely good husbands, though.

Estrella smiled as she continued shelling the shrimp. She didn't know nothin' about husbands. She'd run away from hers in the middle of the night.

At the table Vernette was saying, "How are you going to protect her from Deana Davis?"

"I don't know," Audra admitted.

"Well, you'd better come up with something," Vernette said. "Nobody should find out who her mother is on the six o'clock news. You know where she is. You need to go to her and explain *everything*."

"And lead Deana Davis straight to her? I won't do that!"

Estrella dropped the colander with the cleaned and deveined shrimp in it in the sink with a clatter. It had dawned on her what Audra and Miss Nette were talking about.

Audra had a child somewhere.

Vernette had seen the colander slip from Estrella's usually competent fingers. "Shall we get another mother's opinion?" she asked Audra.

Audra looked at Estrella. "Estrella, would you leave that a moment and come sit with us?"

Estrella was more than happy to. She set the colander in the sink and hurried over.

Wiping her hands on a clean dish towel, she slid onto a chair and gave them her undivided attention. "It's true? You have a daughter, Miss Audra?"

Audra had finished removing the curlers from her mother's hair. She sat down.

Looking Estrella in the eyes, she said, "I'm taking you into my confidence, Estrella. I know this won't go any further."

"Of course not," Estrella immediately answered. "I will take it to my grave."

Audra told her everything.

After which, Estrella advised, "If you can't go to Georgia to speak with her, let Mr. Jonas go in your place. He can charm the birds out of the trees. He'll have her back here with you in no time flat."

As if on cue, the doorbell reverberated throughout the house.

"Speak of the devil," said Vernette.

"I'll get it," said Audra, happily springing to her feet.

Her heart felt light again in anticipation of seeing Jonas.

She fairly skipped through the house.

Vernette looked after her with a smile on her lips. "She adores that boy." She suddenly sprang up herself, gathering the rollers. "I've got to go primp a little."

Estrella rose, too, to go check her hair and makeup.

Three women in the house and they all still enjoyed the presence of a handsome man every now and then.

On the front portico, Jonathan Hawkins had given up on the doorbell and had started knocking on the heavy door. "Open this door, Audra!" he playfully shouted in his deep baritone.

When Audra opened the door she suppressed a groan. She knew exactly why Jonathan was here. The copy of *Variety* grasped in his hand was a dead giveaway.

She stepped outside and pulled the door closed behind her. "Did you make a wrong turn?" she asked. "Miss Freethy lives in a downtown apartment building, doesn't she?"

Jonathan, six-three and a gym addict from way back, flexed the biceps in his right arm as he brought the entertainment newspaper up to Audra's eye level.

She tried not to goggle when she saw her name on the front page. But, by God, she'd never made the front page before! She snatched the paper.

Quickly reading the short announcement of Deana Davis's intentions to make her the subject of her next biography, she couldn't help seething with anger.

Hiding her pique, she looked into Jonathan's handsome caramel-colored face. He wore an expression of utter sympathy. He really was a good actor.

So was she. Smiling, she said, "Thanks for the paper. Did you want anything else?"

"Well," Jonathan began, making his tone as ingratiating as possible. "I know how you feel about her brand of journalism, so I came over to show my support."

His light brown eyes swept over her petite figure. "And to

tell you the truth, I miss you." That sexy voice was known to melt a woman's resolve in a heartbeat.

Audra tapped her small foot on the Italian tile. If he only knew how trite his little come-on seemed to her at this moment. She had more pressing matters to attend to, like saving her daughter from the jaws of a shark.

His charm might have worked on any other day, but not today.

She flashed a disarming smile. "Jonathan, I've had time to think about what you said when you broke up with me in your last e-mail. You're ten years younger than I am. I know you were just being gracious when you said *you* were too immature for *me* at this point in your life. You were trying to spare my feelings. And I truly appreciate it. But the fact is, you were right. You *are* too immature for me. I'm glad you realized it before our relationship went any further."

She turned to go back inside then, but Jonathan had other ideas.

He grasped her by the wrist, jerked her into his embrace and roughly kissed her on the mouth. Audra bit his lip and stomped down hard on his instep.

He let her go and she quickly backed away from him. "Never manhandle me," she said, her voice low and menacing.

Jonathan worried his bottom lip with his tongue, wondering, she supposed, if she'd drawn blood. "I didn't wound you," she assured him. "Your good looks are intact."

"So that's how it's going to be?" he said quietly. "You're never going to forgive me for my dalliance with Marisa?" His eyes, full of regret, continued to appeal to her. "She's boring. We don't have anything in common. We don't have anything to talk about."

"I didn't think talking was high on your list of priorities when you started the affair," Audra returned calmly. She wasn't about to let him know how she'd cried her heart out the first few nights after he'd sent that cold message. Around the fifth night, though, she began to wonder why she was crying. Would she sincerely miss him? Or was she crying because she'd gotten used to having a warm body in her bed?

She had no illusions about her and Jonathan. He was thirty-nine. She was forty-nine.

He had started out as a model and now he was featured in action films that went straight to DVD. She was a veteran who was still sought after. A miraculous occurrence in this town. And she was independently wealthy.

She didn't need him to support her. She definitely wasn't looking to get married and have babies at her age. And, let's face it, if she wasn't in love with him the relationship wasn't worth fighting for.

She'd put it behind her. There would be more Jonathans in her life. If she were really lucky, there would be someone much more substantial. A man who could truly love her for who she was, and not for what she could do for him.

Relationships in Hollywood were so superficial. She was always amazed when she ran across couples who sincerely loved each other and were committed to staying together.

"I made a mistake," Jonathan told her, reaching for her hand like a disobedient schoolboy asking for forgiveness for being naughty in class. "You and I had something special. We clicked everywhere. She's even boring in the bedroom. I have to tell her how to do everything. I never had to tell you what I liked."

"Well, darlin'," Audra said, reverting to the southern accent she'd grown up using. "That's because I taught you everything you know. Now, be a good boy and go home." With that she hurried inside and closed the door.

Jonathan stood there in indecision a few moments. Then he turned and went back to his car. As he drove through the gates of the estate, an apple-red Alfa Romeo entered.

Chapter 2

Jonas drove the brand-new Alfa Romeo straight into Audra's garage, put it in Park, revved the engine because he liked the sound and shut it off. He smiled, remembering his father's last words to him this morning. "Yeah, take any car you want, but don't touch the Alfa Romeo. I just bought it and I haven't really had the chance to open it up on the highway yet."

Jonas, thirty-six, felt like a teenager again, stealing his father's cars and taking them for joy rides. Of course, he had every intention of returning the Italian sports car. As soon as he grew tired of it.

After he left Audra's in a few days, he might drive down to San Francisco just to watch the sun set against the backdrop of the Golden Gate Bridge. He had all the time in the world. Something he hadn't been able to say in years.

Jonas was a consultant. He went to developing countries to help them learn how to grow economically. For the past three years he had been working in South Africa in its three major cities—Cape Town, Johannesburg and Pretoria—teaching serious-minded entrepreneurs how to ensure that their fledgling businesses thrived in a burgeoning economy. Opportunities were rampant in South Africa.

The work had been gratifying for Jonas because every single one of the businesspeople he'd trained had been highly motivated for success. To Jonas, that was half the battle. They had to be self-motivated. He could talk until he was blue in the face, but teaching someone to feel enthusiastic about themselves and their potential was a gargantuan, and often impossible, task.

Now that his charges could stand on their own feet his expertise was no longer needed. He had set his sights on Haiti next, although he was somewhat reluctant because of the country's shaky political infrastructure. He didn't relish getting stuck in Port-au-Prince in the midst of a political upheaval.

As he unfolded his long legs out of the Alfa Romeo, he vowed to stop thinking about business. He had been back in the States for a week. This time was for family.

He'd paid his obligatory visit to his father in the Hollywood Hills. The old man hadn't changed a bit. His work was still the most important thing in his life. His family, his wife, everything else, took a backseat to filmmaking.

Jonas didn't begrudge his father his single-minded devotion to his craft. He simply wished that at some time in his life he'd been made to feel that perhaps *he* was as important to his father as a movie.

Norman Blake was good at evoking emotions on film. But when it came to his personal life, he was batting zero. Take his first wife, Bianca, Jonas's mother, for example. He had ignored the poor woman so completely that she had been dead in their beach house from an overdose of sleeping pills for three days before Norman wondered about her absence and had one of his people look into it.

Jonas had been away at boarding school when it happened. He came home for the funeral. The next time he was summoned home it was to attend his father's wedding to Audra Kane.

Jonas wanted to hate Audra. She was everything his mother had not been. Where his mother had been insecure and dependent upon Norman to give her life meaning, Audra was self-contained and ambitious.

In Norman's absence, she always maintained a full schedule of her own. Norman seemed to be someone she welcomed into her world whenever he was around. Her life certainly didn't revolve around him.

The more Jonas got to know her, the more he wished his mother had been as strong and independent. She might have divorced his dad instead of taking those pills.

He missed her terribly.

Audra didn't intrude in his world when he was home from school. She spoke to him as though he were another adult. She invited him to her soirees. Asked his advice about film roles she was thinking of going after. When he was sixteen Jonas refused to go back to the boarding school in England and insisted on going to a public school there in Beverly Hills. Audra had stood up for him. To this day he didn't know what she had said or done to his father to make him acquiesce.

But that was Audra, always championing him.

He had come to love her like a mother and, in spite of the divorce, he still considered her as such.

Of course, the crazy woman running toward him right now in no way, shape, or form resembled any of his friends' mothers. She was gorgeous even without makeup.

He grinned and opened his arms. Audra ran and jumped into them. After a firm hug and kisses on the cheek, Jonas set her back down.

"Oh, my God, let me look at you," she cried, tears clouding

her vision. She blinked them away and reached up to caress his face with both hands. "What is it with you and traveling? I believe you've spent more time out of the country than in it. You *are* still an American, aren't you?"

Jonas had never been able to adequately explain his wanderlust to Audra's satisfaction.

Like most mothers, she tended to want her children physically closer than several countries away. For Jonas's part, he believed his desire to travel had been ingrained in him when he was a boy. His father, an admitted Anglophile, grew up in England.

His family had come from the West Indies. Norman still spoke with a noticeable British accent. Jonas, who had lived in several countries in his formative years, did not have a discernible accent. He simply spoke English as any well-educated American might.

Jonas spoke four languages fluently and three others well enough to get by anyplace in the world. Hence, he felt at home anywhere. Being adaptable was something he had learned to be since he knew he couldn't rely on his father for emotional support.

He had to be able to rely on himself for everything.

"One of these days I'll settle down somewhere," he said to Audra now.

That earned him a beautiful smile. Then she took his hand and they began walking to the house. "I know you only said that to make me happy," she told him. "But whether you believe it or not, you *will* want to stay in one place long enough to breathe one of these days. You just haven't met the right person yet."

"Let me guess," Jonas said. "You've got someone in mind."

"No," Audra denied. "Not this time. I'm not going to try to hook you up with anyone. In fact, I may need your help with a personal matter. But first, we're going to feed you like a king and catch up with each other's lives."

The cool August morning had given way to a warm afternoon so they had lunch out by the pool. Nearly every night before bed Audra swam laps for exercise in the Olympic-size pool. Today sunlight glinted off its placid pale blue surface.

Jonas ate heartily to the delight of the three ladies who plied him with his favorite foods: seafood and pasta with generous amounts of fresh garden salad on the side.

Audra watched him eat. No wonder he looked so healthy and vibrant, she thought.

His normally golden-brown skin was darker now due to the African sun, and his straight, white teeth looked even whiter as he bit into the shrimp.

He looked more and more like his father every year. The same dark brown, wide-spaced eyes with thick black lashes. A slightly long nose that gave his face a Roman profile. At least, that was her imaginative description. Dark brown, naturally wavy hair that through the years he'd worn long, short and even in dreadlocks. Now it was cut so close to the scalp he might as well have cut it all off. When had he gotten so darned conservative? She was used to his being miles apart from his father when it came to his manner of dress and decorum. Norman was conservative to the point of stiffness. He'd used the same British tailor for thirty years. The same shoemaker, too.

Jonas was wearing his favorite jeans, but his shirt was definitely tailored specifically to fit his muscular body. Being a fashionista herself, she could even tell which designer: Ralph Lauren. The sapphire-blue color complemented his skin.

She noticed he was wearing brown leather Italian loafers, the leather like butter.

Okay, she conceded. He had combined conservative taste with laid-back style.

It looked good on him.

"How long are you home for this time?" Vernette wanted to know. She'd cleaned up nicely after rushing to her room when she'd heard the doorbell earlier. Her short, silver hair was in a

neat bob, and she was wearing a silk pantsuit in emerald-green.
On her small feet were jeweled slippers.

Estrella, too, looked becoming after removing her apron to
reveal the smart navy-blue A-line dress underneath. Estrella
believed women should never wear pants, something her
mother had drummed into her head along with Catholic indoc-
trination.

She didn't understand American women's obsession with
pants. She didn't own one pair of the infernal things. Her
daughter, Maria, had insisted she try on a pair once and they'd
cut into her crotch something awful. Maria had told her she
simply needed a larger size but Estrella had avoided pants ever
since because she didn't want to be reminded she *had* a crotch
after years of divorce and celibacy.

She stuck with her dresses.

"I'm not sure," Jonas said. "I've been invited to go to Haiti
to head up a project there but I'm having second thoughts."

"Isn't it dangerous there right now?" Audra asked. "I heard
over the news that there was violence in the streets during the last
presidential election. At least wait until things have settled down."

Jonas sipped his Chardonnay. "I have friends who live there,
and they say things are probably not going to settle down
anytime soon, Mom."

Audra loved it when he called her Mom. Even when they
were discussing something as serious as whether or not he was
going to risk life and limb by going to try to help an economically deprived people learn how to improve their situation.

In some ways she was extremely proud of Jonas for his dedication to an ideal. He had inherited millions from his mother.
Therefore he didn't need to work a day in his life. However,
he felt duty bound to help others, to give back, to leave the
world a better place than he'd found it.

But she drew the line at altruism when it could very well
lead to bodily harm.

"Just think on it for three months," she pleaded with him.

They had all finished eating. Estrella and Vernette rose and began clearing the table, giving Audra the opportunity to have Jonas to herself. They sensed the conversation was about to turn to serious.

"Thanks for a wonderful meal," Jonas said to Estrella and Vernette. Vernette had prepared southern-fried catfish, another of his favorites.

"It was my pleasure," said Estrella, blushing.

"It was nice to cook for someone who actually cleans his plate," Vernette joked as she collected his plate. She playfully eyed it. "Not a crumb left."

"What's for dessert?" Jonas shamelessly asked.

"We'll be right back with pecan-praline pie," Vernette said. "If we didn't clog your arteries with the shrimp and catfish, that is."

"Pecan-praline pie is worth a clogged artery or two," Jonas said. "I'll jog it off tomorrow morning."

As she and Estrella left the patio, Vernette shook her head at the resilience of youth.

She was sixty-eight and no longer touched pecan-praline pie with a ten-foot pole. Nowadays her richest dessert was vanilla frozen yogurt with canned peaches in its natural juices. And sometimes even that gave her gas. Getting old wasn't for sissies.

In their absence, Jonas reached across the table and clasped one of Audra's hands.

Looking into her eyes, he said, "Something's wrong, isn't it?"

Concern was mirrored in his dark eyes. "You're not sick?" It was one of his greatest fears when it came to Audra and his father, his closest relatives. He had no brothers or sisters. Most of his father's relatives were in Europe. His mother's family resided on the East Coast. He had rarely seen any of them when he was growing up. Only at the occasional family reunion when his father deigned to attend them.

As a result he didn't know any of them well.

Audra and his father were all he had.

Audra laughed shortly. "No, that's not it. It's something more important."

"What could be more important than your health?"

Her mouth suddenly dry, Audra took a big sip of water. "You haven't heard that Deana Davis's next book is going to be about me?"

Jonas frowned. "Damn."

"Damn is right. That harpy from hell has me in her sights and it ain't gonna be pretty when she's done with me."

Jonas's eyes narrowed. "What could she possibly dig up on you? You're the nicest person in this town."

"It's something I did before I hit town that could sell books," Audra said with a resigned sigh.

"What? You posed nude? Everybody and her grandma have posed nude."

"There are no compromising photos of me floating around," Audra said.

"Then what did you do?"

Audra released his hand and hugged herself as if she were cold. "Maybe I should start at the beginning."

Jonas poured more wine into his glass, and patiently waited for her to begin.

"When I was twenty, I fell in love…"

Atlanta, Georgia, Twenty-Nine Years Ago

Audra was flying high. She was portraying Beneatha in Lorraine Hansberry's *A Raisin in the Sun*. The play had been running for the past four weekends on the campus of Spelman College in Atlanta. She'd gotten rave reviews.

The play's final performance had been tonight, and they'd gotten a standing ovation.

She was leaving the auditorium by the back exit with two

other young women who had been in the play when a man's voice called out to her. "Miss Kane!"

Audra looked up and her heart began racing. Her two friends flanked her as he approached. They were not going to let him near her if he turned out to be an unsavory sort. Audra was the shortest of them. Gale and Sienna were both tall and slender while she had curves. She couldn't believe Trent Chapman, a law student, was interested in her instead of one of her beautiful friends.

However, he'd been sending her notes and little gifts for the past two weeks. She knew his interest was genuine.

"Audra, you were wonderful!" he said when he finally stood before her. He reached out to grasp her by the arm, but Sienna stepped between him and Audra.

"Audra, do you know this guy?" she asked, leveling a belligerent look at Trent.

"It's all right, Sienna," Audra said. "This is Trent Chapman. We know each other."

Satisfied, Sienna stepped aside. "Okay, then."

"Trent," Audra said, making the introductions, "this is Sienna Jackson and Gale Brown. They were in the play, too."

"Excellent performance, ladies," Trent graciously said.

"Thanks," the girls said in unison, beaming their pleasure.

Trent handed Audra a dozen red roses. The January air was frigid and his skin was flushed underneath the medium-brown shade. It was obvious to Audra that he was not a Romeo. A simple thing like giving a woman flowers made him blush.

She was utterly charmed by him.

Gale and Sienna cooed over the flowers, then Gale grabbed Sienna by the arm and said, "Audra, if you have plans with Trent tonight, we'll go to the party by ourselves."

Audra was looking up at Trent with stars in her eyes. He had asked her to have dinner with him but she hadn't made up her mind to go with him until this very moment.

"Okay," she said. "Have a good time. I'll call you tomorrow."

She briefly hugged both Gale and Sienna after which they hurried off in the direction they'd been walking before Trent had come along.

Alone with Trent, Audra smiled up at him. "You said something about dinner?"

Trent grinned happily. "Yes, I made reservations for ten." He glanced at his watch.

"We have fifteen minutes to get there."

He offered her his arm. Audra took it and let him lead her to his car waiting at the curb. He handed her in, and trotted around to get in.

His hand shook a bit as he put the key in the ignition. Audra wondered if it was from the cold or if he was nervous being in her presence. All her life men had paid special attention to her. She was used to being pursued by them, wooed by them, and ultimately disappointed by them.

Her own father had abandoned her mother with three children to take care of. Audra had vowed, at an early age, that she would never allow herself to be bamboozled by a man. At the first sign of insincerity, she would be the first to leave.

So far, she'd managed to keep her heart in one piece.

She smiled at Trent and reached over to cover the hand he held the car keys in with her own. "No need to rush. I'm sure they'll hold the table for us if we're a couple minutes late."

Trent regarded her with something akin to adoration in his honey-brown eyes. He took a deep breath, relaxed and turned the key. "Did I tell you how beautiful you look tonight?"

"No, you didn't."

"You take my breath away."

In the present, Audra paused at this juncture in her story. Her mother and Estrella had come back out to the patio with slices of the pie and hot coffee. They sat down and served her and Jonas.

"Thanks, ladies," Jonas said and immediately picked up his fork to begin eating.

Estrella and Vernette watched as the first forkful landed on his tongue. He momentarily closed his eyes, savoring the rich flavor. "It's better than sex," he said.

Vernette guffawed, and Estrella blushed.

Audra continued her story. "From January to May we were inseparable. Except for classes, of course. I couldn't let my grades fall. I was on scholarship. And Trent was in law school at Georgia State. He came from a family of lawyers, and his father was especially hard on him. He had a real fear of his father."

Atlanta, Georgia, Twenty-Nine Years Ago

Trent looked pale, as if he were about to pass out.

Audra was furious with him, with herself. She hadn't even waited for him to have a seat when he'd come to pick her up for their Friday night date.

As soon as he'd walked into the apartment, she'd thrust the slip of paper into his hand and said, "Read that!"

It was the doctor's prescription for prenatal vitamins. Prenatal. If that didn't say it all, she didn't know what else to say.

Trent looked up from the slip of paper, down at her and back at the paper. "You can't be pregnant. We never did it without using protection."

"Well, the condoms failed to protect me!" Audra shouted. She was tiny, only five-three and a hundred and ten pounds to his six-two and two hundred pounds, but at that moment she looked like she could tear him from limb to limb.

"What are you going to do?" Trent asked, still grasping the paper in his hand.

Audra snatched the prescription and balled it up in the palm of her hand. "Have you been listening the past five minutes?" she asked. "I'm pregnant. That means I'm going to have a baby. Your baby." She calmed down a bit. "Our baby."

Trent began pacing. "Wait a minute, Audra. Have you explored all of your options yet?"

A chill came over Audra. Options, he said. He couldn't possibly be suggesting that she do away with their child, because abortion wasn't even in her language. Number one, she'd been raised in the church and she considered abortion to be murder. Number two, her mother would be devastated if she got rid of her own flesh and blood.

Her mother was going to be devastated anyway, when she showed up on her doorstep with a big belly. However, knowing her daughter had had an abortion would be something from which she might never recover. Audra felt that in her heart.

"What do you mean by options?" she cautiously asked Trent.

"Adoption?" he said, equally cautiously.

"You mean you don't want anything to do with this child?" Audra asked evenly.

Trent began talking fast. "Audra, I have another year in law school. Then there's the bar exam, establishing myself in a firm somewhere and extremely long hours of trying to prove myself. I can't get married right now. My dad would kill me."

"Nobody asked for your hand in marriage," Audra cried, indignant. "I don't want to marry somebody who panics at the first sign of trouble!"

"Well, I don't want to marry somebody who screams at the top of her lungs when she should try to be levelheaded and see reason. We are not prepared to be parents. You haven't even graduated from college. You're broke, and my parents aren't about to support us while you have this baby and sit at home taking care of it. So, I might as well be broke, too."

Audra took a deep breath and went into the kitchen to get a glass of water. Trent followed her. "Audra, I will support you no matter what you decide to do. I only wish that you would consider adoption. Or an abortion if you don't want to carry the baby to term. Your choice."

Audra calmly drank half a glass of water before stopping. The coolness of the liquid felt good going down. Something deep inside her was simmering, boiling, threatening to rise to the surface. She feared what she would turn into if she let it escape.

He *had* been thinking of suggesting an abortion. That told her more about him at that moment than she cared to learn. He didn't care that the child growing within her had half his genes. It didn't faze him that if the child died it could very well be his last opportunity to have a child. Something could happen down the line and he could no longer be able to father a child. None of that went through his mind. All he saw was an inconvenience, a mistake that needed to be corrected.

The tender affection she had had for him when she rose that morning turned to ash.

It had been consumed in the fire burning in her gut.

Setting the glass on the counter, she turned to him.

Trent, seeing the sheer fury mirrored in her eyes, backed away from her. "Maybe we should sleep on this and talk more tomorrow," he said.

"Talking won't solve this problem," Audra calmly said. "You've already told me everything I need to know about you. The thought of sacrificing in order to have this child terrifies you. You don't want to disappoint mommy and daddy and you wish this would just go away. I've got you down pat. No need for further conversation."

She walked over to the door and held it open for him.

He looked down at her and said beseechingly, "Audra, please, see reason."

"You mean, see your point of view. Do as you ask. It's over between us, Trent. Whether I choose to have this baby or abort it, there is nothing left of us. As you so eloquently said a moment ago, it's my choice. I don't want you around mucking up my plans, so don't come back."

"You don't mean that. I love you."

"Correction—you love the thought of me. The flesh-and-blood woman who happens to be carrying your child means nothing to you." With that she slammed the door in his face.

"And that's the last I saw of him," Audra said now.

Jonas had finished his pie and two cups of coffee. Estrella and Vernette were fighting back tears.

Audra sighed tiredly. Thinking of it all had emotionally drained her. "I had Sunday and gave her up for adoption. A week after it was finalized, I caught a Greyhound bus to Los Angeles."

"And didn't tell me anything!" Vernette declared, still miffed after all these years. "Honey, you could have come to me."

Audra tenderly smiled at her mother. "I know that, Momma. But at the time you were raising two children of your own. I didn't want to put that burden on you."

"But it took you twenty-one years to tell me I had a grand-daughter somewhere. That really hurt," Vernette said, remembering the day Audra had told her about Sunday.

At the time, Vernette was still living in Atlanta and Audra had come for a visit.

After dinner one night, Audra had come to her mother's bedroom and confessed everything.

Vernette had refused to speak to her for months afterward.

Jonas interrupted them with, "Sunday? Did you say her name is Sunday?"

"That's a long story," Audra said. "You see, the couple who adopted her named her Sunday, probably because she was born on a Sunday. They were an older couple by the name of Kenneth and Jane Adams. She goes by Sunday Adams today. Her friends call her Sunny."

"How do you know all this?" Jonas said.

"Because after she turned twenty-one, I hired a private detective to find her. I was going to get in touch with her. But after what I learned, I couldn't go through with it."

Vernette went and put her arms around her daughter. Audra

clung to her a few precious moments, then Vernette sat back down and finished saying what Audra was too choked up to enunciate.

"You see, Audra was bound by the terms of the adoption not to contact Sunny until she was of legal age. In the state of Georgia, that's twenty-one. But, by the time Sunny turned twenty-one she had been in the system for years. Her adoptive parents had been killed in an accident when she was eight. She spent the next ten years going from one foster home to another. She got into college at eighteen. Audra couldn't face her after learning that Sunny had been abandoned again at eight and she could have done something to save her from years spent in the system."

"I'm a coward," Audra said in a small tortured voice.

"You ain't no coward, baby," Vernette firmly told her. "You made sure she had a scholarship to college. You made sure that she never went without, by making it appear as if she had inherited money and property from the Adamses. She wouldn't be living in Warm Springs, Georgia, now if she didn't believe she'd inherited that house you bought for her. Warm Springs is the only real home she's ever known. That was a brilliant idea you came up with last year."

"Yeah, I'm good at pulling strings behind the scenes," Audra said. "I just don't have the guts to face her and take the hatred, full force, that I'm sure she must feel for me. I abandoned her to a life of misery."

"How do you know that?" Vernette asked. "For all you know, Sunny is a perfectly happy woman."

Jonas had been listening intently, taking it all in. Earlier, Audra had said she might need his help with a personal matter.

He knew, now, what she needed help with.

"You think Deana Davis is going to find out about Sunny," he said.

Audra nodded, tears streaming down her face.

Estrella handed her a cloth napkin.

Audra wiped her face. "It's only a matter of time."

"Then I'd better leave tomorrow," Jonas said.

Audra smiled gratefully, and started crying again.

Chapter 3

Sunny Adams followed the guard down the long corridor. The air was cool and smelled of body odor and disinfectant. No matter how many times she visited her clients in jail she never got used to the claustrophobic feeling it gave her.

The guard paused in front of a steel door with bars in its window. He unlocked it and gestured for her to precede him. "I'll be back with her in a few minutes," he said.

This was always the routine. Sunny would be escorted to the briefing room after which her client would be brought to the room in chains where she would be told to sit in a chair while the guard locked one of her ankle cuffs to a steel bar in the floor.

The guard, this time, a stocky African-American man in his mid-forties with a neat graying afro and kind brown eyes, briefly regarded Sunny with curiosity. "You her new lawyer?" he asked, his hand on the door's handle.

"I'm here to decide that," Sunny told him.

"She needs a good lawyer," he said.

Sunny was aware that guards, who were around the prisoners all day, were often privy to information she might not be. She lent him an ear. "Is there something you'd like to say to me?"

"That husband of hers was a frequent visitor here," he stated. "He was a mean son of a bitch. I just don't think she did it. And if she did, she was defending herself. I'd just like to see her get a fair chance, that's all."

"Tom Chapman and Associates will give her every consideration," Sunny said, sounding stiff and professional. She couldn't be certain whether he was just a concerned bystander or someone who'd become enamored with Kaya Bradley, the woman she had come here to speak with.

Kaya had been here for more than three months awaiting her trial. Accused of shooting and killing her rap star husband, she had been the lead story on every TV station in Atlanta since she'd been arrested. Her trial had been scheduled for next month. However, she'd recently fired her lawyer for incompetence after he had failed to get her out on bond and to get the court to allow her four-year-old son to visit her.

"Tom Chapman?" the guard said, unable to hide the fact that he was impressed. Tom Chapman was the best defense attorney in Georgia. "You must be good if he sent you."

"I try my best," Sunny said crisply, hoping her tone sent the message that she'd like to get this show on the road.

He got the hint and pulled the door open. "I'll be back in five minutes."

"Thank you," Sunny said, this time with a glimpse of a smile.

As he had been trained to do, he locked the door behind him.

Sunny placed her briefcase on the tabletop and sat down in one of the two wooden straight-back chairs. She got a legal pad and a pen from the briefcase.

She wondered why Kaya Bradley had personally requested that she come down to the jail to interview her on the firm's behalf. Perhaps Tom had rattled off the list of associates in his firm, and she'd chosen the only woman because she felt she'd feel more comfortable working with a female.

Tom had filled Sunny in on Kaya's case. However, she had not followed the media frenzy caused by Kaya Bradley's arrest. Her attention had been on a domestic violence case she'd been working on until recently.

Just two weeks ago she'd defended her client in court and won the case. Her client's husband had subsequently been sentenced to five years in prison, and his considerable assets were to go to his wife and children.

Sunny counted the win as quite a coup because rich men were rarely convicted of domestic abuse and sentenced to prison. They were able to afford excellent lawyers who usually got them off with a fine or a slap on the wrist.

As she sat there with her legs crossed and tapping the right heel of her pump on the concrete floor, she wondered if Tom had asked her to consider taking this case because it was rumored that Kaya Bradley had also been the victim of domestic abuse.

It was highly likely.

The guard returned with a petite woman dressed in the jail's signature bright orange jumpsuit. He told her to sit. She readily complied, and he quickly attached the chain of her right ankle cuff to the steel bar in the floor.

He left without another word and locked the door behind him.

Sunny sat up straighter and looked Kaya in the eyes. Kaya Bradley was in her late twenties. Just as she was. She was attractive with creamy brown skin, very dark brown eyes, auburn hair and classically beautiful features. She reminded Sunny of a young Naomi Campbell.

"Oh, my God," Sunny suddenly cried. *"Kayla?"*

Kaya Bradley laughed. "I wondered how long it would take you to recognize me," she said, her eyes tearing up. "I immediately recognized your name when Mr. Chapman came to see me and told me you were one of his associates. I told him I wanted you to assist him with my case. I knew you would save me."

Sunny rose and hugged the smaller woman. Kaya clung to her. Sunny let go of her and they sat back down. Their eyes met across the table. "You dropped the *l,* huh?"

"That was Eddie's idea," Kaya said. "But he had it done legally, so now I'm stuck with it."

"How did you get mixed up with him, Kayla?" Sunny wanted to know. She hadn't meant to sound judgmental, but she knew she had. She smiled at Kaya. "I'm sorry for my tone."

"It's all right," Kaya told her. "I've asked myself the same thing time and time again."

She sniffed and tried to wipe the tears from her face with the side of her hand but the handcuffs got in the way.

Sunny retrieved a tissue from her briefcase and gently wiped Kaya's face. "If I had known that you were Kaya Bradley I would have come to see you before now."

When they were children Sunny had lived with Kaya's family for two years. It had been one of the few positive experiences she'd had in the foster care system. She and Kaya, the same age, had become close friends and had tried to stay in touch over the years, but when they graduated from high school they lost touch. Sunny hadn't seen Kaya in ten years.

"I know you would have," Kaya said softly.

Sunny had to grab a tissue for herself and dab some wayward tears. She cleared her throat afterward, though, and got down to business. Looking Kaya in the eyes, she said, "I realize you've been questioned many times but I need to hear your account of what happened the night Eddie died. I need to hear everything you remember about that night. Every detail, even what might seem inconsequential to you."

She picked up the pen and waited for Kaya to begin.

"Eddie and I had been partying that night," Kaya said, her

words slow and measured. "Another wrap party for a video he'd shot. We had been arguing off and on because I believed he was cheating on me with one of the dancers featured in the video."

"Had you caught him cheating before?"

Kaya sighed and chewed on the inside of her jaw, a nervous habit. When she finally answered, Sunny could see the shame in her eyes. "Yeah, I'd caught him cheating a number of times."

"How many?"

"Do I have to say?"

Sunny narrowed her eyes. "Yes. We don't know what's going to be the catalyst to pull your fat out of the fire. So, yes, you need to be open and honest with me, Kayla. Sorry…*Kaya.* I'll try to remember that."

"Okay," Kaya said to full disclosure. "I know of at least six different women."

"I'll need their names."

"Why?"

"Because I'll have to speak with every one of them."

"I'm ashamed that Eddie was low enough to touch some of those witches," Kaya said. "I don't want it all over the news that he was cheating on me with them."

"Oh, so if he were cheating with respectable women, it would have been okay?" Sunny said. "Listen to me, Kaya. In order to defend you I'm going to need every possible advantage. If I understand your situation correctly, you went to bed when you and Eddie got home from the wrap party. A couple hours later, you heard a gunshot and ran into the entertainment room and found Eddie dead on the floor with the gun in his hand. You said it was suicide. But forensics found your prints on the gun and his blood on your clothing. Am I correct?"

Kaya nodded. "Yeah, I ran to him, pulled him into my arms and threw the gun aside."

"The only thing that gives me pause," Sunny said, "and

makes me believe that you could possibly be innocent of his murder is the fact that there was no gunpowder residue on you. If you had done it, there should have been. Otherwise, I'm going to be brutally honest with you. You sound guilty as sin."

She continued. "Here is how the prosecuting attorney is going to see it. You suspected Eddie of cheating on you again, after six other times. There were rumors that he beat you on occasion. Is that true, as well?"

"Yeah," Kaya said in a soft voice, her eyes lowered.

"Okay, so he was a cheating, abusive husband. You got tired of his crap and shot him. Women have done it before."

"But I didn't kill him! I swear I didn't. Navarre was in the house when it happened. If I'd planned to kill Eddie, I definitely wouldn't have wanted our son to be in the house when I did it!"

"Maybe it wasn't premeditated," Sunny said. "Maybe you snapped."

"I didn't snap, Sunny. I was asleep upstairs and I heard the gunshot and ran downstairs as fast as I could."

"Did you hear anything as you were coming down the stairs? The sound of someone running? The sound of a door closing as someone was leaving the house?"

"No, Eddie had the music blasting in the entertainment room. I only heard the gunshot because it was louder than the music."

"Your son sleeps through loud music?"

"Navarre has been around musicians all his life. Loud music is nothing to him. He could sleep through a bomb."

Sunny was furiously scribbling on the legal pad. She looked up at Kaya. "Who else besides you and Eddie had keys to your house?"

"His manager, Chaz Palmer, and the housekeeper, Ida."

"I can see the housekeeper having a key, but his manager? They were that close?"

Kaya nodded. "They grew up together here in Atlanta. Chaz says if not for him, Eddie would have been a nobody."

"Is that true, in your opinion?"

"Nah, Eddie was super talented. He just let Chaz ride on his coattails because they were buds. Chaz is a lot of hot air."

"Enjoys the notoriety that comes with being the friend of a famous entertainer?" Sunny guessed.

Kaya nodded. "I could sense the desperation in him sometimes. The bigger Eddie got the more other people in the business would drop hints to him that Chaz was dragging him down. That he needed someone with more expertise to watch his back. It's a cutthroat business."

"I imagine so," Sunny said. She rose. "I think I have enough to get started. Have that list of Eddie's women for me when I come again. I'm going to speak with the lead detective on the case to make sure they've looked into the whereabouts of Chaz and Ida on the night Eddie was killed. To make sure they haven't left any stone unturned. It's Friday. I'll come back to see you on Monday at around the same time. Two o'clock?"

"I'm not going anywhere," Kaya joked.

She rose, too. Sunny stood looking at her. She appeared to be the same sweet Kayla she'd known when they were kids and teens. She'd even named her son, Navarre, after the Rutger Hauer character in *LadyHawke,* their favorite film when they were twelve. However, life had a way of changing a person.

Was Kaya Bradley capable of killing her husband in cold blood?

Sunny hoped not.

She gave Kaya a brief hug. "Take care of yourself."

Kaya blinked back tears. "I'll do my best."

Sunny let go of her and went to bang on the door. "Open up, I'm finished in here!"

A few moments later the heavy door creaked open and the same guard smiled at her.

He held the door while she strode into the corridor. Locking it, he said, "Do you think she did it?"

"That's privileged information," Sunny informed him.

He smiled broadly. "I think she's in capable hands."

"May I ask why you're so interested in her case?" Sunny said, glancing up at him.

He was about two inches taller than her five-nine.

"I have a daughter her age," he said.

Sunny smiled. Earlier she'd thought he was only in his mid-forties. He must be in his late forties or early fifties to have a daughter who was in her late twenties.

"I took you for forty-five," she said lightly.

"You're kind," he said. "I'm *fifty-five.*"

"Then you must be doing something right," she joked.

"Eating my wife's cooking every day for thirty years. That woman can burn!"

Sunny laughed. As a matter of fact, she missed home cooking herself. She was looking forward to getting back to Warm Springs this weekend and having a plate of something sinfully southern and delicious at her friend Patty's café on main street.

"Dammit, Caesar, I ought to leave your furry behind up this tree for the rest of your natural-born life!" Sunny snapped at the big gray cat. "You are such a wuss. You'll chase a squirrel up and then look down and wonder how the hell you got up there in the first place. I'm telling you, this is the last time I risk my neck for you!"

Caesar merely looked at her as he sat perched on the sycamore branch. He would not move an inch. The claws of his forepaws were stuck firmly in the branch and his body trembled.

"I'm getting too old for this," Sunny grumbled as she swung her five-nine, one-hundred-and-sixty-pound body onto a sturdy lower branch and began climbing.

The branch creaked. "And maybe too heavy," she added.

She carefully stepped onto a higher branch, her well-worn Keds giving her traction.

Pulling herself up, she said, "I'm coming."

Caesar looked down forlornly at her.

"You *ought* to be sad," she said. "And you owe me. You should fetch my slippers and my paper for a week after this. No, a month. But *no,* you cats act as if you don't know how to help a sister out from time to time. I'm going to get me a dog. That's what I'm going to do."

Caesar meowed as if in protest.

"You never see dogs getting stuck in trees," Sunny told him.

Sunny was so busy castigating poor Caesar that she hadn't noticed Jonas when he opened the gate and came into her yard.

Her two-story, southern-style clapboard house sat on a big corner lot and was surrounded by a white picket fence. She took pride in it. It had recently been painted white and trimmed in yellow. The lawn was neatly manicured, and it was beautifully landscaped with an abundance of colorful, seasonal flowers and plants.

Her home was her refuge after a busy week in Atlanta. In Atlanta she maintained a small apartment, but it was only a place to lay her head at the end of the day. This was home. So she was not liable to take kindly to strangers who had the temerity to come into her yard without being invited.

Finally, she'd climbed high enough to grab Caesar. "Got you," she said triumphantly.

She transferred him from the higher branch to a lower one. Caesar, full of courage and vigor once again, leaped from the branch to the ground and didn't once look back at his mistress as he ran around the corner of the house.

"You're welcome!" Sunny said, laughing. "Ungrateful wretch. See if I come after you again. What a way to start the day. I get up, dutifully give you your breakfast and while

I'm in the shower, you go outside and get yourself stuck up a tree. Patty had better have some of her blueberry pancakes left. I'm starving."

While she was talking to herself, she was steadily working her way down the sycamore. When she got to the lowest branch which was around five feet from the ground, she straddled it momentarily, then swung her legs together and prepared to jump down.

"Careful," said a masculine voice to the left of her.

Startled, Sunny lost her balance and fell off the branch.

Jonas caught her and both of them fell to the ground and rolled down the slight incline a few feet before coming to a stop in a jumble of flailing arms and legs.

They tussled a bit, trying to right themselves.

Sunny ended up straddling him. She quickly climbed off him and stood. "Don't you know not to sneak up on folks when they're trying to get down from a tree without breaking their necks?" she said irritably.

By the time she'd gotten her words out, she had looked into his eyes and the rest of what she was about to say to him suddenly seemed unimportant.

She watched him get to his feet. He was wearing jeans that appeared to be made especially for him for she could see every muscle flex in his powerful legs and thighs as he rose. The rest of him wasn't bad, either. He had a broad chest with clearly delineated pectorals that begged to have her hands all over them.

The hem of his white T-shirt had hiked up a bit, revealing a washboard stomach.

And his arms were nothing short of a miracle, muscular, with beautifully shaped biceps ending in big, strong hands.

It was all she could do not to stare at him like a fool.

His appearance in Warm Springs was so incongruous that, to her, he was like a golden-brown fantasy who'd stepped out of one of her dreams. The trouble with that idea was that she couldn't ever recall dreaming about a man who looked half this good.

Then it dawned on her. He was probably one of those gay guys who haunted Warm Springs on weekends looking for antiques. Yeah, that was it. Some of them were so divinely handsome she and Patty would sit by the picture window in the café and drool over them as they strolled past. It was a sin and a shame for all that male beauty to be wasted on another man.

He'd obviously stopped to ask for directions. Her house was only a few blocks from main street and the myriad shops that sold the sought-after treasures.

"I bet you're lost, aren't you?" she said when he had been staring right back at her for the past two minutes. "You're looking for antiques?"

"No, I'm not lost," Jonas said, smiling at her. He couldn't stop smiling. He hadn't known what he had expected to find when he finally stood face-to-face with her. It certainly wasn't this tall, leggy *goddess*. She had on a pair of pale green city shorts and a simple white blouse. On her feet were white tennis shoes. And her long, thick black hair fell to her shoulders in a mass of loose curls.

She looked nothing like Audra.

Okay, there was something about the large, warm brown eyes with an almost Asian shape to them. Audra's eyes were also shaped that way. And their mouths were similar. Full-lipped and kind of pouty.

But Audra had golden-brown skin and this woman's skin was darker, with red undertones. It was healthy and looked silky smooth. In fact, everything about her was robust and healthy. Those legs and thighs were shapely and full, not skinny.

Her hips were round and shapely. Her breasts… He had to stop himself.

He had not come clear across the country to fall in lust with Audra's daughter.

He took a deep breath and stepped forward, offering her his hand. "Hello, my name is Jonas Blake and I represent your birth mother. She'd like to meet you."

Sunny's eyes stretched and her mouth fell open with shock and surprise. For long moments all she could do was open and close her mouth, with no words issuing from it. Then she blurted, "You're pulling my leg, right?"

Jonas shook his head in the negative. "I assure you, I'm telling the truth."

Sunny snorted. "Sure you are. I'm going to be twenty-eight next month. What birth mother in her right mind waits that long to contact her child? Go on with you!" She turned and quickly went into the house.

Jonas trotted after her. He stood on the front porch. "Miss Adams, please!"

"Get off my property!" Sunny shouted from inside.

He didn't go anywhere.

A couple minutes later, Sunny returned with her shoulder bag clutched close to her side. She glared at him as she passed him on the porch. "I told you to leave."

"I can't do that. I came all the way from Beverly Hills to deliver a message to you, and I'm going to deliver it."

"Don't make me call the police," Sunny warned.

"Go ahead and call them. I'm not accosting you. All I want to do is talk to you."

Sunny stomped down the front steps. "Well, I'm late for breakfast. I get mean if I don't eat, so don't expect me to be civil until after my belly's full."

Jonas took this to mean she was willing to hear him out. He followed her off the porch and onto the adjacent sidewalk. "Breakfast is on me," he said.

Sunny looked up at him as they hurried across the street. "Beverly Hills. Are you saying that my birth mother lives in Hollywood?"

"No, Beverly Hills is not Hollywood. People get the two towns confused."

"Okay, okay," Sunny said impatiently. "I get you. Who is she?" Her narrowed eyes and skeptical expression told him she still was not taking him seriously.

"Audra Kane."

Sunny burst out laughing. She stopped walking in the middle of the street. Luckily traffic was very light at nine on a Saturday morning so they didn't run the risk of getting splattered on the grill of an eighteen-wheeler.

"Honey, you must be an escapee from the loony bin. Audra Kane? I don't look anything like Audra Kane. She's a tiny little thing. She and Halle Berry could be sisters. Do I look anything like Halle Berry?" She peered up at him expectantly.

"I've seen Halle Berry," he said. "And I think you're every bit as lovely as she is. But, no, you don't look anything like her."

"Good answer," Sunny said with a smile and started walking toward the café again.

Chapter 4

Patty Engstrom spotted Sunny when she came into her café. Patty was manning the grill today because her husband, Sven, had injured his right wrist playing touch football with his friends last night.

When they'd opened the café they'd agreed that Sven would be the short-order cook and Patty, since the entire menu was based on her recipes, would do the bulk of the cooking for the dinner guests.

Today, blond, blue-eyed Sven was doing easy duty at the cash register while Patty and the waitresses worked their butts off catering to the hungry morning crowd.

"Hey, Sunny. Who's that good-lookin' guy with you?" she called out before the door could close in Sunny and Jonas's wake.

Diners craned their necks to see to whom Patty was referring.

Sunny, used to Patty's sparkling personality and particular brand of humor, was not in the least embarrassed by the extra attention.

"None of your business," she called back. "We came here to eat, not to gossip."

"Well, my food goes down better with a little gossip," Patty returned jovially. "You have never been in here with a gentleman before. Of course we're curious."

Sunny was directing Jonas to a table next to the window. "Ignore her," she whispered to him. "Keep that up, and I won't bring anybody else in here!" she warned Patty.

Patty grinned, her brown eyes twinkling in her plump brown face. "That isn't the first time you've threatened not to come here again. My fried chicken always makes you eat those words."

"You got any fried chicken this morning?" Sunny asked shamelessly. "Some of your fried chicken and waffles would hit the spot."

"Sorry, fresh out," Patty said. "Hank and H.J. got the last of the chicken."

Hank and Hank, Jr., father and son, were seated at a booth a few feet from Sunny's table. She sent them a baleful look.

Hank Perotti owned a specialty shop in Warm Springs Village that sold leather goods.

He was a tall ruggedly good-looking man with a year-round tan. His son, H.J., was equally tall, with masculine good looks. Besides the specialty shop, they owned a ranch on the outskirts of town that catered to tourists.

"Don't give *us* the evil eye," Hank said, smiling. "You ought to get up earlier. The early bird gets the chicken."

"Don't make me come over there," Sunny said, grinning at him.

"I've been trying to make you come over here since you moved to Warm Springs, but you just haven't worked up the nerve to do it."

Several diners laughed goodnaturedly.

It was no secret that Hank, in his fifties, widowed, still a handsome rascal, and he knew it, had a thing for twenty-seven-year-old Sunny.

"And have every woman of a certain age in this town sending me hate mail?" Sunny said, laughing softly. "No, thank you."

Hank rose and dropped several bills on the table. "Excuses, excuses."

Sunny smiled at him as he and H.J. passed their table on the way out. Hank winked at her. Sunny winked back.

Jonas had been observing her throughout the exchange. She'd been cool and collected.

Thoroughly enjoying herself. He wondered what, if anything, ruffled her feathers.

"I believe he's serious," he said of Hank Perotti.

Sunny met his eyes. "No harm in a man stating what he wants. That's honest. I'd rather that than a lot of pretense and flattery. Hank is a plainspoken man."

"He's also twice your age."

"Yeah, but he's sure well preserved."

"Sunny, how're you doing today?" Ronniece, one of the waitresses, said as she walked up to their table, pad and pen poised in her hands. Ronniece was nineteen and dreamed of moving to Atlanta. Her aunt Patty, who had raised her after her mother's death, was trying to keep her close to home. At least until she finished two years of community college. After that, she could go to any university she was accepted into.

Ronniece had set her sights on Spelman College.

"Hi, Ronniece. This is Jonas. Jonas, Ronniece's aunt and uncle own this café."

"Hi, Jonas," said Ronniece, blushing. She had golden-brown skin that was so clear and unblemished that it appeared almost unreal. Her aunt Patty had nicknamed her Butter but Sunny wasn't about to use her nickname in front of a perfect stranger. It would embarrass the girl.

"Pleased to meet you, Ronniece," Jonas said with a warm smile.

"What'll you have?"

"Some of Patty's scrambled eggs with cheddar cheese, a slice of ham and a short stack of blueberry pancakes," Sunny said. "Oh, and hot coffee. Keep it comin'."

Ronniece looked at Jonas and blushed again. "And you, Jonas?"

"Since I'm new here, I think I'll bow to my host's experience and order the same thing she's having," he answered.

"All right," said Ronniece. "I'll be right back with your coffee."

In her absence, Sunny sighed softly and regarded Jonas with a serious expression.

"Okay, now, come clean. Somebody is playing a practical joke on me. Who is it? Kit? This sounds like something Kit would do. We went to law school together. She lives in Newport News, Virginia, now. But distance never stopped her from trying to pull one over on me."

Jonas pulled his cell phone from his pants pocket. "Wait a minute."

He dialed Audra's cell phone number. She had told him that she would answer it no matter what time he called.

"Hello, Jonas. Are you there with her?" Audra answered, breathless and anxious.

Jonas was looking into Sunny's eyes. "We're sitting in a café in Warm Springs. I'm handing her the phone now."

Sunny smirked as she took the phone and brought the receiver to her mouth. "Hello?"

In Beverly Hills, because of the time difference, Audra was still in bed. She was sitting, propped up on pillows, with her sleep mask pushed up on her forehead. For a moment, after hearing Sunny's voice, she couldn't manage to speak. Then she cleared her voice and said, "Sunny, I can imagine what you think of me, not coming to see you myself, and sending Jonas. But I will explain everything when I see you. Please come. Please. There's so much I have to say to you. Please come."

Sunny held the phone firmly to her ear. The clarity of sound was remarkable. It really did sound like Audra Kane.

"I…I…" she said, confusion and fear evident in her eyes.

Frowning, she handed the phone back to Jonas, got up from the table and fled to the ladies' room.

Jonas said to Audra, "I'll call you back. She's upset. Gotta go."

In Beverly Hills, Audra stared at the phone as the dial tone replaced the sound of Jonas's voice. She flipped her cell phone closed and climbed out of bed. She needed a stiff drink, but she'd given up alcohol more than ten years ago after she discovered her weakness for it. Alcohol was the lonely woman's refuge. She had learned to find solace elsewhere.

She went downstairs to make a cup of hot chocolate instead. Yes, hot chocolate could be addictive, too. But at least you didn't run through a hotel lobby naked after imbibing too much.

As she took the stairs, barefoot, she prayed that Jonas would be able to reach Sunday and persuade her to come to Beverly Hills.

In Warm Springs, Jonas stood at the ladies' room door, speaking consolingly to Sunny.

"I know this is a lot to digest," he said. "A stranger walks up to you and tells you your mother is somebody you've probably known about all your life. It's surreal. You can't quite wrap your mind around it. But it's true, Sunday."

"Nobody actually calls me that," Sunny said through sniffles. "Except in court. Even then I get snickers."

Audra had *told* him she went by Sunny. "It's a lovely name," he said softly.

"Liar," said Sunny, leaning against the bathroom door. "It's a ridiculous name. But it's what my adoptive parents named me. It's grown on me."

She was slowly pulling herself together. When she'd heard that woman's voice on the phone she'd had the only panic attack of her life. Her heart began racing and suddenly she couldn't breathe properly. The busy café with the buzz of human voices, the noise from the kitchen, all seemed like too much sensory stimulation to deal with.

She had to go someplace where she could be alone, if only for a few minutes. Her mind had gone to the ladies' room, and moments later her feet had taken her there.

She didn't feel foolish for reacting the way that she had. Early on, she'd learned that the human mind had many built-in coping mechanisms. Fleeing from an untenable situation was a sound reaction in her opinion.

Crying, however, wouldn't be tolerated.

She walked over to the paper towel dispenser and snatched a paper towel from its jaws. Wiping her face, she peered into the mirror. Her eyes were red rimmed. She folded the paper towel, ran cold water over it, wrung it out, then placed it over her eyes.

She stood there with it covering her eyes while she spoke to Jonas. "I'm okay. I'll be out in minute. Don't let your break-fast get cold on my account."

"I'm not leaving until I see that you're okay with my own eyes," Jonas told her.

She removed the paper towel and peered into the mirror. Her eyes were still slightly red but they looked better. She'd learned that trick from one of the girls she'd met in juvenile court when, at nine, she'd been caught shoplifting food from a grocery store.

In the foster home in which she'd been residing at that time, she was never given enough to eat and was often hungry. To this day she didn't like skipping meals because of it. She knew realistically that she had no reason to associate herself with that half-starved little girl anymore, but somewhere in the back of her mind she did.

The thought of denying herself food repulsed her. To stay in shape she exercised five days a week and ate in moderation but never totally excised her favorite foods from her diet.

She sighed as she threw the paper towel in the trash. She had sworn a long time ago that she would not allow her upbringing, or lack thereof, to make her a victim.

She was the victor. She had survived it all. She had worked hard to make something of herself. In essence, she'd created a life out of nothing. In spite of the fact that she had no one to depend on.

Since her adoptive parents' deaths in a car accident when she was eight and no one in their families had been willing to take on the responsibility of caring for her, she had resolved that she would take care of herself.

She'd done a pretty good job of it, too. She'd made excellent grades, no matter how many times she'd had to change schools throughout elementary and high school. And when it came time for college, she'd won several scholarships. One that she hadn't been aware she'd applied for.

She'd graduated at the top of her classes in high school and in college. Because she had met Tom Chapman at a mixer at the University of Georgia, her interest in the law had been piqued.

He'd jokingly told her that if she passed the bar exam he would give her a job in his firm. He hadn't been smiling when, three years later, she'd walked into his office and taken him up on his promise.

She'd been with his firm for more than two years now.

Sunny smiled as she opened the ladies' room door.

Jonas pushed away from the wall and looked into her face. "I won't say another word until after you eat," he said.

"Thank you," Sunny said, and turned to go back to their table.

In their absence, Ronniece had already brought their orders. They sat and Sunny bowed her head. Following her example, Jonas bowed his.

"Lord, thank you for this food," Sunny intoned. "And please don't let me have another meltdown today. Once a day is enough."

Jonas smiled but didn't say anything.

They ate their food, which, because of Patty's special touch in the kitchen, was delicious. Afterward they contentedly sipped their coffee, stealing glances at each other, thinking neither was the wiser. In fact, they were both aware of it and welcomed the interest, although, at this early date, neither knew where, if anywhere, a mutual attraction would take them. Still, the sensation was sweet.

Patty brought their bill to the table instead of Ronniece. She was a short, stout woman with a pretty face. Her eyes shone with humor. "Jonas, you're welcome here anytime. Bring Sunny with you if you *must*."

"Thank you. I'll be back," Jonas said with a smile.

Sunny got up and kissed Patty's cheek. "Don't ban me from heaven. Those pancakes were as light as a cloud."

"Okay, this time," Patty relented, pleased with the adulation. "But watch yourself or I'll say, 'No pancakes for you!'" She laughed harder than anyone else at her mimicry of the Soup Nazi from *Seinfeld*.

She laughed all the way back to the kitchen.

Jonas placed a twenty on the table. It covered the bill plus provided a very nice tip.

As they walked to the door, Sunny said, "How about a walking tour of the town?"

Jonas smiled at her. "I'd like that."

The temperature was in the high sixties and the sun was shining brightly. Sunny gestured left and they began walking in a southerly direction. Patty's café was a few blocks from the shops that lined the streets of downtown.

"Is this your first time in Georgia?" Sunny asked, peering sidelong at him.

"No, I've been to Atlanta before. On business."

"Oh, what sort of business?"

"I own a consulting firm. I teach people the practical steps in opening and running successful businesses. I'm usually asked to go to developing countries to help them get started."

"Do you enjoy it?"

He smiled down at her. "I do. I get to travel and meet interesting people. I've lived in South Africa for the past three years."

"Wow," said Sunny, impressed. "Tell me about it. I've never been out of the country."

"South Africa is a country of contrasts," Jonas said. "Economically, culturally, you name it, it's diverse in nature. Before apartheid was abolished it was a country where the have-nots had no opportunity to change their status in life. None whatsoever. Now there is the opportunity, but things are moving very slowly. Of course, you can't expect things to change overnight, but there are still so many socially and economically deprived people, it's staggering."

"It makes you realize how fortunate most of us are and don't even realize it," Sunny said.

"Yeah," Jonas agreed. "Education, for example. Kids in the United States go to school free of charge. In South Africa they have to pay, and the fee is often too exorbitant for most families. It's a real struggle to pay their tuition, pay for their uniforms. Even getting to school is an ordeal. But, you know what? They appreciate an education far more than anyone I've observed here in the States."

"I think we all appreciate something we've worked for more than what's given to us on a silver platter," Sunny said. She was speaking from experience. Everything of value she'd gotten in life she'd had to work for. She didn't take any of it for granted.

Jonas felt like a fraud, talking about the struggle of the South African people when he had never gone without a meal in his life. His father had sent him to the best schools, he'd worn designer clothes from birth. Deprivation of any kind was foreign to him.

Yet it wasn't guilt that propelled him forward. He had no time for guilt, because it was a hindrance to action. He helped people because he genuinely believed that the world would never improve until the inequities between poor people and rich people were addressed. The earth had enough natural resources for everyone, with an abundance left over. The wrong people were in charge of distributing the riches, though. Greed ruled the day.

That point was exquisitely driven home in South Africa when a warlord burned down a school in his area because the people weren't paying him the proper tribute.

Jonas had wanted to take a gun and kill the bastard himself.

They had been walking in silence for a few minutes when he said, "Audra worries that you've had a miserable life, but you seem happy to me. Are you?"

His stomach was tied up in knots, awaiting her reply. Although he'd only known her a few minutes, he desperately wanted her answer to be yes. Yes, she was happy.

Sunny smiled at him. "You haven't told me nearly enough about yourself in order to ask me something so personal. I don't even know how you and Miss Kane are related. Did she hire you to come down here? Are you a personal friend? Did you do this out of the kindness of your heart?"

Jonas realized she had a point. He had been so intent on doing Audra's bidding and getting her to go back to Beverly Hills with him, he had done nothing to gain her trust. No wonder she'd handed the phone back to him in the café and retreated to the ladies' room.

"Audra was married to my dad, Norman Blake."

"The director?"

"So, you've heard of him."

"Of course. He's Spike Lee's mentor. Spike Lee's always talking about his influence on his career."

Jonas was well aware of that. Once, the knowledge had rankled. But now his father's generosity in taking someone under his wing and offering wisdom and guidance was seen by Jonas as proof that Norman Blake had the capacity to care about another human being.

"Dad has a way of inspiring others."

"You never thought of following in his footsteps?"

Jonas shook his head in the negative. "After my mother committed suicide, I knew Hollywood wasn't the place I wanted to spend the rest of my life."

Sunny paused in her steps to look up at him with concern. "I'm so sorry."

Jonas continued walking. "It was a long time ago. I was twelve when she did it. I remember feeling rage against my father. He was the reason she killed herself. She lived for him and he neglected her at every turn. She'd been dead for several days before it occurred to him that he hadn't seen or spoken with her in a while. By then it was too late."

At his side Sunny remained quiet, letting him get it out.

"Two years later he married Audra." He laughed shortly. "I was determined to dislike her, but she was so kind to me, she won my heart."

They were downtown now where benches and rocking chairs lined the sheltered streets. The town of Warm Springs sat among rolling hills and freshwater springs.

Located about an hour south of Atlanta, the town first had a close call with fame in the nineteenth century as a spa town because of its mineral springs which maintain a temperature of ninety degrees Fahrenheit year-round. It is known today as the vacation home of former President Franklin D. Roosevelt, who went there in the twenties looking for a way to improve his paraplegia. He found comfort in the warm spring waters of the small Georgia town.

The town is home to the Roosevelt Warm Springs Institute for Rehabilitation, President Roosevelt's former polio hospital, which is a world-renowned center offering physical and vocational rehabilitation to patients with spinal problems.

The hospital was so close to the downtown area that it was not unusual for Sunny to see patients being squired around town in their wheelchairs, getting a little sun, recreation and getting a bit of shopping done in one trip.

"You said she *was* married to your father. They're divorced now?"

Jonas smiled at her. "You know my father, but you don't follow Audra's life closely enough to know they've been divorced for years. Have you seen any of her movies?"

Sunny took offense. "Of course I have."

"Name one," he challenged.

"I can name more than one. *Twilight, Asking for Trouble* and *The Templar.* I have *The Templar* on DVD. I love it."

"What did you love about it?" Jonas asked, amused.

"She totally kicked butt in it," Sunny answered, smiling. "She was like a cross between Indiana Jones and Ripley in *Alien.* Did she have fun making it?"

"She threw her back out," Jonas said ironically. "Twice."

Chapter 5

"Why does she want to see me now?" Sunny was sitting on a park bench with her legs crossed and her body turned toward Jonas. He sat a couple feet to her right.

Around them park visitors played softball in one corner. A martial arts class went through their drills in another. Mothers and fathers watched their little ones romp on a colorful merry-go-round, a swing set and monkey bars on the children's playground.

"Audra wanted to tell you herself."

Sunny was looking into his eyes when he said that. They were pleading with her to understand. But she didn't understand. "Am I supposed to just hop on a plane with you for a reunion with Miss Kane when I don't have all the facts? That's not going to happen. Why the urgency? Tell me, or this interview is over."

Jonas reminded himself that he had to be patient. Audra had not given much thought to how Sunny would react. She'd been too panicked to think, obviously.

"Can we try phoning again?" he asked.

Sunny nodded. "Okay."

She uncrossed her legs and sat up straighter on the bench as Jonas dialed Audra's number. A few seconds later, he said, "Yeah, she's fine."

He handed her the phone.

"Hello, Miss Kane," Sunny said.

Jonas got up and went for a stroll around the park, giving them privacy.

In Beverly Hills, Audra was back in her bedroom after going downstairs to make a cup of chocolate. She was sitting, crossed-legged, in the middle of her huge bed.

"Hello, Sunny," she said softly. "Thanks for agreeing to speak with me. I know you must be confused as to why I've contacted you after all these years. I'm willing to answer any questions you have. No matter how tough."

Sunny took a deep breath. "Do you know what I do for a living?"

"You're an attorney."

"Then you must realize that your behavior has me wondering why you waited so long to come forward. You *do* know that in the state of Georgia you had the right to contact me when I turned twenty-one?"

"I *am* aware of that."

"Then, why didn't you?"

"Because when I had the agency locate you I learned that, due to your adoptive parents' deaths, you'd gone into the foster care system when you were eight. I felt like I should have done something then."

"How could you have known, when you were barred from contacting me until my twenty-first birthday?" Sunny asked reasonably.

"Intellectually I know that to be true. But as a mother I believe I should have known and I should have been there for you."

"I'm not going to argue that with you," Sunny told her. "I'm sure you have a reason for wanting to suffer needlessly. However, I deal in facts and the fact is, you could have come forward when I was twenty-one, and you didn't."

"I was getting to that," Audra said. "When I found out you had to spend ten years in the foster care system I was afraid to face you because I could have saved you from that. I *should* have saved you! But I didn't, and at that point I didn't believe I deserved to be a part of your life. I felt that I would have been intruding on your life instead of adding something to it. If you can understand that."

"In other words," Sunny said, "you were afraid that after my experiences as a ward of the state, I would detest you and not want you to be a part of my life!"

She heard it when Audra broke down into tears. "Yes!"

"Stop that freaking crying," Sunny said, "and listen to me. I don't hate you for giving me up. I had good parents. I have wonderful memories of them. I'm living in their house here in Warm Springs. I inherited it."

Audra did not dare tell her that she'd arranged for the house to go to her. She wanted Sunny to have wonderful memories of Kenneth and Jane Adams, something good from her childhood to hang on to.

"I'm glad," Audra said.

"Jonas hasn't told me why you gave me up for adoption," Sunny told her. "He's tried his best to only do what you asked him to do. But I've been giving him hell."

Audra smiled, and Sunny could hear it in her voice when she said, "He's a good man."

Sunny felt tears rolling down her cheeks. She brushed them away with the pad of her thumb. "Why did you give me up?"

"Because I couldn't bear the thought of aborting you, and I didn't have the means to take care of you by myself."

"The father didn't want me?"

"He was scared. He was in law school at the time. He comes from a family of lawyers and he was afraid of disappointing his parents. He freaked when I told him. I broke up with him and told him I'd handle everything without him."

"What's his name?"

"Chapman. Trent Chapman."

Sunny's breath caught in her throat. "Thomas Trent Chapman?"

It was Audra's turn to gasp. "Oh, my God, you know him?"

"It can't be the same Chapman," Sunny said. "The head of the law firm I work for is named Thomas Trent Chapman."

"Is he black?" Audra asked.

"Yes."

"In his mid-fifties?"

"Yes."

"Over six feet tall with medium-brown skin and honey-colored eyes? He had wavy black hair the last time I saw him. I hope he's going bald now."

"My boss is not going bald. He does, however, have gray in his sideburns. And the rest of your description is dead-on."

"Baby, if Thomas Trent Chapman is not your father then you're working for his twin brother."

"This is so cool!" Sunny exclaimed. "When I woke up this morning, all I was really looking forward to was some of Patty's blueberry pancakes, and look what I've wound up with—a mother *and* a father." She laughed.

Audra was laughing and crying in Beverly Hills. "Are you sure you don't hate me? Do you need to sleep on it and decide tomorrow?"

"Nah," said Sunny. "One thing I learned being a foster kid is to be flexible, go with the flow, expect the worst but pray for the best. Today I got the best of the worst. You could have been a birth mother who was only tracking me down to see what you could get out of me. That's happened to some of my friends.

Okay, one more question and then I'm going to have to go home and go to bed for a couple days to chill out from all the excitement. Why now?"

Audra paused for a few seconds. "Have you heard of Deana Davis?"

"The celebrity biographer? Just a few days ago, as a matter of fact, she was on some morning show. But I had the volume down on the TV while I was getting ready for work. I didn't hear what she was saying."

"She was discussing her next book," Audra said. "It's about me."

Sunny now had the full picture. Audra Kane was going to never contact her because she was too afraid that she hated her. Deana Davis's announcement that she intended to write a bio about her had forced her hand.

"I see," she said now. "You had to get to me first to try and counteract some of the fallout from being exposed in the media as your daughter."

"There's no nice way of looking at it," Audra said regrettably. "As your grandmother put it, no one needs to learn who her birth mother is from the six o'clock news."

"I have a grandmother?" Sunny asked, laughter evident in her tone.

Audra laughed. "You have a grandmother, an aunt, an uncle and many, many cousins. Most of whom live in Georgia. Your grandmother, Vernette, lives with me."

"When can you all come for a visit?" Sunny asked.

"I was going to ask you to come here," Audra said. "Deana has her spies everywhere. I swear there are two strange cars that park down the street every day whose occupants watch every move I make. I know I saw a guy snapping photos of me and your grandma when we were taking our evening stroll around the neighborhood yesterday."

"I'm sorry, I won't be able to travel for several weeks,"

Sunny said with a sigh. "I've agreed to defend a woman I knew when I was a child against a murder charge."

"Oh, no, that poor woman," said Audra sympathetically. "What happened?"

"She's accused of killing Eddie Bradley, the rap star."

"I heard about that," Audra told her. "Well, actually, your grandmother heard about it. She keeps up with goings-on in her home state. One of her granddaughters told her about it and she filled me in. According to Chandra, that's one of your cousins, the wife didn't do it. The manager did. Apparently, that's the verdict on the Internet."

"I can't really talk about the case," Sunny said. "But it's good to know that she has a groundswell of support out there. I'll tell her when I see her on Monday."

Audra sighed loudly. "You can't come here, and I can't go there without leading that witch to you. What are we going to do?"

"Have really long phone conversations?" Sunny suggested.

"I'll think of a way," Audra assured her. "I'm very resourceful."

"So am I," Sunny replied. "I wonder if I got it from you?"

"Perhaps. You certainly got your interest in law from your father's side of the family. I'm amazed that you went into law."

Sunny told her about meeting Tom at the senior mixer at the University of Georgia.

"You don't suppose," she asked when she was finished, "that he knew I was his daughter back then?"

"How could he?" Audra asked. "I was so mad at him by the time I gave birth to you that I didn't put his name on the birth certificate. I let them put, 'father unknown.' He could not have traced you by any records. No, my dear, he is not aware that you're his daughter. I wish I could be there to see the look on his face when you tell him. He will most certainly remember me!"

"I can't believe this is happening," Sunny said in awe.

"Believe it," said Audra. "Oh, one more thing—is he married with children?"

"He's married," Sunny told her. "To a social butterfly. They never had children, though. Rumor has it that they tried but weren't successful. I feel sorry for them."

"So do I," Audra said. "I don't wish him ill. We were both young and scared to step up and take responsibility. I hope you never had to face a decision like that."

"Are you fishing?" Sunny joked.

"For more tidbits about your life? I certainly am. I want to know everything about you now that we're talking. Have you ever been in love? Close to marriage? I've only gotten information piecemeal from the detectives I've hired over the years. That last one I hired didn't even tell me you were working for Thomas Trent Chapman. If I had known that I would have been prepared when you mentioned it earlier."

"Yes, I was in love once," Sunny told her mother. "Or I thought I was. It was when I was in college. He was my first love. Turns out I didn't mean nearly as much to him as he meant to me. He left me with plenty of doubts."

"You don't want to get hurt again."

"I can definitely do without it," Sunny admitted. "Besides, my work keeps me busy. These days, I look, but don't touch."

"Sounds like my philosophy."

"You're a movie star. Surely men are lined up to go out with you."

"You would think that, wouldn't you?" Audra said, laughing softly. "The fact is, when you get to be my age suitors are few and far between. I went out with Jonathan Hawkins for a while, but he just left me for a younger woman."

"He's nuts."

"Yeah, but that's another story. Actually, I'm quite happy to be on my own. Next time, I'll look before I leap."

"So will I."

Audra was silent a moment, then asked, "What do you think of Jonas?"

"He's very nice."

"He's single."

"He's your stepson."

"He's not related to *you*."

"Okay, I find him attractive. He's walking toward me right now, by the way. But it would be foolish to get involved with him. Now that you and I have found each other it's almost like he's my stepbrother."

"Oh, honey, please," Audra said, pooh-poohing her notion. "Jonas is the best man I know, and you're my flesh and blood. If the two of you were to get together I'd die a happy woman."

"Stop that kind of talk, right now," Sunny said, blushing. "He's less than three feet away and he's smiling at me."

"Then smile back at him and invite him to dinner at your place tonight."

"You're incorrigible."

"Yes, I am. And I'm your mother! I can say it at last! I've got to go wake up your grandmother and tell her all about you. Will you call me back this evening?"

"All right," Sunny promised.

"Goodbye, then, darling."

"Goodbye," Sunny said, and disconnected. The word "Mom" had been on the tip of her tongue, but she simply didn't feel comfortable enough, yet, to say it.

She stood and handed the phone back to Jonas.

When he took it, their hands touched and she jerked hers away a bit swifter than was necessary. Jonas noticed and smiled. "Did you get your questions answered?"

Sunny was picking up her shoulder bag from the bench. "Yes."

"Then you believe me?"

Their eyes met. "I do. I suppose you've accomplished your mission now, and you'll be going back to California."

Jonas looked confused. "Do you know something I don't? Because my mission was to take you to Beverly Hills."

"I told…Audra that I can't possibly go to California right now. I have a new client who's accused of murder. Her trial is less than three months away. She fired her former lawyer and I wasn't able to get a continuance, so her court date remains the same. She's already been in jail, away from her four-year-old son, for over three months. I have a lot of work to do between now and then. I can't afford to take a break."

"Then Audra told you why she sent me here?"

"Yes, I realize Deana Davis might track me down," Sunny told him as she placed her bag on her shoulder. She looked him in the eyes. "Don't worry, I'll handle her if she shows up."

Jonas was smiling at her with a great deal of respect mirrored in his eyes. "You're amazing. I don't know if I would have been able to handle this with as much aplomb as you're displaying right now."

"Save your compliments," Sunny told him. "I'm going home to take two Tylenols and lie down. My body's abuzz with nervous energy. If my mind doesn't splinter between now and tomorrow morning, I'll be a lucky woman."

Jonas laughed shortly. "I can't see that happening."

"That's because you love Audra and you think, by virtue of birth, I must be like her. Well, I'm not Audra Kane. I'm just a Georgia girl who had to struggle for everything, and I don't take this kind of drama in stride. Now, if you'll excuse me, I'm going home."

She offered him her hand. "It was nice meeting you, Jonas. Take care of yourself."

Jonas took her hand in his, but he didn't shake it. He bent his head instead and planted a kiss on the top of it. He looked into her eyes. "The pleasure was all mine."

Then he let go of her and walked in the opposite direction. She assumed he was heading to one of the town's hotels where he would check out, get into his rental car and return to Atlanta where he'd get on the next plane to California.

She felt strangely remorseful at the sight of his retreating back.

She was used to goodbyes, though, and soon turned away to head home.

Jonas liked Warm Springs, Georgia. It was a picturesque small town with many things to recommend it. It was a town conducive to walking. The citizens took pride in their homes and businesses. He could see that in how clean and well kept the streets were. The folks he passed eyed him with curiosity. Some greeted him warmly. And there was a nice mix of races. All getting along amiably, it seemed.

What's more, the rolling hills, covered with nature's greenery, was soothing to his soul. He felt at home here.

Plus, if he were being completely honest with himself, he didn't want to leave Sunny Adams. If he could have come up with any excuse whatsoever to stay, he would have. But there had been none.

For a moment, when they'd been looking into each other's eyes, he thought she was going to ask him to stay. He'd hoped she would. Willed it, to no avail. Sunny Adams was not the type of woman to reveal her vulnerable side to a man she'd only known a couple of hours.

He couldn't believe he'd just met her. He felt as if he'd known her for a very long time, as if she'd always been a part of his life. Wishful thinking on his part, he knew.

But it felt so good!

He was nearly back to his hotel when his cell phone rang.

"Jonas, I'm so stupid. I asked Sunny to phone me tonight, but I didn't give her my phone number. Would you be a dear and give it to her for me?"

"Audra, I'm glad you phoned. Sunny told me that you two had worked everything out. She can't come to Beverly Hills because she's working on a murder case, but she's aware of the Deana Davis situation and will handle whatever comes up. Is that right?"

"Yeah," Audra said. "But did she tell you whom she's defending?"

"No, she didn't."

"A woman accused of killing her rapper husband, Eddie Bradley. Have you heard of him?"

"I have a few of his CDs," Jonas said. "He's hard-core."

"*Was* hard-core. He's dead. I was wondering if you think Sunny might be in any danger investigating his death? Rumor has it that his manager's some kind of thug. And kids who buy Bradley's CDs are chiming in all over the Internet, saying nobody killed Eddie but the manager, a guy named Chaz Palmer. I was worried after I got off the phone with Sunny and went and did a Google search on Eddie Bradley. Word of mouth says that Eddie was getting ready to fire Palmer."

"You can't believe everything you read on the Internet," Jonas said.

"I know, but now that I can actively worry about her instead of worrying about her from afar, I'm exercising my rights as a mother. I want to hire somebody to watch her back as long as she's working on this case."

A light at the end of the tunnel.

It was as good an excuse as he would ever get to stick around.

"Don't worry, Audra. I'll keep an eye on her for you."

Audra gave a great sigh of relief. "Oh, Jonas, would you? I wasn't going to ask because you're on vacation and I've already taken up some of your downtime."

"I wouldn't have offered if I didn't want to do it," Jonas assured her.

"Well, thank you," Audra said, gratefully. "Be careful."

"You know I can take care of myself, Audra. Bye for now."

"Bye."

Jonas was smiling as he closed the cell phone. He glanced behind him. He could go to Sunny's house now and deliver Audra's message. However, he had something else in mind.

In Beverly Hills, Audra was sitting on the side of her mother's bed. Vernette was propped up on pillows waiting for the rundown. "Did he bite?" she asked anxiously.

"Like a big ole catfish on my hook!" Audra told her.

"We are so bad," said Vernette.

"Momma, you should have heard Jonas's voice. He was relieved to have a reason to stay in Warm Springs. That boy is smitten."

"It would be nice, wouldn't it?" Vernette said with a wistful expression in her eyes. "Jonas deserves some happiness. And Sunny definitely does. Let's pray."

The two women held hands and Vernette said a short prayer. After which Audra rose, kissed her mother on the forehead and said, "I'll let you get a bit more sleep."

The doorbell rang.

Audra glanced at the clock on her mother's nightstand. "Who could that be at eight o'clock in the morning?"

Vernette went to rise, but Audra gestured for her to remain in bed. "You rest, Momma. It's probably Jonathan again, come to give it one last try."

"If it is, tell him the Beverly Hills Police doesn't take stalking lightly," Vernette advised.

"Believe me," Audra said, leaving the room, "he will get the message this time."

She hurried downstairs and peeked through the peephole in the heavy, intricately carved mahogany door. Her ex-husband, Norman Blake, stood on the other side.

She opened the door and swung it wide. "Well, if this isn't a surprise, albeit an unpleasant one. What do you want?"

Even at eight in the morning, Norman was fully dressed in

a dark blue tailored suit and a crisp white shirt. His handmade shoes shined. Audra looked down for old times' sake. Yes, she could still see her reflection in them.

"Can't you be civil?" he said in his cultured British accented voice.

"I can, but I choose not to be," Audra said, smiling at him. "Once again, what are you doing here?"

"I'm looking for my son. He has something that belongs to me."

"You mean the Alfa Romeo," Audra surmised.

"Precisely," Norman said.

"What? You're going to take it out for a spin on the freeway in Saturday morning traffic? You must be insane."

Norman laughed in spite of himself. "I do miss your sense of humor. My other two ex-wives didn't have much of one."

"What do you mean, your other two ex-wives?" Audra asked, her curiosity piqued. "You've done away with number four already?"

"Sadly, we are in the process of divorcing," Norman said.

Audra couldn't help laughing.

"This is no laughing matter," Norman said indignantly.

Audra was laughing so hard, she was crying. "Norman, has it occurred to you that your son avoids marriage because he doesn't want to end up a royal screw-up like his father? You are a prime example of what *not* to do! When are you going to admit that you're simply not the marrying kind? The only reason you and I lasted for ten years was because I didn't give a damn if you ignored me. I had my own life to live. But I'm going to tell you, Norman, most women won't take that treatment. I think you should have learned your lesson after three failed marriages."

Norman shocked her by sobbing.

Audra went and pulled him into her arms. She realized then that he'd come to her because he knew she would comfort him.

Chapter 6

When Sunny got back home, Caesar had left her a gift at the front door: a dead mouse.

The predator was nowhere in sight. Perhaps he was out stalking his next victim.

By the time she had buried his kill, deep to prevent his digging it up again, she really did need to take something for a headache and lie down.

This had been some weekend so far!

To her surprise, she fell asleep and slept until late afternoon.

Rising, she still felt groggy. Too much sleep did that to her. What she needed was a quick shower.

As she was lathering up in the shower, it all came rushing back to her. It was funny how sleep helped you to forget your troubles, at least momentarily.

Fully awake again, she had to face the facts that Audra Kane was her mother and the man who'd hired her fresh out of law school could possibly be her father. She knew that taking a nap in the daytime, something she never did, had been a way to avoid deciding what she wanted to do about Thomas Trent Chapman. Phone him and say, "Hey, Tom, did you do the horizontal mambo with Audra Kane twenty-nine years ago? Because if you did, I could very well be the issue of your loins."

That ought to give him a heart attack or a stroke, or both. No. When, or if, she told him, she would do so face-to-face.

She was drying off when Caesar sauntered into the bedroom. She almost regretted installing the pet door in the kitchen door. There was no telling what he would drag home from one of his hunts. She was grateful he'd never come home with a snake or a severed human hand.

"You came home when you got hungry, huh?" she said. "Thanks for the mouse, by the way. I can see you're doing your part to keep the house rodent free. I'll rethink my threat to get a dog."

Caesar meowed and turned to run downstairs to the kitchen. He knew she would follow him and, like his dutiful human slave, prepare him a fresh bowl of food and water.

Sunny hummed as she smoothed lotion all over her body and put on underwear.

She slipped into a pair of plaid men's pajama bottoms and a white midriff top with spaghetti straps.

Running downstairs barefoot, she went straight to the kitchen to feed her hungry cat after which she intended to feed her own growling belly. She'd slept through lunch and it was nearly 7:00 p.m.

Caesar was sitting next to his food dish. He looked up at her when she entered the kitchen. "Did I keep you waiting, Your Majesty?" Sunny said.

He looked away as if she bored him.

Sunny laughed and walked over to the pantry, chose a can of salmon-flavored cat food and opened it with the handheld opener she used exclusively for Caesar.

Caesar forgot he was ignoring her when she put the food in his dish, and rubbed up against her leg in gratitude before devouring his dinner.

Sunny left him to it and went to open the freezer to peer inside. She had a theory that if she stood with the freezer door open long enough, something would jump out of it and cook itself.

She was admittedly a lazy cook. She ate out more than in, and if she could manage it she would invite herself to dinner at her friends' houses in Atlanta every weeknight to avoid cooking when she got home from work.

She supposed if she had someone else to cook for she might show more enthusiasm for the task. As it was, she hated cooking for one. She needed to change her attitude, though, because if the past twenty-seven years, soon to be twenty-eight on the seventeenth of September, were any indication, she might be cooking for one for a very long time. What if she never found a man she could live with?

Most of her girlfriends were single and most of them were older than she was.

Katherine "Kit" Larsen, her best friend, was thirty-eight and she'd never married. She had been too busy taking care of an ill mother the first twenty-five years of her life.

Then, after her mother died and she'd been left a bit of money, she decided to go to college. After college, she went to law school. She was thirty-four by the time she'd earned her law degree.

She was standing there in front of the freezer with her face growing cold when it occurred to her that she hadn't phoned Kit yet. Stomach still growling, she closed the freezer door and went to sit at the breakfast nook where a phone sat on the counter.

The phone rang and rang at Kit's house in Newport News, Virginia. Unlike her, Kit had a love life. She was probably out on a date with one of her many boyfriends. Kit believed in spreading the love around. She was a beautiful, full-size woman with a zest for living. She had a lot of love to spread around.

Sighing, Sunny listened as the answering machine finally kicked in.

She waited while Kit's voice finished saying, "Hey, you know who you called. If you don't recognize my voice, you've got the wrong number. If you have the right number, leave me a message. Otherwise I'm going to think your call was unimportant."

"Kit, it's been a mind-blowing day. I heard from my birth mother of all people! Hit me back when you get in, no matter what time it is."

She hung up. She chose not to dial Kit's cell phone number. She didn't want to interrupt her if she were indeed on a date.

Rising, she went back to look in the freezer.

Her hand was on the door's handle when the doorbell rang. Glad for the diversion, she hurried through the house to the front door, her footfalls clearly audible on the hardwood floor. The house, which was built at least a hundred years ago, sat about three feet off the ground on concrete piers. Sunny had learned that when she'd moved in and the man who'd done some renovations had found a family of possums living in the crawl space underneath it. Because the house sat so far off the ground her footfalls had a hollow sound on the wood floors.

When she'd lived in the house as a little girl, she remembered liking the sound of her footfalls on the floor but she hadn't known the reason why her weight on the floor made a sound whenever she walked on it.

She looked through the peephole.

She'd forgotten it was growing dark out. A tall figure stood back from the door.

She couldn't see the person's face so she switched on the porch light.

Jonas. Her heartbeat immediately picked up its pace.

Her hand went to unlock the door, then she let it fall to her side.

What was he doing here? Nervous, suddenly, she looked down at her pajama bottoms and midriff top. She wasn't wearing a bra.

"Just a minute!" she called, turning and hurrying upstairs to get her bathrobe, or something else to cover herself with. She didn't have those pert breasts that weren't discernible under a blouse. Hers were heavy and you definitely knew mammary glands were in the vicinity when she wasn't wearing a bra. They weren't easily hidden under clothing.

A couple of minutes later, she opened the door. She'd hurried into a bra and changed into a more modest blouse.

"Jonas," she said a bit breathlessly. "I thought you were on your way home."

Jonas was freshly showered, too. He was wearing navy-blue cotton linen slacks, a sky-blue polo shirt and brown leather loafers. He smelled divine. She could stand there in the doorway, all night, and breathe in the masculine sandalwood scent of him.

She suppressed a contented sigh.

"Change of plans," Jonas told her as he stepped across the threshold, handing her a bouquet of pink roses as he did so. Backing up, Sunny looked curiously at the roses.

Jonas smiled at her. "They're roses, genus *Rosa*. They have prickly stems so watch out for them."

Sunny smiled up at him. "I know what roses are. I just don't know why you're giving them to me."

Clutching the cellophane-wrapped roses to her chest, she closed the door with her free hand and turned to get his explanation as to why he was there.

"Because it's customary for a man to bring a woman flowers when he's taking her on a date."

Sunny inhaled the heady scent of the roses. "You're purposely talking in riddles. You know—after only knowing me a few hours—that I don't like that!"

Jonas smiled. His beautiful brown eyes held an amused light in them. "Audra told me that you promised to phone her this evening. But she forgot to give you the number. I'm delivering it. After which, I wanted to take you to dinner."

It had slipped Sunny's mind that she had not gotten her mother's number. Too much information in one afternoon, and her brain was bound to block out something.

"That's true, I didn't get her number. Hold on, I'll go put these in water. Sit down. The living room's right through there." She pointed left of the foyer.

"I'll go with you," Jonas said. "There's more."

He followed her to the big kitchen. Caesar had gulped down his food and was licking his whiskers clean. He looked up at Jonas, found him uninteresting, and lazily strolled out of the room.

While Sunny got the vase from the cabinet above the refrigerator, he watched her every movement. How she went up on her toes and stretched that long, lithe, gorgeous body to grab hold of the vase.

Her round, full buttocks undulated beneath the thin cloth of the men's pajamas she wore, and when she stood at the sink running water into the vase, he couldn't help noticing the enticing outline of her breasts pushing against the fabric of her blouse.

"Audra was concerned that you're defending the wife of a very popular rapper," he said as he walked over to the sink and stood beside her, his back to the sink so that he could see her face. "She believes the manager, whom she says the rapper's fans have pegged as the killer, may be dangerous. She wants me to stay close to you until after the trial."

Sunny set the vase with the roses in it beside the sink and looked into his eyes. She saw that he was entirely serious. "That's ridiculous, Jonas. The trial isn't going to begin for nearly three months and there's no telling how long we'll be in court. I can see you're not aware that justice is rather slow. You can't put your life on hold for months. Audra had no right to ask you to do that."

"She didn't ask me, I volunteered," he told her. "I've just

completed a project in South Africa. I've been invited to go to Haiti but I'm still giving it some thought. I prefer to stay here until we're certain that you'll be safe."

Sunny was having a difficult time maintaining righteous indignation when her libido was sending warning signals. Earlier today she had known she was physically attracted to him, so it had been a relief when she'd thought that he was on his way back to California and she no longer ran the risk of embarrassing herself. Now that he was back, looking and smelling so fine, she couldn't control her body's strong reaction to his. Her nipples were growing hard as a result of his nearness. And the rest of her body was flowering, too. Her nostrils were flared. The better to breathe him in.

And, Lord help her, even her vagina was growing moist in expectation of…

"Your staying with me, guarding me, is not reasonable," she cried as she picked up the vase, made a big show of wiping the water from around its base with paper towels, then turned and walked into the adjacent dining room.

Jonas followed.

Walking a bit behind her, he once again observed the sensual movement of her hips. He marveled at how gracefully she carried herself. "Why is it so unreasonable?" he asked after she'd set the vase in the center of the dining room table.

Sunny faced him. "Because I'm a red-blooded girl and having you near is going to mess with my equilibrium, that's why!"

Jonas couldn't believe his ears. His prayers had been answered. She wanted him as much as he wanted her. He closed the space between them in a couple steps.

Sunny refused to run from him. She stood her ground. And there wasn't much ground to stand on because he'd come so close that their bodies were a mere inch apart. The heat of his body made her own tingle with pleasure.

Jonas bent his head. "I thought I was in this alone." His

clean, fresh breath assailed her nostrils. She took a deep breath and went up on her toes. Jonas captured her mouth in a soul-deep kiss. Soft, firm lips moved gently, at first, across hers. Sunny felt herself falling, floating, as if in a kind of sexual delirium. He pulled her closer and enveloped her in his arms. The kiss deepened and Sunny knew that this was past being a mere kiss, it was the beginning of a seduction. The thought frightened her. What was even more frightening was the fact that she had no intention of stopping it.

If she and Jonas made love right there in her dining room she was not going to regret it.

They had to come up for air eventually. When they did, Jonas whispered, "You taste so sweet." He smoothed a lock of curly hair from her face and smiled regretfully at her. "But you're right. This isn't going to work if we can't resist each other. From now on I'll keep my hands to myself. I promise."

Sunny's body had not stopped tingling. She couldn't bear to meet his intense gaze without wanting to kiss him again.

She turned her back on him. Speaking with as much authority as she could summon, she said, "I want you to leave. Go back to California. I'm fully capable of looking after myself. Tell Audra she'll just have to trust that. No, I'll tell her when I phone her tonight." Turning back around, she added, "Give me her number, and then you have to go."

Jonas didn't see any point in arguing with her. He calmly removed his wallet from his back pants pocket and brought out the business card that he'd earlier written Audra's cell phone number on. The rest of the contact information on the card belonged to him.

Sunny gratefully took it. Looking him in the eyes, she said, "Thank you for wanting to look after me, Jonas. But I've been looking after myself a long time and it's a hard habit to break."

She walked him to the door and held it open.

Jonas left without another word.

* * *

On Monday afternoon Sunny went back to the county jail to speak with Kaya again. This time when the same guard, who introduced himself simply as James, brought her client to the briefing room, Kaya looked wan and drawn. There were bruises on the left side of her face and her right eye was nearly swollen shut.

Sunny immediately began interrogating James. "What happened to her? Did somebody attack her?"

James shook his head sadly. "A couple of women jumped her in the shower. She's been moved to solitary, but she can't stay in there for much longer."

"I'll see about that," Sunny said. She would talk to the administrator before she left and if the jail personnel couldn't manage to keep Kaya safe, she would get a court order to have her moved to another facility. The women's prison upstate might be safer because they were set up to accommodate prisoners who weren't safe in the general population. The county jail wasn't designed to hold prisoners on a long-term basis.

Kaya had weeks more to spend in jail before her trial.

"See what you can do," James said as he left the two women alone in the room.

Kaya was smiling at Sunny. "You remember when you beat up Terry Young for hitting me in the face?"

Sunny smiled, too. "He had it coming. He was two grades ahead of us, the bully."

She went into her briefcase and withdrew photos of Kaya's son, Navarre. That morning, she had gone to Kaya's parents' home and introduced herself, telling them she would be representing Kaya from now on. Then she'd asked them if it was okay if she took a few photos of them and Navarre to give to Kaya when she went to see her in the afternoon.

Seeing what they were, Kaya grabbed the photos like a starving person might a plate of food. She devoured the images of her son and parents. Tears sprang to her eyes and she hastily brushed them away because they were preventing her from clearly seeing her son's sweet face.

"He's so beautiful," she said over and over again. "Thank you, Sunny."

She thanked Sunny so many times that Sunny had to stop her. "It was my pleasure. They're yours to keep." Sunny went on with the session as though the woman across from her were not still enraptured with the photos of her four-year-old. "I was able to keep your court date, which is good on one hand, and not so good on the other. It means I'll have less time to prepare your case."

Kaya drew her gaze away from the photos. "Chaz came to see me."

"What for?"

"He said he wanted me to know that he didn't think I killed Eddie. He said there were a lot of people who either hated or were envious of Eddie. He mentioned all of the women that Eddie had used and tossed aside. He told me to tell you that if there's anything he can do to help my case, he's willing to do it."

"How kind of him," Sunny said mildly, hoping to elicit a reaction from her client.

It wasn't long in coming.

"That bastard killed Eddie!" Kaya cried. "You had to be here, Sunny. The whole time he was spouting platitudes and telling me how much he was on my side, he had this evasive look in his eyes. I don't really want to believe he would kill Eddie for money, but three months behind bars has taught me that things aren't always what they appear to be. What if he did it and he's letting me take the fall!"

"Apparently, many of Eddie's fans believe he did it, too," Sunny told her. "Did Eddie ever mention firing Chaz?"

"He said it so often, it was a running joke," Kaya said. "But Eddie wouldn't have fired him. He loved Chaz."

"There's a thin line between love and hate," Sunny said. "Especially when there's loads of money involved. I need to see the contract between Eddie and Chaz. Do you know where Eddie kept his important papers?"

"A safe in the wall in our bedroom closet," Kaya said. "The police didn't even ask."

"Here, write down the combination for me, along with the list of those names you were supposed to get for me." She passed her legal pad to Kaya. "Did you keep a spare key somewhere outside the house in case you got locked out?"

Kaya was busy writing. "Yeah, it's under a garden gnome in the front yard."

Sunny rose. "I think I'll go do that now before nightfall. That is, after I speak to the administrator about keeping you in solitary."

Kaya grasped Sunny's hand. "Be careful, Sunny. Chaz has been in and out of jail for battery. He likes hitting women with his fists."

Less than an hour later, after a brief talk with the jail's chief administrator, Sunny was getting out of her car in a swanky Atlanta neighborhood of brick two- and three-story homes.

It didn't take her long to find the gnome Kaya had mentioned. It was painted with bright primary colors, wore a pointed hat and carried a mug of ale in its right hand.

It was sinfully ugly.

Once in the house, Sunny locked the door behind her. She was relieved there was no alarm system. It was a gated community with a guard on duty 24-7. Perhaps Eddie and Kaya hadn't seen the need for further security.

Besides, from what she'd read in the police report, Eddie had been a serious gun collector. The gun that had killed him had been registered to him. On the table in the room in which he'd been killed there had been gun-cleaning supplies.

It wasn't unreasonable to believe that Eddie had been cleaning his gun and in a fit of depression had turned the gun on himself. That's what Kaya believed, Sunny was sure.

However, Sunny had another theory. What if Eddie had indeed been cleaning his gun and someone had come into the house, they'd argued, and that someone had pulled the trigger, then put the gun in Eddie's hand?

Kaya, who said Eddie was dead with the gun in his hand when she entered the room, had gone to Eddie, pulled him into her arms and, not thinking, had picked up the gun and tossed it away from his body. Sunny could believe Kaya could've been distraught enough to do that.

Sunny went into the entertainment room where Eddie's body had been found.

Someone had cleaned the carpet. There were no telltale signs that a murder had taken place in there. Gone was the blood, the chalk outline of the body and the crime-scene tape.

The room had every conceivable piece of electronic equipment in it, not one but two large-screen TVs, one on each end of the room. They were flat-screen and the center of attention amongst expensive seating groups. Eddie probably loved to entertain in this room. He and the fellas swigging beer and wine and partaking of a toke or two.

Catching the game with his pal, Chaz. A man he'd loved so much he had given him the key to his home.

Sunny left the room, thinking how sad it all was. Eddie Bradley had apparently made a splash in the hip-hop world. He had loyal fans who were clogging up the blog spots online, theorizing about his murder. They sincerely wanted whoever had killed him to be brought to justice.

But could she put a grain of salt in their theory that Chaz Palmer was the culprit?

No, she had to get evidence.

Which led her to the stairs, and up them, to the master suite.

Like the rest of the house, the master suite was beautifully and tastefully furnished.

French Provincial-inspired pieces in cherrywood. A huge canopied bed, and off-white carpeting so thick Sunny's feet sank an inch when she walked on it. Successful rappers certainly raked in the bucks.

She went directly to the closet—well, one of the closets— and began looking for the safe Kaya had mentioned.

There was no safe in the first closet. It must have been Kaya's because it was filled with women's apparel. She hit the jackpot in the other closet. Hidden behind Eddie's fur coats was a steel-reinforced sixteen-by-sixteen-inch safe.

Chapter 7

Pay dirt!

Dunk, so named because of his talent for the basketball maneuver, nearly fell out of his chair when he saw the tall, shapely woman going into Eddie's house. He lowered the binoculars and scratched his itchy testicles.

He let his hand stay in his pants as he tried to decide what his next move should be.

His marijuana-hazed mind moved in slow motion. Chaz had told him that if anyone went into Eddie's empty house, that he should alert him. Alert him. Oh, yeah. That meant Chaz wanted to be told about it right away.

Dunk had been glad to do Chaz Palmer a favor. He was eighteen and an aspiring rapper himself. His dad told him that if he didn't get off his butt and get a job, it was the army for him. Dunk had flunked out of high school. He was the dummy of the family. Both his parents were physicians. His older brother was a systems analyst for NASA. His older sister was the personal assistant to the governor of the great state of Georgia. His parents never got tired of singing his siblings' praises. It made Dunk sick to his stomach.

One day he was going to outshine both of his siblings. Rappers made more money than God. His dad always told him he needed to apply himself. Dunk was going to show the old man.

He dug into the side of the chair for the cell phone his dad was threatening to take.

He'd already put Chaz's number on speed dial. He pressed the number one key.

Chaz answered right away. "Whatcha got?"

"A strange woman just went into Eddie's house, man." Dunk couldn't disguise the fact that he was high. He had to concentrate on clearly enunciating each word.

"I'll be right there," Chaz said, and promptly hung up.

Looking at the phone, Dunk exclaimed, "Damn, man, you coulda said thanks."

Only six blocks away, Chaz grunted as he lifted his great bulk from his chair in his home office. He was six-six and three hundred and twenty-five pounds. Even though getting up was sometimes a struggle, he was in good shape for a guy his size.

He moved pretty quickly, which was evident now as he hurried through the house to the kitchen and then through the garage door. He didn't have time to walk the six blocks. He would have to take the Hummer.

Seven years ago, when he and Eddie had both bought houses in a new housing development, Chaz's house smaller, due to his smaller income, and Eddie's more ostentatious because he was earning big bucks even then, Chaz had never thought of their close proximity as being an advantage. Now he was glad they lived so close.

They'd even exchanged keys so that whenever one of them was out of town the other could keep an eye on his house. Chaz kept the key on his key ring at all times.

Quickly backing the Hummer out of the garage, Chaz cursed. Some kid was skateboarding in his driveway. He had to brake. He blew the horn. The kid gave him the finger and hurriedly skateboarded down the sidewalk.

"You'd better get out of here, you little creep!" Chaz yelled at the kid who looked like he was around fourteen. Bums, Chaz thought irritably. Skipping school. His momma would never have let him miss a day of school unless he was on his deathbed.

He glanced at the clock on the dashboard. It was after three. School was out. The kid had probably not skipped school. Chaz was still angry at him for hindering his exit from the garage.

On the street now, he pointed the Hummer in the direction of Montgomery Lane where Eddie's house was located.

Sunny was in lawyer heaven. In her hands was positive proof that Chaz Palmer had a motive for murdering Eddie Bradley.

Once she'd found the contract in the safe, she had closed the safe and moved the fur coats back in front of it. She wanted to make sure that she put everything back the way she'd found it.

She started reading the contract standing right there in the closet. Like most contracts there was a lot of legalese in it, however she was versed in legalese so it didn't prevent her from understanding it.

In essence, it was very much like a prenuptial agreement. The longer Chaz Palmer remained in Eddie Bradley's employ, the bigger his severance package would be when he was either fired or decided to leave of his own accord.

The contract had been executed nearly ten years ago. In fact, if Chaz had remained in Eddie's employ for a decade, he would have gotten a million dollars in his severance package. Unfortunately, Eddie had been killed before the decade was up. Bad for Eddie no matter how you looked at it. But good for Chaz because the contract stated that in the event of Eddie's death, Chaz would inherit the million anyway. It was a gift of good faith from his best friend. At the time Eddie had signed the contract he had considered Chaz to be a part of his family. You always took care of family.

Sunny was still reading when she thought she heard the sound of the door closing downstairs. She had the contract in one hand and the spare house key in the other. She couldn't imagine who was downstairs but she knew one thing: she didn't want anyone to know she was in possession of the contract.

She was wearing a conservative pantsuit. Navy-blue pin-stripe. Double-breasted jacket and pleated slacks. She coolly slipped the contract down the front of her pants and rebuttoned her jacket.

Then she just as coolly headed downstairs.

The man standing at the foot of the stairs was huge. Rather fair-skinned with a shaved head and a goatee, he was wearing a dark blue jogging suit with a white stripe down the pants leg. On his feet were the biggest, whitest pair of Nikes Sunny had ever seen. They had to be a size sixteen, at least.

"Who are you, lady?" His voice belied his size. It was a tenor, not a bass. As light as Smokey Robinson's, although not as sweet. The malice in his dark gaze prevented Sunny from thinking any sweet thoughts about him.

"My name is Sunny Adams, I represent Mrs. Bradley."

He looked relieved. The scowl turned into a smile. "Oh, yeah, Kaya told me about you. I'm Chaz Palmer. I was Eddie's manager."

Sunny, who had stopped walking at the top of the stairs, continued down. "Yes, she mentioned you had visited her."

When she got to the bottom of the stairs, she offered him her hand. He took it in his baseball-mitt-size paw. Sunny had to call upon her inherited acting skills to present a pleasant face when he touched her because all she could think about was that that was probably the same hand that had killed Eddie Bradley.

"Pleased to meet you," he said as he shook her hand.

"Likewise," Sunny said. Her mind raced. She wanted to get out of there as soon as possible, but if she were too hasty in departing Palmer might think he made her nervous.

What reason could she have for being nervous around an innocent man?

So she went into lawyer mode.

Letting go of his hand, she smiled at him and said, "I was going to call on you later in the week but since we're already in the same room, I wonder if I could ask you a few quick questions about the night Mr. Bradley committed suicide."

She saw in his expression that her reference to Eddie's death as a suicide made him relax further. He smiled at her. "Of course, anything I can do to help Kaya."

They began walking toward the open front door. Palmer had left it hanging open when he had come in. "Did Eddie give you any indication that he was depressed the night of the wrap party? Was he easily angered? Did he keep to himself? Did he drink as if he were trying to drown his sorrows? Anything like that?"

"No," Chaz Palmer answered without hesitation. "You have to understand, whenever Eddie was promoting his work he was always 'on.' Which means that he was wearing the Eddie persona. Nothing distracted him from it. He was all business. Now, if we were in a private setting he might have let his feelings through, and I might have noticed something. Something that would have put me on alert as to his state of mind."

"I understand," Sunny told him. She was looking him in the eyes. She noticed that his gaze lowered several times to her body. She hoped he didn't look too closely at her midriff section. He might see that her jacket wasn't fitting as smoothly as it should have been.

"One more question before I go," she said. "The police believe that Kaya is the guilty party. But she told me that *you* believe she's innocent. Are you aware that Eddie cheated on her numerous times and he also knocked her around on occasion? You don't think she could have gotten fed up with him and shot him?"

"Hell, no!" Palmer said, angry with her for suggesting such a scenario. "Kaya loved Eddie. Cheating is a symptom of the world they lived in. She knew he loved her and Navarre. He wasn't going to leave her for another woman. And as for his hitting her, I've never seen it. That's between a husband and a wife. It's no business of mine."

"But you *do* believe he would commit suicide?"

"Not exactly," the big man said. "I think it was an accident. He didn't mean to do it. I read in the paper that he'd been cleaning the gun at the time. He'd been drinking at the party. He could have stupidly forgotten the gun was loaded."

"Do you honestly believe even a drunk person would pull the trigger of a gun when it was pointed at his forehead? Unloaded or loaded? No, either he did it on purpose or someone killed him and put the gun in his hand."

"Lady, you don't sound as if you're the right person to be defending Kaya. You sound like you're *trying* to find her guilty!" Chaz Palmer yelled at her.

"I am the perfect person to defend Kaya," Sunny yelled back at him. "Because I *do* believe she's innocent. Someone else came into this house that night and shot him. Someone close to him. Someone he trusted. I just don't know who it was. Yet!"

With that, she turned and headed for the door. "Thank you for your time."

Chaz Palmer's face was a mass of frowns. He stared after her. Wanted to pull her back here by her thick ponytail. But he controlled his rage. If he let her tirade get the best of him she would suspect that he had an emotional investment in the outcome of Kaya's trial. He had to appear as if he truly believed

Kaya was innocent and when it was resolved, and Kaya was acquitted, as he hoped she would be, everything would fall into place and he'd get his money. Otherwise, Eddie's will could be in probate for years.

He stood there and fumed.

Sunny walked through the front door. She had been able to maintain her composure throughout their conversation, but now her legs felt weak. As soon as she stepped down onto the first step of the portico, a male voice said, "That went rather well."

She nearly collapsed into Jonas's arms.

As it was, he placed his arm about her waist and helped her down the rest of the steps. "Calm down, lawyer-babe. It's only good old Jonas."

Sunny didn't trust herself to speak without cursing him out, and that would bring Chaz Palmer running to see what the matter was.

She let him escort her all the way to her car at the curb. Then she punched him hard on the upper arm and hissed, "What the hell are you doing here?"

"Keeping an eye on you, like I promised Audra."

She wanted to knock that smile off his handsome face. "How long have you been following me?"

"Since this morning when you left Warm Springs for Atlanta."

Sunny looked up and saw Chaz Palmer leaving the Bradley house. "Well, I guess you can follow me to the police station. I have to see Detective Debarry right away."

Jonas opened her car door, and Sunny slid onto the driver's seat. "I'll be right behind you," he told her as he shut the door.

"I'm sure you will be," Sunny said irritably.

To which he smiled.

"He didn't seem very enthusiastic," Jonas said of Detective Debarry as he and Sunny walked to her car about an hour later. It was late afternoon and the August air had cooled somewhat, but it was still sweltering outside. Sunny was overly warm in her business suit, although the fabric was summer weight. Jonas looked cool in his jeans and a white cotton shirt with a mandarin collar. He'd rolled up the long sleeves for comfort.

"Police are rarely enthusiastic at this stage," she told him. "It's mundane to them. But at least he agreed to look into Palmer's whereabouts at the time of Eddie's death. He'll start snooping around in Palmer's life, and Palmer will get nervous and, hopefully, slip up and reveal his true nature."

They were at the car in the parking lot now. Sunny leaned against the white Jeep Cherokee and tilted her head back to grin at him. "What do I have to do to get rid of you?"

"Are you saying you weren't glad to see me?" He actually looked rather smug.

Remembering how nervous she'd been in Chaz Palmer's presence, Sunny wouldn't lie. "Yeah, I was glad to see you. The sheer size of him almost liquefied my bowels."

Jonas wrinkled his nose in distaste. "That's a little graphic for my taste."

"Speaking of your taste," Sunny said. "I was wondering what a man of the world like yourself planned to do to stop Chaz Palmer if he had, indeed, attacked me."

"Get beat up while you ran for help?" Jonas joked.

Sunny narrowed her eyes at him. "That's not funny."

"I could have handled him," Jonas said seriously. "He wasn't that big. Okay, he was huge. I thought I was a big man at six-four and two-twenty, but he made me look like a boy in comparison."

"He would have beaten you to a pulp," was Sunny's opinion.

Jonas leaned in closer. "But that would have given you the perfect excuse to nurse me back to health."

Sunny laughed shortly. "Honey, there wouldn't have been anything left of you to nurse back to health!" With that, she quickly kissed him on the mouth. "Thanks for coming to my rescue, anyway."

Jonas wanted to make the kiss last but he wasn't about to make the mistake of forcing it. She was stubborn to the core, even when it came to her own protection. He wanted to be able to watch over her as long as possible with her permission.

He would do it with or without her knowledge but he preferred not to have to lie to her. "Where are we going next?" he casually asked.

"I'm going back to the office," Sunny told him. "I don't know *where* you're going."

"Are you positive you're not going to confront another thug?"

"My thug-confronting days are over," she assured him. "This time I'm going to confront my daddy. Thomas Trent Chapman is waiting for a briefing on the Bradley case." She glanced at her watch. It read 4:47. "I told him I'd be there by five."

"Can I buy you dinner tonight?" Jonas asked hopefully.

"If you're willing to bring it to my apartment." She went into her shoulder bag and gave him her personal card. It had her home address and home number on it. "I have to work tonight. How about around seven?"

"Seven's fine," Jonas said.

Sunny unlocked her car door and tossed her shoulder bag and briefcase onto the passenger side seat. "Where are you staying?" she asked.

"I haven't decided yet," he replied.

"You can stay with me. I have a guest room."

"Are you sure?" He looked skeptical.

"We're practically family," was her reply.

He didn't feel like her brother and, frankly, it irritated him that she'd say it. But he wasn't going to pass up the opportunity to be as close to her as possible.

"All right, if you insist. I'll bring dinner tonight, and my luggage."

Sunny gave him a disarming smile. "See you later."

Jonas turned away, confused but already anticipating seeing her again.

Thomas Trent Chapman was on the phone with his wife, Lani, when Sunny knocked on his door. Lani was going on and on about an upcoming charity event. Tom couldn't keep up with them all. However, Lani lived for them. Tom tried to feign an interest in her affairs.

"Yes, darling. It sounds wonderful. Friday night, did you say? No, no I won't stay late at the office like I did last Friday night. I'll be on time. I promise. Darling, hold on a moment, there's someone at the door… Come in!" Tom called.

Sunny walked in and, seeing Tom on the phone, quietly closed the door behind her.

Tom gestured for her to have a seat then spoke into the receiver again. "Sunny is here for our meeting, dear. Let me call you back."

Lani agreed and hung up.

Tom hung up the phone and regarded Sunny with a warm smile. He was fifty-three years old and lean. He worked hard and usually skipped lunch so staying slender came naturally to him. He hadn't meant to become a workaholic like his father, but after he'd married Lani her appetites instilled in him the need to succeed in life.

Lani was the only daughter of an Atlanta millionaire. Her parents had spoiled her all her life. Tom thought it was only fitting to give his wife the kind of life she'd become accustomed to. It was around the fifth year of their marriage that Tom came to the realization that their relationship was going to be based on material possessions and not a deep, abiding love. Lani announced that she didn't want to have children.

It came as a shock to Tom because when they were dating they'd talked about having children. Tom wanted four. Lani wanted only two. They'd compromised with three.

When no child materialized after five years of marriage, Tom suggested they both be examined. There might be a physical reason why she had not conceived. Turned out she was on the Pill and had been from day one of their marriage.

"There are enough children in the world," Lani had said. "I don't want to add to the number of neglected children." Lani's parents had apparently neglected her when she was growing up and she believed she'd inherited their selfish tendencies. She confessed that she had prevented any unwanted pregnancies while they were married and begged him not to subject her to the indignity of giving birth. "Mother's figure never returned to its former glory, and I doubt that mine would, either."

Tom had to admit, Lani was still a size six.

He would not divorce her because he loved her. Furthermore, there had never been a divorce among the Chapman clan and he wasn't about to be the one to set the precedent.

Tom felt that Lani's refusal to have children was the universe's way of punishing him for not being a man when Audra Kane had told him she was pregnant with his child.

He hadn't accepted that child, so the universe was making certain that he had none.

He believed he deserved his sentence. However, because he loved children, he found himself donating to children's charities, taking the time to become a Big Brother and speaking at college functions at his alma mater, the University of Georgia. That's how he happened to meet Sunny Adams, who was sitting across from him now.

"How are you, Sunny?"

"I'm doing well, and you?"

"Lani's dragging me to another charity event this Friday. I'm not doing too well," he joked.

Sunny smiled. "Well, wait until you hear this…"

She went on to tell him about her visit with Kaya, the safe

and the contract, and running into Chaz Palmer in the Bradley house.

"He was obviously watching the place," he surmised. "The question is, why?"

"Because he knew there was something in that house that could cook his goose," Sunny said confidently. "I bet he was starting to get comfortable when the police didn't even question him about his contract with Eddie. Kaya told me they didn't ask her anything about it, either."

"You don't think he suspects you took it?" Tom asked worriedly.

"It's probably crossed his mind by now. Why else would I have been in the house? He was looking me over pretty closely."

Tom sighed. "How many times have I told you to let the private investigators that we keep on the payroll do the dangerous digging?"

"I didn't think going into an empty house would prove dangerous," Sunny said in her defense. She leaned forward in her chair. "What are you so upset about? I'm fine."

Tom's face was thunderous. He angrily got out of his chair. Towering over her, he gesticulated wildly as he accused her of being a hothead. "I hate the way you young lawyers think you have to perform stunts in order to impress your boss and make a name for yourselves. You should have left as soon as Palmer came into the house. Instead you antagonized the man! You practically accused him of murder!"

Sunny rose, too. Sitting, she felt too much like a little girl receiving a dressing-down from her...*father*.

"You *know*, don't you?" she cried.

Tom went still. It was as if the anger had evaporated in a split second.

A moment later Sunny saw in his eyes when the calculating part of his brain took over once again.

She wasn't surprised when he said, as calmly as you please, "Know what?"

Sunny wasn't having it. She took off her pump and started pounding on his antique cherrywood desk with it. If he was going to treat her like a child, she was going to behave like one, and have a tantrum.

"I hate lawyers," she yelled. "You're so used to lying it's become your truth! Who am I, Thomas Trent Chapman? Tell me who I am or I'm going to beat the hell out of your beloved desk." She paused long enough to take off the other pump and brandish it in her other hand. Armed with two shoes, now, the sound became like a drumbeat.

"Who am I?"

Tom's secretary, Margaret, burst into the room. Her eyes stretched in horror when she saw Sunny assaulting the desk. "Wh-what's going on? Should I call security, Mr. Chapman?"

"Get out!" Tom shouted at the poor woman.

But Margaret lingered in the doorway with her hand on the doorknob, unsure of what to do. It appeared that both her boss and his favorite associate had gone nuts.

"Don't yell at her," Sunny yelled at Tom. To Margaret, she said, "We're okay, Margaret. We're just having a difference of opinion. Close the door on your way out."

Still puzzled, Margaret said, "Well, okay." She left.

Sunny resumed her musical number on the desktop. "Say it, Tom. I want to hear you say that you already knew who I was when we met."

"All right, all right," Tom cried at last. "Although I couldn't care less about that damn desk. Just be quiet, please, and I'll tell you everything."

Sunny immediately desisted. She dropped her pumps to the floor and wriggled her feet back into them. Eyes on Tom again, she said evenly, "Talk."

Tom collapsed into his chair as if he'd just ran the Boston

Marathon. Exhaustion marred his handsome features. Indeed, he was tired of maintaining the ruse all these years.

He gestured for Sunny to sit back down.

She sat.

"I didn't know who you were when I met you. But the moment I saw you I began to wonder about you. You see, you have a very strong resemblance to the women in my family. They're tall and golden-brown-skinned like you, with meat on their bones. And you've got their hair, too. Thick, black, curly and nearly down your back. I couldn't keep my eyes off you. After meeting you, I questioned one of your instructors at length about you. She gave me your basic story. How she'd heard that you'd grown up in the system. From there it was a matter of checking your records and that was easy enough."

"How'd you manage that? Audra told me…"

"You've met Audra?" His voice squeaked.

"No, I've only spoken to her over the phone. This is all new to me. I learned she was looking for me over the weekend. She sent someone to find me."

Frowning, Tom's sharp mind appeared to be processing data. Or perhaps, Sunny thought, he was remembering Audra and how he'd abandoned her in her time of need.

"Audra told me," she continued, "that she didn't put your name on the birth certificate. How did you find out when I was born and to whom?"

"Audra was naive," Tom said. "She didn't put my name on the birth certificate, true. But she used her real name."

"I thought you were not supposed to have access to records that didn't concern you. And those didn't have your name anywhere on them."

"It was illegal, true, but I had to know. I paid somebody to find out for me."

"Why didn't you come to me once you'd found out?"

"I didn't think I deserved to be a part of your life. I had abandoned Audra. I felt guilty for that. Plus, I know this sounds ridiculous to you, but I had Lani to consider. She didn't want children, and I felt certain that she would behave badly if I came up with a child from a past relationship. She might have made your life a living hell."

"She never wanted children?" Sunny asked, shocked. "We all thought you two had tried to have kids but were incapable of conceiving. We felt sorry for you."

"I appreciate the sympathy," Tom said sadly. His eyes bored into hers. "I wanted children but when Lani never got pregnant I, at first, thought it was God's judgment of me for what I'd done to Audra. Then, Lani told me she'd prevented any pregnancies and I knew I was cursed. Cursed to love a woman who didn't want to bear my children when I'd had a woman many years ago who had loved me and would have borne my children if I had let her."

"Damn," said Sunny. "I have a couple of guilt-ridden idiots for parents."

Tom laughed nervously as he rose. "You mean you forgive us for being guilt-ridden idiots?"

Sunny went to him and hugged him. It was the first time she'd ever done it. She didn't go around hugging her boss. "It's all good, Tom. Last week I didn't have any living relatives, and today I've got a mom and a dad. How can I be angry about that?"

Tom fiercely squeezed her in his arms, grunting with the sheer pleasure of holding his child in his embrace.

When they drew apart, smiling, to look into each other's eyes, Sunny asked, "What about Lani? Do you think she'll accept me?"

"She can like it or lump it," was her father's response. After which he hugged her again.

Chapter 8

Tom wanted Sunny to go home with him that evening so that the two of them could tell Lani the news together. Sunny declined, saying she thought it would be better, and less nerve-racking, if she weren't there when he told Lani. After some lively debate he agreed, and Sunny left the office.

When she got home, Caesar ran to her and writhed adoringly around her ankles.

She wasn't fooled by his display of affection. He was just hungry.

She put her briefcase and shoulder bag on the hall table and picked him up, cuddling him. She needed the affection, even if he didn't.

Carrying him back to the kitchen, she cooed, "Miss me today? I'm sorry I had to rush in here and drop you off before work, but I didn't want to be late. You're a commuting cat, you should be used to it. You didn't sharpen your claws on the sofa to get back at me, did you?"

Caesar, half-asleep and looking so comfortable in her arms, purred. "No, not you. You're a good cat." She would, nonetheless, go check the sofa after giving him his supper. When Caesar had found her two years ago he'd been nearly feral, living on the streets, eating out of garbage cans, yowling at the moon near her back window.

Every morning, as she left her apartment building, he would be waiting on the front stoop. She started having conversations with him. He would be waiting again when she got home from work and would try his best to follow her inside.

After weeks of this, one night when she arrived home late she simply bent down, picked him up and carried him inside with her. He surprised her by actually liking the bath she gave him, unusual for a cat. Whereas, she complained the entire time that she must be nuts to take in a stinky stray cat. She'd never had a pet before.

The next day, Saturday, she found a vet who worked on the weekend and let him examine the gray-furred, green-eyed, slightly battered cat. The veterinarian told her that he was around two years old and was healthy. Then he gave her some well-meaning advice. "Watch him. Cats who've been surviving on the streets tend to be more predatory than your average coddled kitty. He might bite or scratch on occasion, but with patience I think he'll be a good companion."

Since then Sunny had been scratched a few times but hadn't been bitten yet.

She set Caesar on the floor and chattered as she went to the small pantry to get his food. "We're going to have a houseguest for the next few days, so I want you to be on your best behavior. That means no pouncing on him, and no scratching or biting. If you do, I'll have to shut you in the laundry room and you don't like the laundry room."

The laundry room had no windows. Caesar liked to sit on windowsills and look outside. Sunny suspected he was meant to be a country cat. In Warm Springs he was content roaming the grounds and the other yards in the neighborhood. Her neighbors were mostly elderly people who'd been in the neighborhood for years. They welcomed Caesar in their yards because they believed he helped to keep down the rodent and snake populations.

Sunny was just glad her Warm Springs neighbors didn't have conniption fits every time Caesar set foot in their immaculate yards. Unlike Mr. Tanaka, her next-door neighbor in her apartment building. He swore that he had a cat allergy and whenever Caesar strolled past his apartment door his fur would shed enough to give him an allergy attack.

Sunny thought he was just lonely, and arguing with her about Caesar was the highlight of his day. So she indulged him.

After she fed Caesar, Sunny went back to the foyer to collect her briefcase and shoulder bag. She took them with her to her bedroom where she hung the shoulder bag on a hook behind the closet door and put the briefcase on the computer desk in the corner. Her room was sparsely furnished. Only a queen-size bed, a bureau, a dresser with a mirror and a nightstand on each side of the bed. It was the biggest bedroom in the two-bedroom apartment. It had its own bath. There was another bathroom down the hall next to the spare bedroom.

She sat on the bed and removed her three-inch-heeled navy-blue pumps. Wriggling her toes, she felt the muscles in them loosening up. What she wouldn't give for a good foot massage or a full-body massage. A full-body massage administered by Jonas.

She immediately ditched that idea. Letting her lust—yes, lust—for him get the best of her was unwise. Hadn't she been listening when he told her that his work took him all over the world? The man was a rolling stone. Whereas, all she'd ever wished for was a family to call her own. Men like him didn't settle down.

But who would be the wiser if she simply enjoyed him while he was in her neck of the woods? A no-strings-attached kind of agreement between them that would leave both of them physically satisfied and still capable of seeing each other at family functions without being embarrassed?

"Who are you fooling?" she said as she rose and started removing her clothes for a long hot shower. "You don't have that kind of cold-blooded sophistication. So it's best to just keep your hands off him."

She glanced at the clock on the nightstand before going into the adjacent bathroom.

It was 6:35. That shower would have to be shorter than she had anticipated.

Audra didn't know what to do about Norman. After he'd broken down and sobbed in her arms it seemed that she'd somehow become his patron saint. Saint Audra.

He'd spent Saturday night in one of her guest rooms. On Sunday he'd made himself at home and shared both breakfast and lunch with her and her mother. Estrella, who was still mad at him for divorcing Audra, wouldn't deign to eat with him. She stopped short of refusing to be civil to him when she came home from visiting her daughter, Maria. She had weekends off.

When it became apparent to Audra that he planned to stay Sunday night as well, she had pulled him aside and said, "Norman, go home. I know you feel safe here because I'm like an old shoe, comfortable and a good fit. But I will not be your shelter from the storm your life presently is. You have to face Chandelier…"

"Atelier," Norman corrected her.

"You're joking, right?"

"No, it's Atelier," Norman said.

"Her parents named her after an artist's studio?"

"Is that what it means?"

"Yes, it's a workshop or a studio."

"I don't think she knows what it means. She's very proud of it."

"Well, don't tell her what it means until after the divorce."

Norman laughed. "I won't." Then he'd looked into her eyes with such warmth and gratefulness that Audra had felt her heartbeat quicken. "I'll go. I'm sorry to have been so needy. I don't know what came over me."

"Everyone's allowed a breakdown every few years, Norman. Yours was way overdue. I'm glad to have been the one you were with when it happened."

Soon after that, he'd left her house. But here it was Monday, after sundown, and he was calling with, "Audra, would you have dinner with me tonight?"

Audra hadn't eaten yet, so she said, "Sure, where and what time?"

"Atelier's in Bermuda. I'll have *my* chef whip up something nice for you."

"Oh, no, I'm not having dinner with a married man at his home. Pick a restaurant, Norman."

He chose Spago Beverly Hills. "May I at least pick you up?"

"Certainly, if your chauffeur is driving. You and alcohol don't mix."

"You run *one* car into a tree and you're never allowed to live it down!"

"Be that as it may…"

"Uh, oh, Audra's on a roll," he said, knowing he was in for a tongue-lashing.

"Be that as it may," Audra said again, "I'm not getting into a car with you unless you can tell me you've joined AA."

"I haven't joined AA because I don't have a drinking

problem. Two glasses of wine per day does not make a man a drunk."

"You had more than two glasses of wine the night that tree stepped in front of your car," Audra returned saucily.

"I won't drink at all tonight," Norman said. "I'll show you I don't need it."

"Okay then, you can drive."

Norman sighed. "Thank you, Mother Teresa."

Her phone beeped, denoting she had an incoming call. "You're welcome," she hastily said to Norman. "I've got to go. See you at ten?"

"Fine, a late supper it is," said Norman. "Goodbye."

"Bye," Audra said, and pressed the button that enabled her to answer the incoming call. "Hello?"

"Audra, I'm sitting in my car outside of Sunny's apartment building. I'm phoning so you can talk some sense into me. She invited me to stay with her, and I accepted. I thought it would be a good idea then, but now I'm not so sure."

"Jonas, you're there to watch over her. Living with her, you can be nearby at night. I won't be satisfied until the trial is over or they've caught the real killer. Until then, please, stay close to her."

"Audra, you don't understand, I…"

"You have a love jones for her," Audra finished for him. "I get that, Jonas. I can hear it in your voice. But you're a grown man and she's a grown woman…"

"A volatile combination," Jonas inserted.

"What I meant was, you're both mature enough to resist getting involved until this is resolved. Now, get on upstairs and tell her hello for me. I've been trying not to bug the child too much. So, I phone her only once a day."

Jonas, sitting in his rental car, a brown paper takeout bag on the seat next to him, smiled at Audra's comments. Sometimes she didn't know what she was talking about.

But she always said it with conviction.

He knew that if Sunny didn't want him, he most definitely wouldn't force himself on her. But if she consented, he was not about to resist her, either. Therefore Audra's reasoning was unsound.

They *were* adults in every sense of the word. *Consenting* adults.

A middle-aged Japanese man came out of the apartment next to Sunny's just as Jonas was preparing to ring the bell. He held a bag of garbage away from him as if there were something toxic in it.

He eyed Jonas contemptuously.

Jonas could never resist speaking to people who gave him that kind of look. "Good evening," he said pleasantly.

The man's head bobbed up and down like a nervous bird's as he took Jonas in. "Good evenin'," he said in a southern-accented voice. "You're a friend of Miss Adams?"

"Yes, I am," Jonas said. "Jonas Blake, pleased to meet you."

"Hiro Tanaka," the man said, his expression softening. He looked at the garbage. "If you'll excuse me, I need to dispose of this."

"By all means," said Jonas. "Have a nice evening."

"You, as well," said Mr. Tanaka. "Tell Miss Adams the new shampoo she is using on her cat is working. I haven't had an attack for days."

"I'll be sure to tell her," Jonas said.

Mr. Tanaka continued down the hallway.

Jonas rang Sunny's doorbell.

In the apartment Sunny was hurriedly pulling on a pair of well-worn jeans. She'd barely had time to dry off after her shower. Jonas was prompt.

The jeans fastened, she quickly put on a bra and an old University of Georgia T-shirt.

Caesar appeared in the bedroom doorway and meowed.

"I heard the bell," she said. The doorbell agitated Caesar. He didn't like the sound, and he expected her to protect him from all annoyances as any good human owned by a cat should.

"He only rang once," Sunny said, passing Caesar in the hallway. As she was walking, he ran between her legs, almost tripping her. "What's gotten into you? Chill out, or I'll give you one of those cat tranquilizers Mr. Tanaka gave me for you. You don't want to get hooked on drugs and wind up back on the streets, do you?"

Ignoring her, Caesar ran ahead of her. He was sitting by the door when she got to the foyer. Sunny took a deep breath before peering through the peephole.

As soon as she saw it was indeed Jonas, she got that crazy, sick feeling in the pit of her stomach. She opened the door and stood aside for him to enter. "Welcome!"

Jonas stepped inside. "Thank you."

She closed and locked the door behind him and took his suit bag which he'd placed across his arm. He was holding a large overnight bag in one hand and the brown paper takeout bag in the other.

Sunny took the overnight bag as well. She deposited both bags on the hall table.

"We'll come back for those later when I show you to your room."

Holding the takeout bag only now, Jonas held it aloft and said, "I asked someone where I could find the best fried chicken in Atlanta and they directed me to a little soul food place."

"Momma Sook's?" Sunny asked hopefully. The tiny restaurant was a mainstay in Atlanta. The original Momma Sook was no longer living. These days the proprietor was her great-grandson.

"How'd you guess?" Jonas said, grinning.

Sunny took the bag. "That aroma's unmistakable. It's my favorite. This way."

As Jonas followed her through the apartment, he wondered if she'd painted those jeans on. They were hitting every curve of her voluptuous body. He would have followed her to hell. He was getting a hard-on just looking at her.

This wasn't going to work.

In the bright, open kitchen, Sunny placed the bag on the counter and began removing items from it. Jonas had gotten a bucket of chicken, the spicy kind, baked potatoes, green beans and, for dessert, sweet potato pie.

Jonas wasn't half in the kitchen before she went over to him and planted a quick kiss on his mouth. A habit that Jonas was getting used to. "You're a man after my own heart," she joked.

Sunny didn't wait for his reaction. She busied herself by getting plates and glasses from the cabinets and placing them on the kitchen table. She talked as she worked. "While I do this you can wash up if you like. The bathroom's down the hall. The first door on the left. Your bedroom is next to it."

Jonas gladly took the opportunity to leave the room for a while. It would give him time to calm down. "Okay, I'll be right back."

When he left the room, Sunny gave an exaggerated sigh. Safe from his overpowering sensuality. At least for a little while. What was it about him, anyway, that made her libido go haywire? She'd been around handsome men before. Men who were bent on getting her in bed. She resisted them all because not only were they handsome, they *knew* it! Every last one of them had been conceited.

Maybe that's why Jonas turned her on. He was gorgeous but the fact didn't seem to cross his mind. He had an easy manner about him. When he looked you in the eyes when you were talking to him you could see that he was actually hanging on your every word. That was sexy to a woman, a man who listened.

Plus, the fact that he would do Audra such a huge favor by coming down here to see her on her behalf was endearing. It demonstrated his capacity for love and caring.

It also told her that he cared about family, no matter how much of a rolling stone he might be.

She heard the fan come on in the vent in the bathroom. It was too loud. She'd been meaning to have the superintendent take a look at it, but she stayed busy during the day.

Weekends, she hightailed it for Warm Springs.

"Nice place," Jonas said when he returned and sat down across from her at the table.

"It's just someplace to lay my head," Sunny said. "Home is in Warm Springs." She smiled at him. "Would you say the blessing?"

"Thank you, Lord, for this day," Jonas said. "Thanks, also, for this meal and my lovely dinner companion. Amen."

"Amen," Sunny intoned. Their eyes met and held across the table. "That's the first time I've ever been mentioned in a blessing."

"What's wrong with the men of Georgia? If anyone's a gift from God, it's you. They should be thanking Him for you every day."

Sunny laughed shortly. "I can see the next few days are going to be interesting."

She dug into the food, sampling some of everything. But with Jonas sitting across from her, her appetite simply wasn't what it should be. The anxious feeling in the pit of her stomach overwhelmed her hunger.

Jonas ate heartily, though, proclaiming that, "Momma Sook knows her way around a chicken and a sweet potato pie."

"Yeah, it's definitely down-home," Sunny agreed. "Although I think Patty wins for best fried chicken. You'll have to try it before you go back home."

"What do you do on your off days?" Jonas asked. He drank some of his diet cola as he awaited her answer.

"Warm Springs," Sunny told him. "I was awarded the house last year when my adoptive mother's sister passed away. She was supposed to have been keeping it for me until I turned twenty-one but nobody informed me until I was twenty-seven. A lawyer contacted me and told me I owned the house I'd lived in with my adoptive parents from birth to eight. It revived me. Gave me something from my past to hang on to. I thought everything had been lost from that time. I love it there! Several of the neighbors remembered me and my parents. It's funny, though, they don't remember the sister of my adoptive mother. I guess she didn't come around much. Just made sure the house was aired out from time to time, and the yard didn't become a jungle."

Jonas felt bad listening to her rhapsodize about the house when he knew Audra had purchased it for her and had the lawyer give her a bogus history about the house. In fact, the house had been sold to pay off her adoptive parents' debts when they were killed. No aunt had been keeping an eye on it for her until she turned twenty-one.

But it wasn't his place to set her straight. Audra would have to be the one to do that.

"Why aren't you married?" he asked, changing the subject.

"Why aren't you?" Sunny returned, giving him a saucy look.

"I always said that if I ever met someone like Audra, I'd marry her in a split second," Jonas said with a smile.

"You had quite the crush on your stepmother, huh?"

"Not in the sense of being physically attracted to her, no. It was her spirit that I loved. One of my favorite sayings is by a much-overlooked president, Calvin Coolidge. He said, 'Nothing in the world can take the place of persistence and determination.' That defines Audra for me. If not for her example, I might have turned out to be a disaffected youth. Instead, because she was in my life, I got the chance to know someone who had literally come from a very poor background and changed her life. The world I grew up in no longer held any appeal for me. I got as far away from Hollywood as I could and decided that I'd make my life mean something or die trying."

"Have you ever come close to dying in your attempt to

make your life meaningful?" Sunny asked. She wasn't being facetious. She truly wanted to know. Here was a man who'd been born with a silver, no, a platinum spoon in his mouth, and he was spouting altruistic views. She wanted to know if he'd ever really suffered.

"Don't tell Audra," Jonas said, "because she'll kill me if she finds out how close I came to dying one day in Lagos, Nigeria."

He painted a vivid picture for her as they continued their meal.

In a small warehouse twenty-five women worked feverishly packing up various handmade wares they'd fashioned themselves. It was their first shipment to the United States and a placed called Hartford, Connecticut.

Jonas had spent months helping to form an alliance between the Nigerian women and a women's cooperative in Hartford whose aim was to help Nigerian women gain financial independence. Baskets, pottery, handwoven rugs and blankets, scarves of such intricate design and beauty that the American women were in awe of the Nigerian women's craftsmanship.

Jonas had already done his part. He'd set up their business plan. A plan that benefited both the group in Lagos and the group in Hartford. It had the potential to be a completely successful long-term enterprise.

What Jonas hadn't figured on was organized crime. The local crime lord wanted his cut of the action. It was nearing sundown when five men burst through the doors of the warehouse armed with rifles.

The women screamed and, wanting to gain control in a hurry, one of the gunmen fired a few rounds into the ceiling. "Silence!"

The women huddled together in fear, but they managed to stop screaming.

Jonas had been in the office in the back with the group's bookkeeper, going over a computer program that she needed explained to her.

He immediately got up from his chair and told her to stay there and to stay down.

The man who had told the women to be silent was now setting forth his demands.

"Mr. Agbani requires fifty percent of your earnings or he will burn this warehouse to the ground," he said in Yoruba, their native language. He stood looking them over with a leer colored by pure evil and satisfaction at being able to frighten them. "Do I make myself clear? I shall return in exactly thirty days to collect your gift to Mr. Agbani and thirty days after that from now on. If you cooperate all will be well. If you do not, one of you will die each time I come to collect and you do not comply. Do you understand me?"

At that moment Jonas entered the huge work floor with his hands in the air to demonstrate that he was unarmed.

"I don't understand Yoruba," he said to the lead man. "Would you kindly translate what you've said into English or French or German or even Swahili? I speak fairly good Swahili."

Incensed, the man ran up to Jonas rather heedlessly with the intention of knocking him in the head with the butt of the rifle. Jonas's movements, however, were so quick that the man didn't even see the butt of the rifle coming to connect with his own noggin as Jonas disarmed him, gave him a good lick on the side of the head and held the dazed man by the throat with the stock of the recently liberated rifle.

"Put down your guns, or I'll kill him," Jonas threatened the other four men who were standing with their rifles pointed at him and his hostage.

One of the women translated what Jonas had said for those who didn't understand English. The men, then, one by one laid down their weapons and lay facedown on the warehouse floor.

The women promptly tied them up and phoned the police.

"That was quite the James Bond move," Sunny said now. "What happened to the women and their business?"

"Here," Jonas said, "is the difference between being a do-gooder as I was being that day and someone who truly understands the customs of a country he is a stranger in. When the police got there, they immediately let the men go. Lucky for me, the one I'd disarmed was the son of this Agbani character. Otherwise the other four men would have cut down me and the man I held by the neck. The local authorities actually cooperated with the shakedown artists in the area. They negotiated an agreement between the women and Agbani. The women got off with paying twenty-five percent instead of fifty and Agbani never bothered them again."

"That's incredible," Sunny exclaimed. "Where was the justice?"

"Sunny, your justice is not their justice. The women had to survive the best way that they could."

"It would have helped if you'd known the customs before you made like a superhero and almost got your head blown off."

"Exactly," Jonas said, taking a sip of cola. "That's why I don't want you to tell Audra. My actions were foolish. I could have been killed."

Sunny smiled at him. "She really is like your mother, isn't she?"

"To be honest, I never knew my birth mother well. She hustled me off to boarding school as soon as she could. Even before that I was taken care of by a nanny."

"You had a nanny?"

He smiled. "Didn't everybody have nannies when they were children?"

"Seriously. I've never met anyone who had a nanny. Was she British?"

"Yes, a black woman from London. I mimicked her all the time. It drove my mother crazy. She was American. My father is from Britain. He chose the nanny."

"You sound rather generic to me," Sunny said. "No noticeable accent at all. Except American. You sound like someone with no regional accent. On the other hand, I have somewhat of a southern twang."

"Not very pronounced," Jonas said. "It's sexy, sultry. Kinda makes me sweat."

Sunny reached over, picked up a forkful of sweet potato pie and put it in his mouth. "Eat up. You're talking too much."

Jonas chewed and swallowed the pie, his eyes never leaving her face. He licked his lips. "That's sweet. But not as sweet as your kisses."

"Look here," Sunny said. "If this is going to work we have to get a few things straight. You can't look at me the way you're looking at me right now. You can't say things like that to me. And, for God's sake, don't come out of the shower with just a towel around your waist. Put on a bathrobe!"

He was smiling at her.

"You do own a bathrobe?" she asked nervously.

"I don't even own pajamas. I sleep in the nude."

"You're not making this easy for me."

"You invited me to stay without asking anything," he reminded her.

"Yeah, but I didn't know you were a barbarian!"

"Because I sleep in the nude?"

"No, because you keep saying things to incite me to anger."

"Are you angry?"

"Yes. This isn't going to work."

"Aren't you *really* afraid of this working between us a little *too* well?"

"What do you mean?" she asked, becoming increasingly indignant.

"You should see yourself, you're blossoming right before my eyes." He lowered his eyes to her chest. Her nipples had hardened. She was hoping he wouldn't notice.

Meeting her eyes again, he said, "You want me, Sunny. Why don't you face the fact? Then we can learn how to move around each other in such close confinement without turning each other on. If that's humanly possible."

Sunny wanted to throw him on the table and ravish him right then and there.

Instead, she rose, picked up her still-quite-full plate in one hand and began clearing the table with the other. Looking down at Jonas, she said, "Earlier in the evening I thought you were unique because you weren't conceited. I was wrong, because you're both conceited and delusional if you think I would have sex with a man I've just met."

"I don't want to simply have sex with you, Sunny. I want to make love to you. There's a difference. One day, soon, I'll demonstrate the difference to you."

"There's that conceit again."

"That wasn't conceit. That was a promise."

He rose and picked up his empty plate. "I'll wash."

Chapter 9

"I met your neighbor, Hiro Tanaka, tonight," Jonas said as they stood at the sink washing the few dishes they'd used. "He says that new shampoo you're using on your cat is working. He hasn't had an attack in days."

Sunny laughed softly. "I didn't change shampoos, I only said I did to placate him. For some reason he's obsessed with Caesar. I'm the only person on the floor who has a pet and I think he must have a problem with them. Or maybe he's just lonely and complains about Caesar to have someone to talk to. I let it go in one ear and out the other."

"He seems nice enough," Jonas said. "I was surprised to hear that thick southern accent of his."

"Why, because he's Japanese?"

"Well, yeah," Jonas admitted.

"And you're a world traveler?" Sunny ribbed him. "His

family has probably lived in the South for years. Of course he has a southern accent."

They were done with the dishes. Sunny turned off the light over the sink and put the dish towel on the rack inside the cabinet under the sink. "Come on, I'll help you take your things to your room."

"Then you're not going to toss me out on my ear for flirting with you?"

Sunny turned to leave the kitchen. "Don't make me regret this. I agreed to your suggestion because I don't want Audra to worry about me. After knowing her only three days, I can see she's an obsessive-compulsive. Now that I'm in her life, it's her duty to ensure my safety, as much as she can from Beverly Hills."

They were in the foyer now. She grabbed his suit bag and handed him the overnight bag. Looking into his eyes, she said, "Okay, so we're attracted to each other but we both know jumping into bed would be a bad idea. I don't know you from Adam. You don't know me from Eve. And that spiel about, 'I'll tell you anything you want to know,' won't work for me. I've got to gradually learn who you are. I've got trust issues. That's why my door will be locked tonight even though I *believe* you to be a good man like Audra says."

He followed her down the hall. He assumed they were sharing their faults, so he told her, "I've got commitment issues. My old man has been married four times. He's getting ready to divorce number four, and I've always avoided real commitment because of that."

"What a crock!" Sunny said.

She opened the bedroom door and went inside. The room was large with a queen-size bed, a dresser with a mirror, and nightstands on each side of the bed. Similar to the setup of her room. But the occupant had to use the bathroom down the hall.

Jonas stood in the doorway with his overnight bag in his hand. "What do you mean by, 'what a crock'?" he asked.

"That's a perfectly reasonable explanation for my not being married at thirty-six."

Sunny went to the closet and hung up his suit bag. Coming back out, she smiled at him. "Growing up in the system, I met people who'd been abused in lots of ways. One girl I knew when I was seventeen had a mother who pimped her out for drug money. That girl, today, is the mother of three little girls and she's a wonderful mother. She didn't let her own mother's bad behavior affect the kind of mom she is. It's the same thing to me when a man says he's a womanizer because his dad was a womanizer, therefore, he can't help himself. Yes, he can. He can choose to treat women better."

"I agree with you to an extent," Jonas said. "But our parents leave an impression on us whether or not we want them to. They're the first people we imprint ourselves onto. We mimic them. We look up to them. It's impossible to come away from childhood untouched by your parents. I bet that woman you mentioned fights every day to continue to be unlike her mother."

"The bathroom down the hall has fresh towels and washcloths. The linen on the bed is fresh. The thermostat's set at seventy-five. If that's too cold for you, there are blankets in the linen closet in the hall," she told him. To his theory about parents, she said, "Maybe I am being too judgmental. It's another of my faults that you should know about. I didn't have parents to pattern my behavior after. And I shouldn't go around making blanket statements like that. I apologize. Everything that I am, I had to create.

"And since we subconsciously judge others by our own experiences, I tend to believe that we control our own fates. That no matter which direction life pushes us in, we are always free to change course and do something entirely different."

Jonas had dropped his overnight bag onto the bed. He stood now, staring at her.

She was like her mother in more ways than she could ever

imagine. Audra, too, had created herself. Audra could have made that speech she'd just given him. In fact, he could recall a time when Audra had told him that he didn't have to follow in his father's footsteps. He was his own man.

He sensed she wouldn't thank him for pointing out her similarities to Audra, though.

She would have to find out for herself when she met her mother.

"No need to apologize," he said. "I love your passion."

The smoldering look he gave her told her he liked more than her passion for life.

"I'll leave you alone," she hurriedly said. "I have work to do. Good night."

"Good night?" Jonas cried. "It's only eight."

"I know. Sorry, but I need to do some paperwork before I go to bed and I have an early day tomorrow."

He went to her and kissed her cheek, his lips lingering a moment.

Sunny raised her eyes to his as they parted. In his she saw the longing that must have been more than evident in her own. Backing away, she said, "Sleep well."

"You, too."

She closed the door behind her.

Jonas sat on the bed and pulled his overnight bag closer. He dug in it and found his cell phone's charger. Rising, he went and plugged it into the wall socket and then put his phone in the slot. After which he went to the bathroom to take a shower.

It had been a long day. He should sleep like a log. But with Sunny only a few feet away in her own bed he figured he was in for a night of tossing and turning.

When Sunny got to her bedroom, she put on her nightgown, put on her favorite Otis Redding CD and sat in the swivel chair at the computer desk in the corner. Opening her briefcase she pulled a large manila folder from it and opened it. There were three other folders that contained paperwork pertaining to the

Kaya Bradley case, but this particular one held a copy of Eddie's contract with Chaz Palmer. She intended to go over it with a fine-tooth comb. Until her eyes were grainy. Until images of Jonas stopped running through her feverish brain.

Norman was always assured a table at Spago. He had been going there for years.

Why he hadn't remembered that they closed at ten-thirty on weeknights when Audra had suggested ten o'clock escaped him.

"But for you, Miss Kane, Mr. Blake, we will gladly make an exception," said the maître d' when they arrived. He could not help smiling at Audra.

"You will do nothing of the sort," Audra said, returning his smile. "You and the rest of the staff have lives outside of this restaurant. Please ask Chef Heftner to put together a picnic basket for us. We trust his judgment. We'll dine at home."

Norman liked the thought of having her completely to himself. "That's a splendid idea," he said, pressing a generous tip into the palm of the maître d'. "We'll have a—" he glanced at Audra "—mineral water at the bar while our meals are prepared."

"Very well," said the maître d' with one last glance at Audra. "I'll go inform Chef Heftner of your request."

Norman placed his hand on Audra's lower back, directing her toward the elegantly appointed bar.

Spago Beverly Hills was very popular among people in the business, and Norman and Audra could not pass a table without someone calling a greeting.

Audra was sure tongues would be wagging all over town because she and Norman had been seen together. The two of them had done a good job of avoiding each other at social functions since their divorce.

Norman pulled out a chair for her, and once she was seated, he sat down across from her. "You look *beautiful*, Audra."

Audra was wearing an off-the-shoulder sheath in forest-green. It had long sleeves and fitted her body perfectly. Her hair was glossy and combed back in a simple but sophisticated style. She wore a minimum of makeup and jewelry, choosing to wear only one-carat white diamond stud earrings.

Norman wore a dark blue tailored suit and a white silk shirt. She almost stared when she realized he wasn't wearing a tie. In her experience, Norman felt naked without a tie around his disciplined neck. But then, he'd already been naked with her this weekend, telling her his woes, confiding that he didn't want to be alone as it seemed life was conspiring to make him.

"You've already told me I look beautiful twice, Norman," Audra said, smiling at him. "Shall we talk about something else? Like your son and my daughter?"

"I still can't get over the fact that you never told me you had a daughter," Norman said in low tones. He knew that in this town secrets were one of the most valuable commodities. "I thought we were quite open with each other."

"Get over it," Audra said. "I'm sure you didn't tell me everything about yourself when we were married. And I was protecting her, not myself."

"I understand all that," Norman said, reaching across the table to caress her hand. "But if I had known I could have done something."

"Like what?" Audra asked out of curiosity, not derision. The sincere expression on Norman's face told her that he truly believed he could have done something back then.

"I could have helped you get her back," he said. "At least my money would have gone to something other than divorce settlements."

They laughed.

"You know, I like it when you laugh, Norman. We didn't have enough of that when we were together."

"I know," he said regrettably. "I was so intent on proving that I was just as good as anybody else in this town, I didn't take time to enjoy life. I intend to correct that mistake. From now on I'm going to stop and smell the roses."

Audra snorted. "I'll believe it when I see it. I bet you've got one movie in production, two in the can and one waiting in the wings. Am I right?"

"I've got three in the can, one waiting in the wings, but I am not presently working on anything. I finished a movie less than three weeks ago. About the time you wrapped up filming in Morocco."

"You've been keeping tabs on me?"

"I've always kept tabs on you, Audra."

"Because we're divorced?"

"No, because you're the only one of my ex-wives who didn't leave me. I messed up on *you.* It took me exactly three months to start regretting the day I ever thought of cheating on you."

"It took you three months to come out of the sexual haze, huh?"

"Middle-age panic," Norman said. "I was approaching fifty and a twenty-five-year-old made me feel like a sexual god."

"Priapus," said Audra with a smirk on her lips.

"Pria-what?"

"He's the Greco-Roman god of procreation. He is often depicted with an erect you-know-what. The word priapism, which is a persistent and painful erection, was derived from his name."

"You always did read a lot. You're an anomaly in this town, Audra. A smart actor."

"Stop propagating lies," Audra said. "Actors are smart. We know to kiss up to you directors if we want to work."

Norman laughed. "Is that what you're doing tonight, kissing up to me?"

Audra laughed abruptly. "Honey, I've ignored you for the past ten years. What makes you think I can't continue to ignore you? No, I'm here because I want to be here. Besides, the only time we worked together was a disaster and you know it!"

"*Second Chance,*" Norman said. "The only bomb in my body of work."

"Let's not forget that sci-fi flick you did," Audra reminded him.

"You had to bring that up," Norman said. "I'd almost convinced myself somebody else had made that stinker."

"No, darling, it was you. And your Actor's Studio stint was hilarious when a student stood up and said it was her favorite movie. You almost fell off your chair."

"You saw that?"

"I've kept up with you, too," Audra said. "A little. Most of the time I rued the day I ever met you!"

"Ouch! Did you really rue the day you met me? What about the good times we had?"

"You sound like a Motown song," Audra told him, not giving an inch. "Look at it from my point of view. I was still in love with you. I never really expected you to actually love me back, but I did expect you to show me some respect after a decade together. But you were running around with future-ex-wife-number-three as if you were already divorced from me. That hurt, Norman."

"I'm sorry, Audra. All I can say is I'm not led around by my hormones anymore. I did manage to grow up in the intervening years."

"Then why are you divorcing wife number four?"

"To give her the chance to have children with someone younger. I'll be sixty-one on my next birthday. I don't want to be a father again. I told Atelier that, before we married, but apparently she didn't believe it. And since she's only thirty I don't believe I should hold her to our marriage. Let her find someone who'll be a good father to her children."

"I thought you said I was the only one you'd ever left. It sounds like you're leaving her, to me."

"This is what happened—after she told me she wanted to have a child, I reminded her that that wasn't in our prenuptial agreement. I could sue her for breach of contract. When she heard that, she rushed to her lawyer and he told her she had to file against me before I filed against her, otherwise she would lose at least two million in the settlement. Atelier is a practical girl."

"Practical and soon to be very rich," Audra quipped.

Norman smiled. "I can always make more money but I was not going to bring another child into the world. I haven't been the best of fathers."

"Tell me about it!"

"You could offer sympathy instead of turning the knife in my back!"

"*You* stuck the knife in," she lightly accused.

Norman sighed. "I regret not being there for Jonas, but he was always so self-sufficient."

"You taught him that by your neglect," Audra said. "He would have leaned on you more if he'd been assured of a shoulder to lean on."

"That's what I always liked about you, Audra. You don't mince words."

"I don't see any reason to sit here and lie to you, Norman. We both made mistakes as parents. The good thing is, neither of us is dead. We can make up for it."

Norman smiled at her and affectionately squeezed her hand. "Sunny's willingness to forgive you for your actions has certainly turned you into an optimist. What if Jonas isn't as forgiving?"

"Jonas loves you. A sincere apology from you would wipe out all those years of neglect, believe me."

Frowning, Norman peered into her eyes. "How would I go about it?"

"Well, you can't do it over the phone," Audra said. "So you

have a while to give it some thought. He'll be in Georgia until Sunny's murder case is resolved."

Norman's ears pricked up. "Listen to that. It's our song." His eyes shone with excitement. "Dance with me, Audra."

Audra looked around them. "There's no dance floor."

The bar area was nearly empty of other diners. A sole gentleman sat at the bar and a couple sat at a table in the corner. The piped-in music was low and seductive. The tune was Nat King Cole's "Mona Lisa."

"I don't care," said Norman taking her by the hand.

Audra was pulled to her feet by Norman's magnetism as much as his strong hand. They went into each other's arms, and for precious moments everything else ceased to exist except the look in their eyes.

The maître d' came into the bar area while they were dancing and stood watching them with a rapt expression on his face. He had always been a sucker for love.

When the song ended, Audra smiled up at Norman and asked in a soft voice, "What was that all about?"

"Magic," said Norman.

In Atlanta, Sunny, who was having trouble sleeping, got up to get a glass of water.

Caesar, nocturnal by nature, met her in the hallway and followed her to the kitchen, where they found Jonas with his head in the refrigerator, looking for something to eat.

"There's plenty of leftover chicken," Sunny said.

Jonas jerked up so abruptly he hit his head.

Immediately regretful that she'd spoken and startled him, Sunny went to him and gently rubbed his head. They stood close with the light from the refrigerator providing the only illumination in the kitchen, she in a short, see-through nightgown with nothing on underneath except a pair of hip-hugging panties, and he in jeans.

Jonas hadn't sustained any injury from his lick on the head, but having Sunny so near, her warm lush body smelling so wonderful, was making him dizzy with need.

He'd been bending down to grab the bucket of chicken, but now the last thing he wanted to nibble on was chicken. He wanted to nibble on Sunny.

"I'm so sorry," she was saying, and he couldn't concentrate fully because when she breathed on him, as she invariably would this close to him, her warm, sweet breath reminded him of that kiss they'd shared in her house in Warm Springs.

She hadn't really kissed him since then. A quick peck here or there. He was a growing boy and he needed more sustenance.

"Sunny, kiss me." He was still a gentleman and thought asking was worth a try.

Sunny dropped the hand she'd been massaging his head with and tilted her head to the side, staring at him. "Okay." Her voice was barely a whisper.

Jonas groaned softly, bent down and claimed her mouth. Her arms went around his neck and he pulled her more firmly into his embrace. It didn't matter that his back was pressed against the open refrigerator. Their combined sexual heat kept both of them nice and toasty.

Sunny felt like a revelation to him. If he'd ever kissed anyone as delicious tasting, he couldn't recall it. Her taste was intoxicating. Her body was fully feminine and soft. He just wanted to plunge into her and stay awhile.

Somewhere in the back of Sunny's mind she was aware this behavior would bring her nothing but trouble. But, dammit, if he was trouble, so be it!

He whipped her into a wonderfully sensual frenzy. Her female center was throbbing madly and her nipples begged to be sucked. Yet, he only kissed her. His hands did not travel below her waist as he held her to him.

When they came up for air they were both slightly dazed with passion.

"We need to stop," she said.

He nibbled on her bottom lip and claimed her mouth again. She melted into him.

A minute later he raised his head and said, "Okay, let's stop now."

But the sight of her swollen lips, heaving breasts and general aura of blatant sexuality made him kiss her again. He felt like he was nearly bursting out of his jeans when they parted this time, he was so hard.

Sunny backed away from him on shaky legs. "Please move aside," she told him.

Jonas moved away from the refrigerator.

Sunny grabbed a bottle of water and quickly left the kitchen. "Enjoy your chicken," she called as she turned the corner.

Jonas laughed softly. If her kisses were any indication of what sex was going to be like with her, he was truly looking forward to it.

He took the bucket of chicken from the shelf in the refrigerator, closed the door and took it to the table. For now, though, he would have to satisfy his hunger with a piece of Momma Sook's best-in-Atlanta fried chicken.

Ansley Park was three miles from downtown where the offices of Tom Chapman and Associates was located. Tom had driven the distance for ages it seemed. But today, as he drove through lunchtime traffic, he felt trepidation for the first time.

Last night when he'd gotten home, Lani had surprised him by announcing that her cousin Barbara and her husband were going to be dining with them. Lani loved to spring surprise guests on Tom. She called it "keeping life exciting." He called it a pain in the ass. Of all nights!

It took every ounce of his strength to remain civil to her cousin Barbara and her loudmouthed husband, Henry. Barbara was a perfectly lovely woman. Tom felt bad for wishing she'd just go home last night. But he felt no such remorse for wanting to drop-kick Henry back to their Buckhead neighborhood.

The man talked incessantly about finances. He was the type of relative who always wanted to know how much everything in your house cost. And he was sure to say, "You paid that much? We have one just like it and we paid a lot less. Tom, old man, do you know how the rich stay rich? We never pay full price for anything!" Then he would laugh longer and louder than anyone else in the room.

Tom felt like getting his shotgun and putting some .05 buckshot in Henry's hind quarters before the evening fizzled out.

To top it off, Lani went straight to bed afterward saying she had a monstrous headache. Would he be a dear and not read too long in bed tonight? The light hurt her eyes.

This morning, when he got up to start getting ready for work, she was snoring like someone who'd spent hours at hard labor instead of someone who barely lifted a finger all day. He was loath to disturb her.

That's why he was driving home for lunch. He'd phoned her from the office and warned her that he needed to speak with her about something important.

"Darling," she'd said, "I already have a lunch date with Christine."

"Well, cancel it!" he'd bellowed. He rarely raised his voice to her.

"This sounds important."

"I just told you it was."

Then she'd gone into her concerned-wife mode. "Tom, you're not ill, are you?"

"I'm healthy as a horse. It's something else and I'm not discussing it over the phone. I'll be home at twelve-thirty."

"Okay, dear," Lani had finally conceded, her tone worried.

Now, as he turned onto the long driveway that led to the three-story house in Ansley Park, Tom suddenly felt elated. No matter how Lani took the news that Sunny was his daughter, he knew it would bring him a sense of peace. If Lani couldn't accept Sunny he would simply exclude her from his time with Sunny. It wouldn't be the first time a daughter and her father's wife didn't get along. But Lani was not going to stand in the way of a relationship with Sunny.

He parked the Lexus in front of the house and got out. Lani must have been looking out for his car because she had the door open before he could climb the steps.

She was immaculate in a white silk pantsuit and a pair of white sandals. Every summer found her glowing. She had golden-brown skin and caramel-colored eyes. Her hair was light brown with blond streaks. On her the color was believable. Tom was six inches taller than she was and he loved it when she tiptoed to kiss him.

She did that now. Her perfume enveloped him in a sensuous cloud. There was no doubt he loved this woman. The question was, what price love? He'd given up ever having children with her to keep her happy. He'd made so many concessions over the years.

Today there would be none.

Lani closed the door.

Tom had left his suit coat in the car. It was too hot for it anyway. September was proving to be as hot as August.

Lani seemed at a loss. Her eyes darted from him to the hall closet, as if she had to put something in there every time he came home from work. If not his coat, then what?

Tom noticed and thought how limited Lani had made her life. Catering to him. Being the perfect wife. The beautiful social butterfly whose sole purpose was to make him look good. It was that type of devotion that made his tone gentle when he took her by the hand and said, "Come with me, darling."

He led her upstairs to their bedroom. There were two servants in the house, the cook and the live-in housekeeper. They were instructed to never bother them unless there was an extreme emergency when they went into the bedroom and closed the door.

In the bedroom, Tom led Lani over to the seating group near the big picture window.

From the window you could see the park, one of the parks in Ansley Park, anyway.

He gestured for Lani to sit down in one of the plush armchairs. He sat down across from her in a matching chair. Clearing his throat, he began. "Lani, you and I have been together for twenty-five years. We've had our ups and our downs. But we always managed to work through them."

Lani shook her head, her face a mask of concern.

"I have something to confess," Tom continued. "It's about Sunny Adams. I'm…"

Lani burst into tears and threw herself onto his legs, wrapping her arms tightly around them and holding on for dear life. "Tom, don't leave me!" she cried, looking up at him with pleading eyes. "I can change. I'll be more demonstrative. I'll lose weight!"

"Good God, woman, if you lost any more weight you'd disappear," Tom said, laughing.

He got up and pulled her to her feet. "What makes you think I was getting ready to say I was leaving you for Sunny?"

Lani was still crying. "I've seen the way you look at her when you think I'm not noticing. There's real affection in your eyes. You love her. You're proud of her. She's your favorite in the firm. Deny it!" She was regaining a bit of that Lani gumption.

"I'm not going to deny anything," Tom told her passionately. "I do love Sunny."

Lani's face fell. She started sobbing with more force. "I knew it!"

Tom smiled gently. "Because she's my daughter."

Lani's mouth fell open in shock. Then she had trouble drawing a breath. She hit herself in the chest as if she were jump-starting her heart, which had stopped when he'd said Sunny Adams was his daughter.

"What!"

Tom held her by both arms to keep her from toppling. He thought he'd just as well get it all out before she fainted dead away. "More than three years before I married you I was involved with Audra Kane."

"The movie star?"

"Yes."

"You're lying!"

"No, I'm not. Audra is Sunny's mother. She put her up for adoption. She recently contacted her and after they got acquainted, she told Sunny that I'm her father."

Lani's brain was in working order again because she'd put two and two together and came up with, "You've known all along. And you never said anything to me."

Tom nodded. "Yes, I met Sunny several years ago, before she got into law school. It was then that I started looking into her background and I found out that she was my daughter."

"That's why you hired her."

"That's one of the reasons. She's a damn good lawyer."

Lani gave a relieved sigh. She looked up at him. "Well, she comes from a family of lawyers."

Tom was amazed by the change in her. "You're okay with this?"

Lani smiled weakly. "I've regretted not having children for years now, Tom. But what could I do? Come to you and say I was an idiot for putting those stipulations on our marriage? I was past childbearing age by then. I was so selfish. I can see now that our life together would have been much richer if we'd had children. We might have been grandparents by now. Can you ever forgive me?"

Tom pulled her into his arms. "I forgave you years ago. I love you, sweetheart."

Then he kissed her.

Lani clung to him.

Chaz sat at a table in an interrogation room in the Atlanta Police Department waiting for Detective Milton Debarry to return with the coffee he'd gone to get for them. Chaz knew, instinctively, that Debarry hadn't really been dying for a cup of joe. He had left the room to give him time to reflect on what had already transpired in this room.

Debarry had told him that they had found the contract in a safe in Eddie's home. The contract, they said, was proof that he had a reason to want Eddie dead. One million reasons. For over an hour Chaz had coolly denied any reason to kill Eddie. He was going to get his million anyway. All he'd had to do was wait another month or so.

"Not if Eddie was going to fire you before the time limit in the contract was up," said Detective Debarry with a self-satisfied smile. Chaz had wanted to knock his teeth out. And he could have done it with one punch to the mouth. Detective Debarry was a skinny weasel of a man with prominent teeth and bloodshot eyes. Chaz could have beat him until he begged to die. The anger he felt right now was at the boiling point.

It had been nobody but that lawyer bitch who had found the contract. He'd been suspicious of her when he'd caught her in Eddie's house last week. He bet she'd had the contract hidden somewhere on her body while she'd stood there and asked him, "a few quick questions." He had a few quick questions for her, and she wasn't going to like them. Especially since he'd be asking them with his fist.

When Detective Debarry returned to the room, two plastic cups of coffee in his hands, Chaz was ready for him. "Hey, look, dude. Either y'all charge me with a crime or let me go. I know where this is going. You want to pin Eddie's murder on me. Well, unless you've got a witness who saw me enter or leave that house, you can kiss my ass!"

With that he got up and left. Detective Debarry just sat there and sipped from one of the cups of coffee. It was as if he'd expected this very reaction from him.

Chaz didn't give a damn. They didn't have any physical evidence that he was the one who had shot Eddie. If they did, his big butt would have been locked up by now.

Chapter 10

Chaz had calmed down by the time he drove across town to the recording studio where another artist he handled, T-Man, was laying down tracks. The red light over the door of the sound booth was off, denoting no recording was going on. He was greeted exuberantly by everyone in attendance: T-Man, the engineer who handled the technical aspects of the process, and T-Man's girlfriend, Tanya, who was seven months pregnant.

T-Man's name was derived from Tanya's Man, something Chaz had tried to talk him out of. The rap community didn't take kindly to rappers who were whipped by their women. The man had to be in control. So far they'd been able to keep the meaning of his name a secret from the fan base T-Man was growing here in Atlanta.

Chaz thought T-Man showed a great deal of promise. A year or so more performing in and around Atlanta, then he'd think about taking him out on the road. If everything went well after that, who knows, T-Man could blow up and then they'd all be rolling in dough.

T-Man stood up and gave Chaz a perfunctory hug, flashing his many silver teeth.

Chaz made a mental note to talk to him about the teeth. They were so yesterday. These days the rappers who succeeded were also women magnets, and while women who were attracted to thugs liked the gold and silver teeth, most preferred their men with clean, white teeth. Image was everything in this business.

T-Man was still raw material. When Chaz was finished with him, he would be a star.

Just like Eddie, that ungrateful bastard.

Chaz smiled at Tanya, the impact of Eddie's betrayal lessening when he glanced at her swollen stomach. Chaz loved kids. Always had. If he'd ever married he would have had a houseful. "How're you feeling, little momma?" he asked affectionately.

"Ready to pop," Tanya joked. Her gaze rested on T-Man. "But happy."

"Good, good," said Chaz jovially. "That's what I like to hear."

He regarded the engineer. "Terrance, what it sound like?"

"Sounds like a hit," said Terrance, beaming.

"Excellent," said Chaz. Turning to T-Man, he said, "Are you ready for your gig Friday night? Got everything tight?"

"Yeah, man, everything's been flowing like it oughta. I'm cool."

"All right, then," Chaz said, sounding thoroughly satisfied with T-Man's explanation.

"Can I see you outside for a moment, my man?"

"Sure," said T-Man. His Adam's apple moved up and down in his scrawny neck.

Being alone with Chaz made him nervous. Especially when Chaz was in a seemingly good mood. That's when the stuff generally hit the fan. He could swear the big man had a split personality, one part good, the other evil.

As he suspected, Chaz wasn't as pleased with his progress as he'd seemed to be when they were in the sound booth. "Listen, here, *Nestor,* I've got a lot riding on your performance Friday night. There are going to be some heavy hitters there. If you embarrass me, I won't be happy." He grabbed T-Man by the scruff of the neck.

"I've spent months trying to work a deal for you. Don't you let me down."

"I ain't gonna embarrass you, Chaz. I swear, my stuff's tight."

"It better be," Chaz said through clenched teeth.

He let go of T-Man's collar. Patting T-Man on the cheek, he smiled at him. "You're a good kid and, if you work hard, you're going to make it in this business."

T-Man tried to control the quaver in his voice when he said, "Thanks, man."

Chaz turned away. "I've gotta roll now. Go back to work."

It wasn't a suggestion. It was an order. T-Man wasted no time going back into the sound booth.

Chaz left the studio.

When he got behind the wheel of the Hummer his mind was more settled. Intimidating someone did that for him. He no longer wanted to pound the lawyer. He smiled as he started the engine. They had nothing on him. There was no reason for him to worry.

He headed home.

Sunny had been waiting in the outer office of Judge Leah Mayfair's chambers for more than an hour. She was there trying to get Judge Mayfair to rethink her decision not to allow Kaya to get out of jail on bail or, in the event the former wasn't granted, to allow her son, Navarre, to visit her in jail.

She'd had all the paperwork delivered to Judge Mayfair yesterday, Monday. She was here today to learn the judge's decision on the matter.

"You can go in now, Miss Adams," said Judge Mayfair's secretary.

Sunny rose and smoothed the skirt of her cream-colored suit before confidently walking into the judge's chambers.

Judge Mayfair was a tall, stately African-American woman in her early fifties. She had an attractive medium-brown face with dark brown eyes and silver hair that she wore in dreadlocks. She reminded Sunny of the author, Toni Morrison.

"How are you, Sunday?" asked Judge Mayfair, a smile causing crinkles to appear at the corners of her eyes.

"Good, and you?" said Sunny, returning her smile.

"I'm overworked and underpaid, as usual." She got right down to business after the pleasantries. "I see that you've come up with another suspect in Eddie Bradley's murder. I admire your hard work, but that still doesn't mean your client isn't a flight risk. She has a lot of money at her disposal. You can't be certain she won't skip town with her child. Even if she *is* innocent. Any sane person who has spent three months in jail never wants to return. She could panic and flee the country just based on that. So, no, I'm not going to overturn my decision to deny bail. But she *can* see her son. I want that child protected from the environment as much as possible when he goes in there. Jail is no place for a four-year-old."

Sunny made no effort to protest Judge Mayfair's decision. She knew from experience that arguing at this point in the process made the ornery jurist dig her heels in further.

"Thank you," she said.

Judge Mayfair smiled. "You're welcome. Now, get out of here so I can go to lunch."

"Good afternoon, Your Honor," Sunny said in parting.

"Good afternoon, Counselor," said Judge Mayfair.

Sunny hurried out. Her next stop was the county jail.

In the main-floor lobby of the courthouse she picked up her

shadow, Jonas, whom she had left reading an old copy of *Time* while she had gone upstairs to see the judge.

"How'd it go?"

"Her son can visit her."

"That's good, right?" Jonas asked as they walked toward the exit.

Sunny smiled up at him. He'd dressed according to her schedule today, wearing a business suit and dress shoes. The light gray suit and crisp white shirt made him look like any number of businessmen who haunted these hallways. *Any devastatingly handsome businessman,* she tacked on. The man was yummy, no matter what he had on.

She'd almost forgotten what he'd said to her before she started daydreaming. "Yeah, that's good. I didn't really expect to get bail. I was hoping for it, though."

Jonas opened the door for her, letting her precede him. "If the police could find some physical evidence that incriminated Palmer, they'd let her go, right?"

"If it was really good, yes, they'd have to release her. But it would have to be irrefutable proof."

On Wednesday, Dunk sat on Chaz's stoop wishing he had one of his dad's beers in his hand. The old man had started keeping tabs on his beers, and Dunk knew better than to drink them while he was at work.

After today he'd have the money to finance his own beer buzz. What money he had went toward his ganja habit. He had his priorities. He looked down at the crumpled newspaper in his hand and smiled. He had never paid much attention to the paper before, but something had caught his eye in this morning's paper when he'd glimpsed it in his dad's hands during breakfast. His parents made him get up and have breakfast with them before they went to work. Even though he didn't have anywhere to go.

His dad read the paper while he ate his cereal.

His mom gave him a list of chores to complete before they got home from work.

This morning Dunk had tried to concentrate on what she was saying, but all he could think about was smoking another joint that would take him away from there.

That was when he'd seen Chaz Palmer's name on the front page of his dad's newspaper. He experienced an earthquake in his brain. That's what he called the bursts of clarity he sometimes got when he'd been off marijuana for twenty-four hours straight. This earthquake, however, had been caused by a sudden inspiration.

On the stoop, he wiped a trickle of sweat from his brow with the hem of his T-shirt. He had not smoked any marijuana all day. He needed to have a clear head in order to do what needed to be done.

But, man, he sure craved a hit. The big man wasn't going to like what he had to tell him. Imagining what Chaz would do to him made the sweat on Dunk's forehead pour faster from his pores.

He didn't have time to imagine much longer, though, because Chaz's Hummer was pulling into the driveway.

He nervously got up and waited while Chaz got out of the car and began walking toward him. "Hey, Chaz!" he called much too brightly.

The much bigger Chaz glowered at him. "What the hell do you want? I paid you. Our business is done."

Chaz had given him a hundred dollars for calling him when he'd spotted that tall, shapely woman going into Eddie's house. Chaz had not been generous with information, though. Dunk had found out more about what had been going on in Chaz's life lately from the article in this morning's *Constitution*.

Dunk's legs had gone weak with fear when Chaz had yelled at him. It took him a few seconds to gather his courage and say, as he held the paper out to Chaz, "H-have you seen this?"

Chaz snatched the paper out of Dunk's hand and tossed it over his shoulder. Pages scattered on the lawn. Dunk smiled, which came out like a grimace. "Okay, I guess you've seen it." He nervously cleared his throat. "The thing is, I think I might be able to help you beat the cops."

"You don't know what you're talking about, junior," said Chaz derisively. He leaned in. Dunk automatically took a step backward. Chaz's breath smelled like onions. The scent, combined with his cologne, nauseated him.

Dunk had come here for a purpose, though, so he forged ahead. "I saw you the night Eddie was killed. I couldn't sleep so I got up to smoke some weed. I can't do that when my parents are in the house. My mom has a nose like a blood-hound's. I went outdoors and that's when I saw you park your Hummer on the curb. I thought it was strange that you'd visit that late. It got me curious. So I watched you walk up to Eddie's house and use your key. It must have been around three in the morning, maybe later. While I was standing outside enjoying a smoke I was gonna call some friends and shoot the bull. That's why I had my camera phone with me."

Chaz grabbed Dunk and dragged him up onto the stoop while he unlocked the door with his other hand. "You and I need to talk," he ground out menacingly.

When the door was open, he shoved Dunk inside and locked the door behind them.

Dunk, pretending he wasn't so scared that he was about to wet his pants, looked around the house. "Dude, you do okay for yourself, don't you?"

Chaz hit him in the mouth so hard Dunk was out cold before he hit the floor.

Chaz then bent, picked him up and carried him to the sofa in the great room. There, he laid him down with his legs raised on the arm of the sofa.

Winded now, he went to the kitchen to get a beer.

He came back out a couple minutes later and sat in the chair opposite the sofa.

Dunk recovered consciousness soon after, abruptly jerking up as if someone had thrown a glass of water in his face. "Wh-what happened?"

Chaz leaned forward and showed him his huge fist. "You got hit by this truck. And it's going to run over you all afternoon unless you give me those pictures."

Dunk was gingerly testing his teeth with his tongue. He thought he felt a couple of loose ones. "Can't do that, dude. I sent them to some buds over the Net. Told them if anything happened to me, to give them to the cops."

Growling like an angry bear, Chaz lunged for Dunk, but Dunk, who had youth and agility on his side, easily eluded him. "Chill with the violence. You clocked me once but you ain't gettin' your hands on me for a rerun."

Chaz chased him around the great room until he could chase him no longer. *Three hundred and twenty-five pounds does not a marathoner make.* "Okay," he said at last, out of breath. "What do you want?"

"I want to be bigger than 50 Cent," Dunk said without hesitation. He kept pacing, although Chaz had to sit down. "I'm eighteen. I figure by the time I'm twenty I should be able to afford me a crib like this."

He decided a tour was in order. "Where's the kitchen, dude? You got any more of that beer?" He turned and disappeared around the corner.

Chaz didn't say a word. The little creep had him in the grip of panic. His heartbeat was erratic, and suddenly his stomach had turned sour. How could this happen to him?

Just the day before yesterday he'd told Detective Deberry that the police could, in effect, stuff it. They had nothing on him.

He'd been so careful. The fact was it hadn't been premeditated murder. When he'd gotten up that morning he'd never have entertained the thought of killing his best friend.

He was in bed with a woman he'd brought home from the wrap party when Eddie phoned *him*. After ascertaining that it was Eddie calling he climbed off the woman—they'd been going into round two, anyway—and asked her to leave. He was particular about whom he let hear his business.

While she was getting dressed in the master bedroom, he walked downstairs to his office. "Okay, Eddie. I'm alone now. What's up? Is something wrong with Kaya or Navarre?"

"Nah, nothing like that," Eddie said. Chaz could tell by the quaver in his voice that he was distraught. "I was just cleaning my piece and thought how easy it would be to just put the gun to my head and pull the trigger, then I wouldn't have to live with it."

Chaz laughed nervously. "Don't talk crazy, man. You're about to be bigger than you already are! The future looks bright. It's just another lowdown dirty bout of the blues. You been takin' your medication?"

Eddie was a manic-depressive.

"That stuff makes me sluggish. Can't handle it."

"Are you really cleaning guns?"

"Just my favorite handgun."

Chaz knew which one he was talking about. It was smaller than the others, had smooth action, and the recoil didn't practically throw your shoulder out of joint when you fired it. It was a beauty, all right. Chaz had given it to him.

"Listen, Eddie, I want you to put the gun down and get up and go upstairs to Kaya. I'll come over, let myself in and lock the gun back in the case. Will you do that for me?"

"That's funny," Eddie said. "I phoned you to ask you to do something for me."

"Anything," Chaz said. "You know I'd do anything for you."

"No, no, I can't do this over the phone. You gotta be here for this."

"I'm on my way," Chaz said. "Stay on the line."

"No prob," said Eddie. "I'll just hold the phone on my shoulder while I load the gun."

"Don't load the gun, Eddie. Leave the bullets in the drawer."

Eddie kept his gun on display in a lighted gun case there in the entertainment room.

He kept the bullets in a locked steel cabinet in the garage.

"Already went and got some," he told Chaz.

Chaz was running back upstairs to get something to put on. He passed the woman on the stairs. At that moment, he couldn't even remember her name. She looked at him as if she expected him to say something about the night they'd shared. "I'll call you!" he told her, still sprinting.

"Yeah, sure," she said as if she'd known he would say that. She continued downstairs and left the house, leaving the front door open. What did she care if a thief walked right in? He'd disrespected her. At least that's what Chaz figured she must have been thinking when he got back downstairs, dressed, saw the door hanging open and headed out.

He burned rubber over to Eddie's house, six blocks away, and let himself in with his key. The sound system was blasting some other rapper's CD. Chaz's mind was in such turmoil he didn't recognize the artist.

He knew exactly where to find Eddie, and ran to the entertainment room. Eddie sat at the table in front of the gun case. He had his gun-cleaning accoutrements in front of him: oil, soft cloth, tiny hard-bristle brush. Chaz didn't know why, but Eddie found the act of cleaning his guns relaxing. He wondered why he was in an agitated state tonight.

He sat down in a chair at the table. Sweat had broken out on his face. He wiped at it with his shirtsleeve. "Okay, I'm here. What's up, Eddie?"

Eddie calmly placed the gun on the table between them. "Man, what would you do if you were dying of something that's going to eat away at you until you look like a damned skeleton? A disease that can't be cured and is going to make you suffer like a *mother* before it finally kills you?"

Chaz looked nervously at the gun on the table. He wanted to snatch it up, but he was certain that was what Eddie was waiting for him to do. He sat still.

"Are you sick, Eddie?"

"Full-blown AIDS, man," Eddie said, his eyes in a world of pain.

Chaz's heart seized in his chest. "Does Kaya know?"

"Naw, man, I can't tell her. I did make her get herself checked, though. Told her it was better to be safe than sorry. Plus, she's been making me wear condoms for a while now." He laughed bitterly. Meeting Chaz's eyes, he said, "She's healthy."

Tears welled. "She's my heart, man. Both of 'em. I know where I got it from, though. A groupie who knew she was carrying. She's dead now but I guess she got some sick satisfaction out of infecting the great Eddie Bradley. Ain't that something, man? Using sex as a deadly weapon." He picked up the gun. "And it's gonna kill me as dead as this gun will. Only this gun will be quicker."

He put the gun down on the table and pushed it across to Chaz. "You're my friend. You and me go all the way back to the fifth grade. I know I can trust you to do the right thing and put me out of my misery." His gaze lowered to the gun, then back to Chaz. "Go on, pick it up." He pointed to the space between his eyes. "Put one right here."

Chaz began to cry as well. "I can't do that, Eddie. I love you, man."

"I love you, too, man. That's why I know I can count on you. My will's made out. Kaya and little man will be taken care of. And you got the contract between us. My lawyer will honor it. You'll get your million. I know you need it, man. I ain't stupid.

You let your family get away with murder. You just can't say no when they come beggin' for money. They gonna bleed you dry."

It was true, Chaz was hurting financially. He was counting on Eddie's new album going platinum in a hurry.

"What do I need with a million dollars if I'm in prison?" Chaz managed to get out.

"Naw, man, you'll make it look like suicide. I know the insurance company won't pay off on my policy if it's suicide but Kaya won't need that money. You know what a frugal guy I am. I've managed to salt away three million for her and Navarre. They'll be set for life."

Yes, Chaz knew Eddie was good with money. Eddie had been a nerd in school.

At the top of his class. Everyone thought he would become a doctor or a lawyer. No one had known, at the time, that he had a poetic soul. He was also keenly aware of the world around him. That, coupled with his talent for the written word, made him turn to poetry. From poetry, he'd tried rapping, and the rest was history. He was one of the true artistic talents in the world of contemporary rap music.

But the rap world had changed the quiet, studious boy Chaz had known. Fast money, women, drugs, people bending over backward to please him, all went to his head. He started cheating on Kaya. After a while he'd become desensitized to the guilt associated with having sex with other women. He still tried to keep it from Kaya in order to spare her feelings, but even when she found out, he wouldn't stop.

Once or twice that Chaz knew of, he'd even hit her when she wouldn't stop nagging him about his infidelity.

Chaz had to admit that the life they were living had changed him, too. He'd become hard-nosed over the years. Living up to the rap manager's generic stereotype of being a thug, he started dressing like one, speaking like one. He began bullying the people he managed, keeping them in line with an iron fist.

It had all become second nature to him. He felt powerful. Even though he was a son of a bitch, aspiring rappers routinely sought him out because he was Eddie Bradley's manager and Eddie was at the top. The most successful rapper ever to come out of Atlanta.

Now here they were sitting across from each other: one of them dying from AIDS and the other faced with a dilemma. To kill his best friend or to watch him die a horrible death.

"Are you positive that nothing can be done?" he asked hopefully, almost prayerfully. "There's always talk about new medicines. Can't you go on the cocktail?"

"Hell, man, I've been on the cocktail for months. It only makes me sicker. Haven't you noticed I'm losing weight?"

Chaz *had* noticed but he figured it was because Eddie was working too hard. Eddie had never been a big man like himself, anyway. He was only five-ten and had never weighed more than one-sixty. Chaz used to joke that the baggy clothes Eddie liked to wear weighed more than he did.

Eddie was looking pleadingly into Chaz's eyes. Chaz hated to see him suffering like this. This was some serious nightmare!

Suddenly, Eddie raised the gun to his forehead. "Tell Kaya I always loved her."

And he pulled the trigger. He and Chaz both fell backward, their chairs crashing to the floor almost simultaneously. Chaz was screaming. Blood spatter was on his hands and on the front of his white T-shirt.

He ran to Eddie. Eddie was gone. For some crazy reason, Chaz had expected him to be twitching on the floor, not quite dead. But the bullet must have gone directly into the brain and instantaneously stopped all bodily functions. Not a muscle twitched.

At that point Chaz's mind clicked to what Eddie had said. Make it appear as if it were suicide. When Eddie had fallen backward he'd released the gun and now it lay a couple feet away.

Chaz took off his T-shirt and used it to pick up the gun and put it back in Eddie's hand, then he ran. It was all he could do. His friend was dead. If he were caught at the scene of Eddie's suicide, he would be blamed.

As he ran to his car, it suddenly dawned on him that his being there had given Eddie the strength to pull the trigger. At least he hadn't died alone.

Chaz thought that was the least he could have done for his best friend.

Now he was in deep trouble because a teenager with a picture phone had seen him go into Eddie's house and had assumed that he'd killed Eddie. There was nothing he could say to convince the little blackmailer that it had been suicide. He might fry for something he had not done.

Dunk came back into the room, a long-necked bottle of beer in one hand and a bag of nacho cheese tortilla chips in the other, and plopped down on the sofa. Chaz looked at him for a moment then decided to give the truth a try.

"I didn't kill Eddie," he told Dunk. "Eddie killed himself. He just picked up the gun and shot himself while I was sitting across from him. I couldn't stop him."

Dunk laughed as he opened the bag of chips. "Man, not even Johnnie Cochran, God rest his soul, could get you off with that excuse!"

Chapter 11

On a Thursday afternoon, Sunny knocked on Tom's door.

"Come in!"

She strode in talking. "You wanted to see me?"

Tom was instantly on his feet and walking toward her. After Sunny closed the door, he pulled her into his arms for a warm hug.

Releasing her, he smiled. "I just got off the phone with Audra. She says hello."

Sunny laughed shortly. "She must have phoned you right after she phoned me. I know what you're going to say. My birthday is coming up and she wants to throw me a party but I can't go there and she says Deana Davis's people have all the local airports staked out. If she gets on a plane, someone will follow her here. So she can't come here. She talked *you* into doing it, didn't she?"

"She didn't have to talk me into anything," Tom said. "Lani and I would be proud to host your birthday party at our house. Just give me a list of people you'd like to invite and it's done."

"No!"

Tom looked disappointed. "Why not?"

"Because!" Sunny didn't mean to shout but Audra and her father were smothering her with gifts or the desire to bestow gifts on her. Case in point: the party. She knew they believed they were doing it to make up for lost time, but she suspected they were doing it out of guilt or the need to buy her love. Which wasn't for sale. She wanted to get to know them gradually, to slowly be integrated into their lives. Furthermore, they didn't seem to understand that her head was still spinning.

To go from being alone in the world to suddenly having more relatives than you could shake a stick at was overwhelming.

Plus, there was a certain six-foot-four man in the bedroom down the hall that she wanted to kick out of her apartment one minute and jump into bed with the next.

To say nothing of trying to get a childhood friend cleared of a murder charge.

She was mentally burnt out. She didn't need a big party. She needed a vacation.

"I'm just not up to a big party," she told her father.

She sat in the plush leather chair in front of his desk. He went to lean on the cherrywood desk while he listened to her explanation. "I've had a lot of excitement the past two weeks—learning about you and Audra and working on Kaya's case. I was thinking that a small dinner would be nice. Just you and Lani and Jonas and me at your place, if you like."

"My parents want to meet you so badly," Tom said, his tone a touch pleading.

Sunny could not deny him when he was looking at her like that. "Okay, I want to meet them, too."

His father, Major Thomas Chapman, Sr., was a retired judge. His mother, Valorie Evans Chapman, was a retired professor of English. Sunny felt nervous at the thought of meeting them. All her life she'd worn a hard shell of sorts that protected her from other people's opinions of her. Now she found herself actually hoping someone would like her.

Take Lani, for example. The woman had barely tolerated her presence before.

Sometimes, at company functions, Sunny would catch her looking at her with a jealous, distrustful expression. And whenever she deigned to speak to her it was always with the briefest of exchanges as if she could barely stand to be around her.

Now, Lani, like her mother, phoned her every day just to say hello. And she'd started calling her sugar. Sunny was afraid that she had two mothers now. Both intelligent, competitive women who didn't like to lose and who were going to vie for her attention and, eventually, her loyalty. A terrifying thought to a woman who'd been eight years old when her mother figure was taken from her.

"Then there is your uncle and aunt and their children," Tom said hopefully.

Sunny shook her head. "Don't put too much on me. I might chicken out altogether."

"Okay, okay," said Tom hurriedly. "Just your grandparents." He had been leaning toward her, now he straightened. "Um, Sunny, I've been meaning to ask about Jonas's intentions toward you. I know you'll soon be twenty-eight, and it's none of my business. But the man's living under your roof!"

"I told you why," Sunny said patiently.

"I know that, but I've seen the way he looks at you, and it's not the way a bodyguard should look at the person whose body he's guarding. If you know what I mean."

Sunny blushed. "We're not sleeping together."

"Not from lack of trying on his part, I'll bet!" Tom said a bit testily.

Laughing softly, Sunny pushed herself up. "How do you know I'm not the aggressor?" She stepped forward and kissed him on the cheek. "Gotta run."

She hurried out.

"Sunny!" Tom called to her retreating back.

"It's after six, Dad. My love slave and I have things to do."

Tom opened his mouth to protest again, but closed it when he realized she'd just called him Dad.

He grinned like an idiot.

Sunny closed the door behind her and stood there for a few seconds, frozen. She'd called Tom Dad. Was it too quick? She had liked him from the beginning. Otherwise she certainly wouldn't have remembered his promise to hire her should she get her law degree. She'd kept that promise in her mind for years.

It was an easy transition for her now, to think of Tom as her father. She'd known him for years. Not like Audra. She was worried that when she met Audra she wouldn't feel as warm toward her as she did Tom. She was a complete stranger. With a face she'd known for years, to be fair. However, how many times had she looked at an Audra Kane movie and said to herself, *That woman looks like good mother material?* Never!

When she got back to her office, she found Jonas sprawled on the leather sofa, sound asleep. She took the opportunity to observe his square-shaped face in repose.

Long black lashes lay flush with his high cheekbones. He had a noble nose. Kind of long, but she liked it. And what a mouth! Lush and full-lipped, she loved kissing him. She was tempted to do it right now.

For the past thirteen days, which was how long he'd been staying with her, they had managed to stay out of each other's beds by following certain logical rules. They did not walk around in a state of undress. And after that kiss in front of the open refrigerator door they'd agreed that kissing when they were mere feet away from a bed was inadvisable.

If they were going to see this through, they had to abide by those rules. No tantalizing apparel, or lack thereof, and no kissing near a bed.

So far it was working for them.

However, kissing in the elevator, in the car, at restaurants, walking in the park and, once, at a pet grooming shop, was permissible.

Jonas opened his eyes while she was looking at him.

"Am I pretty when I sleep?"

"You're a slobbering mess," she joked.

He quickly raised his hand to check if he had indeed dribbled while he'd slept. He had not. Sitting up, he grabbed her around the legs and pulled her onto his lap. He nuzzled her fragrant neck, then planted a warm kiss there. "What time is it?"

"After six. You want to get out of here?"

"Sounds like a plan," he heartily agreed. "But first…"

Sunny melted under his intensely sensual gaze. She anticipated the taste of his kiss before his mouth actually descended upon hers. Her imagination paled in comparison.

He had a way of moving against her mouth that invited pliant abandon. His tongue gave her such pleasure that her natural desire was to *give* in return.

She lay back on the big couch. He moved on top, spreading her legs as he did so.

Sunny was wearing loose-fitting slacks. Her hands were on the backs of his arms. The play of muscles against the palms of her hands turned her on even more.

She could imagine how his body would feel, totally nude, on top of hers.

As the kiss deepened, she felt his erection at the junction between her thighs.

They pressed closely.

Her nipples ripened and grew slightly painful. Her female center throbbed. It was sublime torture. All they had to do was remove some items of clothing and complete the act. She was more than ready.

Jonas broke off the kiss and peered into her smoldering eyes. "Marry me, Sunny."

Sunny climaxed. It was the most pleasurable and, at the same time, the weirdest sensation she'd ever experienced. While in the grip of sexual release, all she wanted to do was get up and slap him for asking her to marry him after knowing her for only two weeks. Was he *crazy?*

Jonas felt her minute convulsions. He gently held her close until she let out a soft sigh and went still in his arms. Then he continued to hold her and nuzzle the side of her neck. "I love you so much. I know it sounds insane to you, but I think I fell in love with you the moment you fell for me."

"I fell for you?" she asked softly.

"When you fell out of the tree." He kissed her neck. His warm breath on her skin was turning her on again. "It's corny as hell, but I don't care." He looked deeply in her eyes. "You're everything I want in a woman, a wife, a lover, Sunny. You're smart, brave and funny. Any man would be lucky to have you at his side. I just hope I'm the lucky man you choose to be with."

He dug in his pocket and withdrew a ring. He gave it to Sunny. Stunned at the five-carat white diamond solitaire, Sunny sat up and stared at him. "Where did you get this?"

They were sitting close on the couch now, eyes locked.

"Atlanta's a big town. There are quite a few jewelry stores. Do you like it?"

"It's beautiful, but…"

"No buts. Try it on. Here, let me."

He took the ring and slipped it onto her finger. It fit perfectly, a coincidence that spooked Sunny even more. She stared alternately at him and the ring.

"You're making me nervous with your silence. Say something other than but!"

Sunny's mind was racing. She felt like her life had been in fast-forward ever since Jonas had come into it. He had brought with him all the possibilities that she'd ever wished for: a Prince Charming who would love her for whom she really was; a real family; a future spent with someone she wouldn't mind growing old with.

However, the logical part of her mind was telling her it was impossible to know that you loved someone after *two weeks*. She *wanted* to believe. Life had never shown her that fairy tales exist, though. She had no faith in them.

Nothing in her life had come this easily for her. From the moment she'd met him, he was right: she'd been falling for him. Falling, to her, meant you were totally out of control, and decisions shouldn't be made when you were not in control of your faculties.

She kissed him.

She could feel the relief in his body as he relaxed against her. While she was kissing him tears sprang to her eyes. When they parted, he was not surprised to see them. He thought they were tears of happiness.

Sunny removed the ring from her finger and placed it in his palm. "I wish I was that woman you described a minute ago. But I'm not brave. I don't believe in love at first sight. I don't believe in a lightning bolt out of the blue. I know that I *want* you. But I don't know that I *love* you."

She hated saying that to him because she was aware he had a fear of commitment.

It must have taken a great deal for him to let down his guard and propose to her. Yet, she couldn't lie to him.

Jonas's eyes seemed to look right through her. She could tell when he drew up a wall between them. She felt it go up as surely as she knew the couch was solidly below her.

She stood up. "I'm sorry, Jonas."

Clearing his throat he rose, too, and smiled at her. "Don't be. Somebody had to be the sane one, right?" He pocketed the ring. "Come on, let's get out of here. I'll cook for you tonight."

Sunny didn't know what to say. He was willing to swallow his pride and remain by her side after she'd turned down his proposal. She couldn't even look him in the eye as she turned and hurried to the door. "I...I've got to go to the ladies' room first. Be right back."

Jonas was glad for some time alone to figure out the emotions warring for prominence within him. He felt as if his heart had been ripped from his chest. How could he have been that far off base about Sunny's feelings for him? Yes, the physical time they'd spent together was short but he'd never been as affected by any other woman in his life.

She challenged him to be a better man with her zest for living. She stimulated him intellectually. He would not grow tired of talking to her if they lived to be a hundred.

And the sexual heat between them could melt the polar ice caps.

The crazy thing was, now he knew why his dad had married so many times. And divorced so many times. It wasn't because he *didn't* believe in love. It was because he *did*. He believed in it so much he was determined to keep trying until he got it right.

He was actually beginning to think of his dad as a hero instead of a serial womanizer.

Okay, that was pushing it. His dad had some serious issues to work through.

But, at least, he thought he understood him better. In marrying and divorcing, Norman Blake was brave enough not to give up on love.

Jonas picked up his suit coat and straightened the cushions on the couch. By the time he'd done that, he heard Sunny returning. Meeting her eyes across the room, he could tell she'd been crying while she was in the ladies' room.

She smiled faintly. "Ready?"

"Yeah," said Jonas. He was indeed ready. Ready to never

give up on her. She'd turned him down today but that didn't mean she didn't love him. He felt kind of foolish because the thing growing within him felt foreign to him. It was hope.

Sunny, who tended to chatter when she was nervous, said as they left the office, "I think you should rethink your offer to cook for me tonight. I don't have much of an appetite. It'd be a waste of your talents."

"Come on now, lawyer-babe, your appetite hasn't failed me yet. You'll get it back once you wrap your lips around my grilled salmon and pasta."

"Fresh salmon?"

"Of course."

"With a little Cajun seasoning?"

"The hotter, the better."

"Deal."

He put his arm about her shoulder companionably. "I knew you'd come around."

It was as if the proposal had never happened. They went back to their routine.

Friday evening, right after work, they got on the road to Warm Springs. As Jonas drove, Sunny closed her eyes for what she thought was a moment, only to awaken as they were pulling up to the house.

Parked on the street in front of the house was a black Jaguar convertible with tan interior. "What is Kit doing here?" Sunny wondered aloud.

How long Kit had been there was questionable because she had a key to Sunny's house in Warm Springs. Just as Sunny had a key to her home in Newport News, Virginia.

"Your best friend?" Jonas asked.

Sunny had told him the basics about Kit: occupation, where she lived, how long they had been friends. There were a few things she had neglected to tell him about her.

Thanks to daylight-saving time, Jonas was about to get an eyeful.

Kit came bounding out of the house, screen door slamming behind her. She was wearing a short, sleeveless yellow dress that accentuated her bosom and long legs. Two of her best assets. Mounds of naturally curly auburn hair made a halo about her beautiful face. Deep dimples were carved into caramel-colored cheeks. And a bow of a mouth opened to scream, "Sunny! I was wondering when you would get here. I've been here since two o'clock. I took the day off."

"Kit! What a surprise!" Sunny said as she and Jonas got out of the car.

Kit stopped in her tracks when she saw Jonas. "Damn! Is this Jonas?"

Kit had been walking toward Sunny but suddenly changed directions. She couldn't get to Jonas fast enough. And Jonas, Sunny was quick to note, was smiling.

Okay, what was the man going to do, frown at her best friend as if she were something Caesar had dragged in? Ridiculous. She couldn't recall ever feeling jealousy whenever Kit had met any of the other men she'd dated in the past. She and Jonas weren't even officially dating and she didn't want Kit with her voluptuous body, beautiful face and winning personality within a hundred feet of him.

Sunny cut Kit off at the pass. She stepped in her path and hugged her before she got to Jonas. "Kit!" She nearly squeezed the breath out of her. "It's so good to see you. Why didn't you tell me you were coming? I would have tried to get here earlier."

Kit looked up into Sunny's eyes. She was three inches shorter. "I had to see him with my own eyes," she whispered. Then she turned her head to regard Jonas with blatant admiration. "Aren't you going to introduce us?"

Sunny supposed there was no way around it.

Jonas was standing only a couple feet behind them holding

Caesar, whom he'd taken out of his pet carrier while Sunny and Kit had been hugging.

Both of them went to stand in front of him. "Jonas," Sunny said, "I'd like you to meet Katherine Larsen, my dearest friend."

Kit offered Jonas her hand for shaking and Caesar took a swipe at it. In the two weeks Jonas had lived with Sunny, Caesar had become quite attached to him. On the other hand, he had never warmed to Kit who didn't like cats. To him, she smelled like the dachshund she kept as a pet.

Sunny took Caesar from Jonas and put him on the ground. "Go inside."

Caesar sauntered toward the white picket fence, looking back at her once with his emerald-green eyes as if to say, *I was trying to do you a favor!*

Sunny laughed shortly as she turned back around to her houseguests. "He didn't scratch you, did he?"

"No," Kit said. "I'm used to his evil ways." She smiled up at Jonas and offered him her hand once again.

Jonas took it. "It's a pleasure, Kit. Sunny's told me some wonderful things about you."

"Oh, has she?" Kit asked, glancing at Sunny. "She hasn't told me nearly enough about you. For example, she didn't tell me you were such a gorgeous tall drink of water!"

"Well, she told me how beautiful you were, and she wasn't exaggerating."

Kit soaked up the compliment while simultaneously turning up the charm level. "How sweet. I have a feeling I'm going to enjoy every minute of this weekend."

She took him by the arm as they walked to the house, leaving Sunny to bring up the rear. "Do you like shrimp, Jonas? I picked up some at this quaint little fish market on the way here. I knew Sunny wouldn't have anything edible in the house. She hates grocery shopping. She's a pretty good cook when she sets her mind to it, though. She does a scrumptious shrimp boil. Do you know what that is, sweetie? You don't sound like you're from the South. Not that they can't have shrimp boils where you're from, but we're kind of known for them down here."

"I cook a little myself," Jonas told her. "Do you put Irish potatoes and corn on the cob in yours so they'll soak up the spices in the water?"

"You do know what I'm talking about," Kit said delightedly. Looking over her shoulder at Sunny, she said, "I figured you should be here pretty soon so I've already shucked the corn for you and washed the potatoes. All you need to do is work your culinary magic and add the right spices and we'll be set. Hurry up, would you? I'm ravenous." She smiled up at Jonas. "Why don't you and I get better acquainted while Sunny puts supper together?"

"I've gotten used to helping Sunny in the kitchen," Jonas said. "Maybe we could all pitch in, and supper will be prepared that much sooner."

Kit wrinkled her nose at him. "Oh, I like a decisive man."

Sunny was appalled by Kit's behavior. She was appalled by her own thoughts, as well. She needed to chill out because she was beginning to imagine kicking Kit's tight little rump all the way back to Newport News.

Once in the house Sunny saw that Kit had left her belongings lying around the living room, as she usually did. Her overnight bag was open on the floor in front of the couch, a frilly piece of lingerie sticking out the top. She'd had a fast-food burger for lunch and the wrapper, bag and empty paper cup were on the coffee table.

Since Sunny had lived with her when they were in law school she was used to Kit's untidiness, but it irked her. She wouldn't go to her house and leave things lying around her living room.

Not wanting to embarrass Kit, or herself, she didn't mention it in front of Jonas.

"In all the excitement, I forgot my things on the backseat," said Sunny, spinning on her heel to head back outside.

"Let me," Jonas offered. "I still have the keys."

Kit seemed to be loath to let go of his arm. But one look from Sunny and she did so.

In Jonas's absence, Kit laughed softly. "You should see your face."

Sunny could imagine what she looked like: narrowed eyes, pursed mouth and flared nostrils. Yeah, she was irritated with her best friend.

"What is it with you?" she asked Kit. "You're a flirt of the first order but you've never flirted with any of my boyfriends before!"

"Just a little experiment," Kit told her, walking around her and observing her as she did so. Her light brown eyes were amused. "There's something different about you. I just can't put my finger on it. Oh, yeah, I've got it. You're in love."

"Kit, I'm going to tell you once—don't interfere in my relationship with Jonas. Things are kind of iffy right now. You're probably imagining that we're having sex every night and thoroughly enjoying living together, but you'd be wrong. It's complicated."

"I like complicated," Kit said, unfazed. "And I like you and Jonas together. So, I'm going to stop flirting with him and champion your cause instead."

"Oh, no, that's even worse. It's like trying to pawn your cousin off on somebody. I'd look pathetic. Believe me, I make myself look pathetic enough in his eyesight without your help."

"Then what can I do?" Kit asked, pouting. "I didn't plan this surprise weekend for days so that I could come here and do absolutely nothing. You're my girl, and I want to see you happy before I go back to Virginia."

Sunny went and hugged her. "I know you do. But the best thing you can do for me and Jonas is nothing."

"Hell, I could have done that over the phone." She brightened. "I did get to see him in the flesh, though. He's delicious in every sense of the word. And did you notice how he jumped to your defense when I tried to banish you to the kitchen so I could have him to myself? He's a gentleman. The best kind of man to have in your bed."

Sunny put an arm about Kit's shoulder, directing her to the hallway. "Let's get supper going. We can talk in the kitchen."

Minutes later, when Jonas joined them, they were companionably chopping onions at the counter. "I put your things in your room," he told Sunny.

Sunny looked up at him and smiled. "Thanks, Jonas."

"What can I do to help?" he asked.

"We've got it under control," Sunny said. "Sit, have a drink."

Jonas went to the sink and washed his hands. He pulled a paper towel from the rack over the sink and dried his hands. "So, did you talk about me while I was outside?"

Both women laughed.

"What other topic is there?" Kit asked. "We already know everything there is to know about each other. You're it, fella."

Jonas got a bottle of water from the refrigerator. He sat at the table and uncapped the bottle. "That makes me very uncomfortable." He certainly didn't look uncomfortable. He seemed to be enjoying their exchange. Eyes on Kit, he said, "Are you sure you know everything there is to know about Sunny?"

"Do you want to quiz me?" Kit challenged.

"Okay," said Jonas, smiling wickedly. "What's her favorite color?"

"Blue," said Kit. "Too easy."

"Her favorite song of all time?"

"She's got this love, lust thing going on for Otis Redding. She'll try to deny she's in love with him, but don't believe her. It's 'These Arms of Mine' by Otis. Turns her to jelly every time she hears it."

Jonas's eyes met Sunny's and she blushed to the tips of her ears. "Guilty," she said. "Otis is my all-time favorite singer."

"I knew that," he said.

"How?" she asked, her voice soft with wonder. She'd never told him.

"His is the only music you'll play while you're working," Jonas answered. "He soothes you."

Sunny was amazed by his observation. She hadn't been aware he was paying such close attention to her habits. "That's true," she said.

"More questions," Kit said, smiling as she transferred chopped onions from the cutting board to the pot on the stove. "This is fun."

"Has she ever climbed a tree to save Caesar?" Jonas asked. He was looking directly into Sunny's eyes. She didn't know how he was aware of the fact that she'd never told Kit she had risked broken bones to rescue Caesar. Perhaps because he'd witnessed Caesar's reaction to Kit and assumed Kit didn't care for the cat therefore Sunny wouldn't waste conversation time with Kit discussing Caesar. At any rate, he was very astute and that turned her on.

Kit narrowed her eyes at Sunny. "She'd better not climb a tree for that fur ball!"

"Sorry," said Sunny. "But I've done it many times."

Kit smiled and shook her head in disbelief. "There's no accounting for love of one's pets. I once got between a pit bull and my dachshund. Now, will you two stop looking at each other as if you were both something good to eat? It's, frankly, making me miss my boyfriend who couldn't come with me this weekend."

"Boyfriend?" said Sunny, astonished. "You mean you've chosen between Earl and Harper?"

Kit laughed. "There was no contest, really. Harper sings to me in bed afterward. What woman can resist that?"

"It depends on how well he sings," Sunny joked.

"Let's put it this way," Kit said. "To me, he sounds like Otis."

"Well, all right," Sunny said, beaming. "He's a god among men."

Chapter 12

Early the next morning, Sunny and Jonas met on the back porch to stretch in preparation for their run. In addition to her shorts, sleeveless tee and Adidas athletic shoes, Sunny had tied a jacket around her waist. September mornings were cool in this part of Georgia.

Jonas wore knee-length athletic shorts, a short-sleeved T-shirt, both navy-blue, and white Nikes. He was wearing his jacket. After living several years in South Africa he'd become acclimatized to warmer weather.

"Kit doesn't run, huh?" he asked as they did hamstring stretches.

"She used to, but her knees started bothering her. She walks."

"The knees do go if you're not careful," Jonas said. "All the continuous pounding. I'm going to have to find an alternative to it soon myself. I've been running since I was in my teens and my body's beginning to tell me to quit."

"But you're hooked," Sunny said knowingly.

He smiled at her with his eyes. "You, too?"

"It's the endorphins. They're mood enhancers. Then, too, you start competing with yourself and the next thing you know you're running forty to fifty miles a week. Yeah, I know how it is. I've had shin splints, torn ligaments. Now I only run two or three miles a day. I get my high, but don't punish my body."

His gaze swept over her. "Smart girl. I wouldn't want to see your body injured in any way."

Sunny's left heel was touching her left buttock as she grasped the ankle. Holding the stretch, looking out at the deep backyard as if she were daydreaming, she said, "Nor I yours."

That was the final stretch.

Sunny ran down the back steps, Jonas behind her. Caesar shot through the pet door from the kitchen and sprinted ahead of them both. He'd done the same thing last weekend when they'd been in Warm Springs.

"That's some neurotic cat you've got there," Jonas said, laughing softly. "He runs with you. He loves baths. Normally, cats hate getting wet."

"He's just showing off now," Sunny said. "He won't last a half mile."

They ran around the corner of the house and onto the front sidewalk and across the empty street. The houses they passed were a mixture of architectural styles, a few bungalows, neat cottages, a handful of clapboard treasures like her house, and even a stately brick mansion with ancient live oaks on the grounds.

"He's not really a cat," Sunny said, picking up the thread about Caesar.

"He looks like a cat to me."

"That's just his disguise. He's really the reincarnation of Julius Caesar. Hence, his name."

"What makes you think he's Caesar?"

"If he's not Caesar then he's some other long-dead king. Have you ever met a more imperious creature?"

Jonas laughed shortly. He usually didn't give cats a second thought, but he liked Caesar. How could you not like an animal that insinuated itself into your life whether you wanted it to or not? The first few days, Jonas tried to ignore Caesar's overtures.

He would walk into a room and Caesar would walk over to him and meow as if he were saying hello. Jonas would walk around him. Caesar would give him a disdainful look and walk in the opposite direction.

Five days of this and Jonas figured the cat wasn't going to give up, so he picked him up. Caesar purred and rubbed his head against Jonas's chest. From then on they were pals.

"I like him," Jonas said to Sunny as they changed directions and headed downtown to one of the main parks. "But he's just a cat."

Caesar suddenly cut in front of Jonas, resulting in Jonas having to jump over him.

"That crazy cat!"

"Don't let him hear you say he's not an emperor again, or there'll be hell to pay," Sunny joked.

Jonas laughed. They were passing the supermarket and Caesar veered off toward it.

"Told you he wouldn't last," Sunny said.

"You're just going to leave him on his own?"

"They know him at the supermarket. The meat department manager will probably give him a piece of fish and send him on his way. He'll be at home when we get back, looking smug and happy."

"I'd like to talk about something serious now that we're alone," Jonas told her.

"Shoot!"

"What do you want for your birthday?"

"I wish you wouldn't get me anything," Sunny said. "Audra and Tom are already throwing a party I'm not looking forward to."

Curious, Jonas pursued the issue. "What is it you don't like about parties?"

"I have nothing against parties for other people. It's parties thrown in my honor that get under my skin."

"Why?"

Sunny picked up her pace. "I'm really having a difficult time running and talking this morning. May we please just run?"

Her tone was clipped and irritated.

Jonas was intrigued. What sort of woman didn't like having her loved ones around her singing her praises and giving her expensive gifts? It was patently unnatural.

He didn't want to make another misstep so close to the debacle that had been his proposal, however, so he dropped the subject.

"Fine, we'll run in dead silence."

"Thank you."

He tried not to let her attitude bother him, but he was still bruised from the pounding she'd given him when she'd refused his proposal. Now she was unwilling to talk about her feelings with him. What would be next?

They ran in silence.

When Sunny started running toward the highway, Jonas knew he had upset her and she required a longer run this morning. He hadn't said another word since she'd asked him to be quiet, but he was bursting with questions.

He watched her out of the corner of his eye. She ran with purpose, her face a mask of frowns. He was sorry he'd brought up the birthday party if it had put her in such an apparently foul mood.

Wanting to apologize, he cleared his throat.

Sunny glared at him.

He was not a coward, but the expression in her eyes scared him.

They ran on.

Thirty minutes later they arrived on the grounds of the Roosevelt Warm Springs Institute for Rehabilitation. As in many buildings in Georgia the hospital was constructed of red brick. Georgia was known for its red clay.

The entrance was characterized by huge white Doric columns.

Sunny ran to a group of stone benches underneath the spreading boughs of huge live oak trees whose branches were heavy with moss. Because she knew it wasn't advisable to simply come to a dead stop after jogging several miles, they ran in place beside the benches.

"My adoptive parents worked here. He was a physical therapist and she was a nurse." She stopped running and walked in circles, her finger on the side of her neck, monitoring her heart rate. Jonas did the same, although he didn't feel the need to monitor his heart rate. He never thought about it.

As she walked, Sunny told him about her parents. "Kenneth and Jane Adams were already in their fifties when they adopted me. Mom told me that the agency kept them waiting for me for so long that she was afraid they weren't going to allow her and Daddy to take me home for fear they were too old to become parents. But the adoption finally came through. They had been married more than twenty-five years. They had lost hope of ever having children."

They walked around each other. Sunny looked him in the eyes as they tangoed.

Or it seemed like a dance to her. She was still somewhat angry that he hadn't wanted to leave well enough alone when she'd said she didn't care for birthday parties. Now her eyes dared him to pay anything less than strict attention to what she had to say.

Jonas was enthralled. He couldn't look away from her expressive eyes. It was as if he had to be a witness to her pain.

"Do you know what a happy childhood is?" she asked. She didn't expect him to answer. "It's having parents who cherished you from the moment they held you in their arms and let you know they loved you every single day of your life. In little ways.

"I wasn't spoiled. From the start, I knew the value of working for what I wanted. I learned to clean my room. My mom taught me how to prepare simple dishes from the age of six. She taught me to garden. When I turned seven she bought me a used sewing machine and began to teach me how to sew pillows and curtains and other simplistic patterns. I loved all of that because I was doing it with her. My dad was quiet. He enjoyed puttering in the detached garage. He had a workshop out there. He wasn't very physical. I don't think he liked sports. But he loved books and would take me to the library every Saturday morning.

"We didn't even own a TV. I didn't miss it. I had school and the library, and my friends, and most of all my parents who believed that the best things in life were free. Every year they would go all out on one thing: my birthday party. When I was six there were pony rides. When I was seven they hired a clown. When I was eight they set up a mini carnival in the backyard. I had so much fun that Saturday afternoon I couldn't sleep when I went to bed. Then the following Monday morning they were killed on the way to work. A truck driver fell asleep at the wheel of his semitrailer."

She broke eye contact. "I know I shouldn't associate my birthday with their deaths, but I do. I haven't had a birthday party since then, and I don't want one! But I also don't want to have to tell Audra and Tom what I just told you. They'll only feel guiltier for having given me up for adoption."

Jonas went and pulled her into his arms. She resisted at first, but then let him. He held her for several minutes without speaking.

Momentarily he said, "Don't you think your parents would be appalled that you associate your birthday, something they obviously got a great deal of pleasure out of celebrating, with their deaths?"

Sunny had sincerely never thought of it that way. "I felt as if I was honoring their memory by refusing to celebrate without them on my birthday," she said softly.

"You can honor their memory by simply being *happy,* Sunny. Because by being happy you would be acknowledging the fact that the foundation of love that they laid in your early childhood gave you the strength to carry on after their deaths. They loved you. It stands to reason that they would want you to celebrate your life!"

Remembering how much her parents had enjoyed themselves right along with her and the rest of the children at her birthday parties, Sunny had to agree.

But old habits were hard to break. "I'll give it some thought."

Jonas smiled at her. "You do that."

He took her by the hand. "Let's walk back to the house, shall we? You've worn my old legs out."

Sunny laughed. "Yeah, you are pushing forty."

"I'm not pushing forty. I'm only thirty-six."

"That's closer to forty than thirty."

"Oh, hell, woman, let's run," Jonas said, and took off, leaving her in the dust. "I just wanted a little quiet time with my woman and you're giving me lip."

Sunny ran alongside him. "Am I your woman, after I turned you down?"

"Did you think I would stop loving you just because you said no?" he asked incredulously. "Sunny, until I met you I'd fooled myself into believing that love, true love, didn't exist. I was wrong. It does. And it looks remarkably like you."

Sunny beamed her pleasure. "I'm glad you're not giving up on me because I'm growing more attached to you every day. I would miss you if you went away."

Jonas smiled at her. "Well, that's something," he said, trying his best to keep the sadness out of his tone. Sunny reached out and grasped his hand in hers. "Let's walk back home."

So they walked.

When they got home, Caesar was sitting on the back porch daintily eating a nice piece of pink salmon.

Kit, who was in the kitchen preparing breakfast, heard them coming through the door. "There you two are." Her gaze targeted Sunny. "Sweetie, your mother phoned."

Her eyes sparkled. "I got to chat with Audra Kane. I can die happy!"

Sunny went directly to the refrigerator to get bottles of water for her and Jonas.

Handing Jonas his, she asked Kit, "Why did she call?"

Kit seemed to have short-term amnesia. She screwed up her face, trying to recall the salient points of her conversation with the famous actress. "Oh, yeah, she said she finally came up with a way to foil that Deana Davis woman. She's going to drive to Georgia!"

Sunny and Jonas looked at each other and burst out laughing. Kit laughed, too, although she didn't quite understand why her best friend and the man she loved were laughing. Audra Kane had sounded perfectly serious to her.

Kit regarded Jonas. "She also said your father's coming with her."

"What!" cried Jonas, no longer laughing.

Four days later at 6:00 a.m., Beverly Hills time, the Kane household was in constant motion. A distinguished black gentleman pulled up in a cherry-red Alfa Spider, the sportiest of the Alfa Romeo models, and blared the horn. A delicate beauty came out of the house, loaded a few bags in the trunk that the distinguished gentleman had graciously popped for her, and then she climbed in beside him and they were off.

As the Italian sports car glided through the gates of the estate and pulled onto the street, two unremarkable cars that had been parked on the street fell in line behind it.

Moments later, at the Kane residence, the garage door opened and a black SUV with tinted windows pulled out, went down the tree-shaded lane, through the gates of the estate and turned in the opposite direction the Alfa Spider and the two cars that were trailing it had gone.

"I think we fooled them," Audra happily said from the passenger seat.

"If those actors you hired scratch my baby, I'm not going to be pleased," Norman, who was driving, griped. "I haven't even had the chance to open her up on the road yet."

"Oh, hush, Norman," said the backseat driver, "and watch your speed. You don't want to be stopped while driving black in Beverly Hills."

Audra turned to smile at her mother. "Georgia, here we come!"

On Monday, September 15, two days before Sunny's birthday, she and Jonas tracked down the remaining woman on Kaya's list of Eddie's lovers. They'd had no luck with the previous four women Kaya had named. Of those four only one was still in Atlanta, and she had been in the hospital recovering from surgery when Eddie had been killed. She had the hospital bills to prove it. A phone call to her physician, put on speaker, with her giving permission to her doctor to give Sunny the dates of her surgery and hospital stay, further corroborated her alibi.

Now down to one, Jonas pulled to the curb in front of a modest home on the south side. It was around two o'clock and the neighborhood was relatively quiet with little traffic on the street, and a few pedestrians, but no children in sight. School hadn't let out.

Sunny and Jonas strode up the short walk to the house. Sunny, holding her briefcase in one hand, rang the bell with the other.

Both she and Jonas were dressed in business attire and wore sunglasses.

"Who's there!" shouted a woman's voice.

"Hello, my name is Sunday Adams and I represent Kaya Bradley. I'm here to see Miss Joy Chambers."

The door was unlocked but the chain was left on. A middle-aged black woman with coppery-brown skin and sandy colored hair peeped at them. "Let me see your ID, baby."

Sunny quickly went into the shoulder bag and produced both her driver's license and her business card. She showed the woman the driver's license and handed her the card.

After a few seconds of careful perusal, the woman took the chain off the door.

"Come in," she said pleasantly.

Sunny and Jonas went inside. Sunny quickly introduced Jonas to her, then the woman locked the door. She was wearing bronze slacks, a black short-sleeve blouse and bronze flats. Her home, they saw as she directed them to the living room, was immaculate.

Modest on the outside but evidently she was an interior decorator of some skill.

Every surface, from the ceramic tile in the foyer to the hardwood floor in the living room appeared as if it had been newly laid. Pristine beige leather living room furniture and wooden African accents with few knickknacks that took up space provided the small room the illusion of space. No clutter. Sunny liked it. "You have a lovely home," she told the woman.

Frances Chambers smiled up at Sunny. "Thank you. It was my Joy who knew her way around a room. She made everything beautiful."

Sunny's hopes of meeting Joy fled. The woman had used the past tense when she had referred to her.

Frances gestured for them to have a seat. Removing their sunglasses, they sat down.

After all three of them were comfortable, Frances said, "I'm Frances, Joy's mother. I'm afraid you're not going to be able to speak with her, Miss Adams. Joy died of respiratory failure more than five months ago."

This time, not only were Sunny's hopes dashed, but her

sense of calm was compromised, as well. Respiratory failure, in a twenty-five-year-old African-American woman. She'd heard the term used too many times in the past when a family was trying to explain what a loved one with AIDS had died of. No one liked to use the term AIDS. It had too many negative connotations. Like the black plague. Even the mention of it struck fear in people's minds and hearts.

Sunny looked at Frances Chambers with sympathy. "I'm so sorry for your loss."

"Thank you," Frances said. She blinked back tears. "You're Kaya Bradley's lawyer? I've been following that on the news. Why would you want to question Joy about Mrs. Bradley? As far as I know, Joy didn't know her."

Sunny dreaded having to ask a grieving mother about her daughter's love life. But there was no way around it. "It's not concerning Kaya, Ms. Chambers. It's about her deceased husband, Eddie."

Frances Chambers lowered her eyes. "I don't want to talk about him."

Sunny had no recourse but to shock Frances Chambers into loosening up. It was a gamble, but if it worked, it meant Kaya's life. "I have reason to believe that Eddie had AIDS, Ms. Chambers. If he did, then he could have passed it on to his wife and any number of other women. Now, you've just told us that your daughter died of respiratory failure. That is one of the causes of death when someone has AIDS."

Sunny softened her tone. "Please, if that's what Joy died of, you must tell me. You say you've been following Kaya's story on the news. If so, you know that she believes Eddie committed suicide. The police don't buy her story. However, if Eddie did have AIDS and inadvertently gave it to someone else, that would give the jury reasonable doubt in regards to Kaya's guilt. You could save her life."

Frances closed her eyes. Tears spilled from the corners of

the shut lids. Looking at Sunny once more, she said, "Joy never meant to hurt anyone. Something happened to her when she was diagnosed. Her heart hardened. She felt as if God had abandoned her so she in turn abandoned Him. She got it from a man she thought loved her. But he didn't. He was only using her. What's more, he was having sex with other men.

"When she told him she had it, he laughed in her face. He said he was dying, why the hell should he die alone? Something broke in Joy that day. She didn't care about anything anymore. Anything, or anyone. She started picking up guys, something she'd never done before. Her preference was cheaters, men who had wives and girlfriends at home yet never seemed satisfied. Always had to have another woman. She was a beautiful girl up until the last few months of her life. It was easy for her to seduce them. She felt like she was judge and jury. She was punishing them for their sins."

She paused to reach for a tissue. Sunny moved the box that was sitting on the coffee table within her reach. Frances wiped her eyes and smiled wanly at Sunny. "You remind me of her. She was tall and big-boned like you. And smart. Smart as the day is long. She used to write all the time. She kept a journal. That's why I know all of this. After she died, I read all of them. Eddie Bradley is mentioned in one. I think it's the one from 2006."

Sunny couldn't believe her luck. "May I have a look at it, Ms. Chambers?"

"Yes, of course," Frances said, rising. "I'll get it for you."

In her absence, Sunny turned to Jonas who was sitting beside her on the couch. "If Eddie had AIDS," she whispered, concern written all over her face, "Kaya could very well have it. This is *awful!*"

Jonas reached for her hand and squeezed it reassuringly. "Don't get ahead of yourself. Kaya may be perfectly healthy."

Sunny looked heavenward. "God, I hope so."

Jonas raised her hand to his mouth and kissed the top of it. "Have faith."

Frances returned with a bundle of black-leather-bound books in her arms. She sat down in the chair across from Sunny and Jonas and placed the journals on the coffee table. She picked up one and handed it to Sunny. "I earmarked the page where Eddie Bradley's first mentioned. Practically that whole year is about him. I think she started falling for him in spite of everything."

Sunny opened the journal and read.

"I met Eddie Bradley at a club. He started salivating like a dog the moment he got a good look at me. I was with Lanette and she thought he was looking at her from down the bar. But then he got up and came over. He totally ignored Lanette. As per our agreement, Lanette found another way to get home that night. As for me, I went to a hotel with Eddie. He was insatiable. He didn't even notice when I slipped the condom off him. He was kind of drunk, to be sure. But, come on, a man should have better sense than to take a strange woman to a hotel and then let her take care of putting on the condoms. He got what he deserved."

Sunny met Frances's eyes. "Do you know if Lanette is still in Atlanta?"

Frances nodded. "Yes, she's here. I'll give you her number." She got up again and disappeared somewhere in the back of the house.

When she returned, she sat down again and handed Sunny a slip of paper with a phone number written on it. "She works during the day so you should call her in the evening."

"Thanks, I will," said Sunny. She looked down at the journal in her hand then back up at Frances. "May I…"

"Take it," said Frances, anticipating her question. "If it will save Kaya Bradley from either the chair or life in prison, take it. I believe Joy would want to correct some of the wrongs she committed when she wasn't in her right mind."

"Thank you," said Sunny, and impulsively reached across the table and grasped Frances's hand. Frances gratefully squeezed Sunny's hand.

After which, Sunny rose and she and Jonas were seen to the door by Frances. "Keep me posted," she said in parting.

"I will," Sunny promised. "And when this is over, I'll return Joy's journal."

Once outside, Sunny wanted to hug Jonas in celebration but didn't think it was appropriate to do so when a grieving mother could be watching. But when they were in the car, and Jonas had pulled away from the curb, she let out a low-decibel scream, in deference to Jonas's eardrums. "Yay! Finally, we're getting somewhere. They ignored the contract, but they can't turn a blind eye to this. They will have to admit it as evidence and admit that Eddie could have killed himself, just like Kaya said!"

Jonas grinned at her enthusiasm as he drove through the south side neighborhood.

"Job well done, lawyer-babe. Where to next?"

Sunny curbed her enthusiasm, remembering what her mother had told her over the phone that morning. "Our parents are due in today. They have reservations at the Four Seasons. We're supposed to meet them at eight, remember?"

"Yeah, but that's hours away."

Sunny glanced at the clock on the dashboard. "It's nearly three. I'm going to need five hours to get ready."

Jonas laughed. "Don't tell me you're nervous."

"Okay, I won't tell you."

"But they're your mother and your grandmother. They don't care what you'll be wearing when they meet you. They simply want to hold you in their arms for once in their lives."

Sunny scrunched up her face much like a tomboy might

when told she had no choice but to wear a dress to the church social. "I just don't know if I'm going to live up to their expectations. Audra is feminine and petite. I'm gangly and, let's face it, pants, not frilly dresses, look better on me."

Jonas begged to differ. "Hell, no, they don't. The first time I saw you I thought you had the most gorgeous legs I'd ever seen."

"I'm not saying I'm awkwardly shaped," she explained. "I'm just saying that I'm not the type of girl who'll ever be comfortable in expensive dresses."

"Just be quiet, Sunny. You're about to make me stop this car and spank you."

"That might be interesting," Sunny said, giving him a saucy grin.

"I'm ignoring that for now," Jonas told her. "Because I have a surprise for you."

Sunny squinted at him. "I thought I told you I didn't want a birthday present."

"It's not a birthday present, it's a I'm-going-to-meet-my-mom-for-the-first-time present and you can't refuse to accept it. I got us a suite at the Four Seasons. On a different floor than your mother's. And now that you've decided you're not going back to the office and you need the next five hours to get ready, we're going shopping for that frilly dress you claim to be so uncomfortable wearing."

"A suite at the Four Seasons must cost an arm and a leg. I can't let you do that."

Jonas gave her an angry sidelong glance before returning his attention to his driving.

"I've had enough of you, Sunday Adams. What do you think I am, your driver? Do you think that because I've been living under your roof for the past three weeks that I can't afford to give you an extravagant gift if I want to? I've been with you, as I've told you many times, because Audra was afraid for your safety. Not because I needed a free place to live!"

"Don't blow a gasket," Sunny cried, laughing at his outburst.

"I don't like to talk about money. It's never brought me happiness. My mother killed herself in spite of being an heiress worth millions. It didn't do her any good. Maybe I have gone overboard with the wanderlust bit, but I'm not sorry I don't own a house anywhere, or even a car. Things start to own you instead of the other way around. But that doesn't mean that one day I won't buy a house or a car, or want to marry and father children. I want that. But for now, I'm happy as I am."

"As well you should be," Sunny cried, smiling still.

"Don't patronize me, woman!"

"I'm not. Seriously, Jonas, I admire you." She schooled her expression. "There, is that better?"

"You make me feel so inadequate," Jonas said softly.

"Is that what this was all about? My making you feel inadequate?"

"I've done a lot of good over the years teaching people who truly need to understand how the economic system works. But lately I've been using the traveling as an excuse for not having a home base. Just as I used my father's inability to find one good woman as an excuse for my inability to do the same. Then, I met a woman who told me to my face what a crock that was. I really needed to hear that. So now, Sunny, I'm not going to go quietly back to my old life when I know I could be living a fuller, richer life with someone like you. You've made it clear that you don't love me. I accept that. But knowing you taught me a valuable lesson about myself. I do want the wife, the family and the house in the country. And I'm going after it. You make me feel inadequate because you seem to have known what you want out of life for a very long time, while I'm playing catch-up."

Sunny looked at him long and hard, then she burst out laughing. "I sure have you fooled, don't I? No wonder you proposed to me after only two weeks. You think I'm something I'm not!"

"You're peerless, Sunny." He said this with a sublimely happy expression on his face.

"I'm a neurotic mess!"

"You are not."

"I ought to know myself better than you do. I've lived with me for twenty-eight years. You've only lived with me for three weeks."

"You're a perfectly sane woman."

"I haven't had sex since I was twenty-one."

That shut him up.

They had come to a stop at a red light. Jonas looked into her eyes. "I'm sure you have a good reason for that."

"I do. I was a senior in college and it was my first time being in love, or I thought it was love. You have to understand that as a female growing up in different foster homes there were times when males in the household tried to sexually molest me. It happens all the time. I learned how to protect myself at an early age. I learned to associate sex, too, with something dirty. So, when I met Kirk, and he slowly convinced me that sex was a wonderful thing that two people in love shared, it was a big deal for me. We made love and it *was* beautiful. While it lasted. Kirk grew tired of me and moved on. I was left wondering what I'd done wrong. Since then I've dated, but whenever things got hot and heavy I found a way to break it off. Until I met you."

"I really messed up when I told you I loved you," Jonas surmised.

"It brought back memories of Kirk," Sunny admitted. "But not for long because I know you're nothing like him. He and I were too young for a commitment back then. He was sowing wild oats. He simply didn't let me in on it. I was too immature to see it. But now, Jonas, I'm going into our relationship with my eyes wide open. I want to make love to you, even if I'm not in love with you. The problem is, after I told you I couldn't marry you I felt you pulling away from me. I haven't pushed it because I figured you would reject me for rejecting *you*."

Cars blew their horns behind them. The light had changed to green.

Jonas continued driving. The sound of her voice and the mere fact that she hadn't been made love to in nearly seven years was wreaking havoc with his libido. He felt like going and checking into the Four Seasons right now. Forget the shopping spree.

He gripped the steering wheel tightly. "God, Sunny, I want to make love to you so badly that I'm going stiff as I speak. If that's what you want, I'd be more than happy to give it to you."

Smiling up at him, Sunny touched his thigh. "Tonight?"

"I won't be able to concentrate on anything else," he assured her.

"Neither will I," Sunny said huskily.

Jonas pointed the car toward an upscale shopping mall he was familiar with. The sooner they got the shopping over with, the sooner they could go to the hotel.

Sunny could hardly contain her excitement. Seven years of celibacy. Seven years of running instead of sex. She remembered it fondly, even if her experience with Kirk had left her with bitter under notes. Like ethereally beautiful music at a concert interrupted by a too-loud latecomer.

She knew that with Jonas, she would find the rhythm once more.

Chapter 13

"You can't tell me you don't like that one," Jonas said, exasperated. Sunny had tried on and rejected half a dozen dresses and pantsuits. They'd finally settled on Lenox Square Mall in Buckhead and they were presently in Bloomingdale's.

Sunny turned this way and that in front of the full-length mirror adjacent to the dressing room. She smiled at her reflection. The sleeveless royal-blue dress was a close-fitting sheath with a square bodice that nicely displayed her cleavage. The hem fell two inches above her knees. Focusing on how she looked from behind, she had to agree, in it she looked good going and coming.

She smiled shyly at Jonas, who wasn't trying to hide the effect the dress had on him.

He was undressing her with his eyes.

"I love it," she told him. "But judging from the way you're looking at me it's not the sort of dress I want to wear when meeting my mom and grandma for the first time. I'm going to have to pass."

"Over my dead body!" Jonas said. "I'm buying that dress whether you wear it tonight or not. Choose something else more virginal if you want, but that dress is coming home with us."

Sunny didn't protest. They were in public and their fighting required privacy. The smirk on Jonas's face told her he was counting on her being less prone to argue when in a public place.

"Fine," said Sunny huffily, spinning on her black patent leather pumps to return to the dressing room. "But don't pull that anymore this afternoon."

"I don't know what you mean," Jonas said, laughing softly.

"Yes, you do," she said over her shoulder, and closed the curtain of the dressing room.

Jonas's cell phone rang.

Pulling it from his coat pocket, he peered at the display. It was Audra phoning.

"Hello, Little Momma," he joked. "How do you like your suite?"

"It's the Presidential Suite," Audra said with a short laugh. "Do you think your father is trying to impress me?"

"He ain't no dummy," was Jonas's considered opinion. "I'm worried about you two. I plan to have a talk with him."

"We're both way past the age of consent, darling. But don't worry, I don't have affairs with married men. He knows that. Until he's free there will be nothing going on in the bedroom except television viewing."

Jonas loved Audra's tendency to speak plainly. "I'm more worried that he's clinging to you simply because he doesn't want to be alone. He's hurt you once. I'll kill him if he hurts you again."

"Miss Nette has already given him that speech," Audra told him. "Where is my daughter? I love saying that!"

"We're shopping. She's in the dressing room right now choosing another outfit to model for me."

"Oh, she's modeling for you?" Audra said, sounding

pleased. "Well, would you please put her on the phone when she comes out? I want to ask her what she'd like for dinner. We're going to dine here in the suite. The dining area seats twelve, can you believe it? This place is beyond gorgeous."

"I see Dad succeeded in impressing you," Jonas said.

"He went to check out the gym, so he isn't here to overhear how much I like the suite." She took a deep breath. "Jonas, I'm so nervous, I don't know what to do. What if she takes one look at me and decides she was too hasty in forgiving me?"

"She's definitely your daughter," Jonas told her, smiling. "She's nervous about meeting you, too."

Sunny came back out. She and Jonas made eye contact and she gave him an askance look. "It's Audra," he said. "She wants to speak with you."

He handed her the phone.

This time Sunny was wearing a simple white cotton eyelet dress with band straps.

The neckline was rounded and didn't show much cleavage, but it molded to her breasts in a delightful way, as far as he was concerned. Cinched at the waist, the hem fell an inch above her knees. The skirt was somewhat flared and it flounced when she moved. She was sexy as all get-out in it. Chaste and sexy, a wicked combination.

He watched her as she spoke with her mother. Her beautiful eyes became animated, and her smile melted his heart. He was happy to see her mother was able to put that expression on her face.

Something magical was going to happen when those two were finally face-to-face tonight. He knew it.

After a quick run by Sunny's apartment to feed Caesar and pick up a few things to take with them for their overnight stay at the Four Seasons, Sunny and Jonas drove to midtown Atlanta.

The Four Seasons Hotel was on Fourteenth Street in the

middle of a historic residential neighborhood. It was a breath-taking, neoclassical, multistoried edifice of rose and marble granite.

Walking up to it, Sunny craned her neck to take it all in. "How many floors do they have?"

"Your mother's on the nineteenth," Jonas said. "I believe that's the top floor."

"I often pass this place but I've never been inside. It's beautiful."

She admired the marble-and-glass lobby as they approached the desk. The woman who greeted them was very efficient. She found Jonas's reservation in seconds. "I'm so glad you phoned to say you were checking in later than the normal check-in time, 3:00 p.m., Mr. Blake. Your suite is ready."

A few minutes later Sunny and Jonas walked into a one-bedroom suite on the sixth floor. There was a guest powder room in the foyer. A full living room and an intimate dining area for two.

While Jonas tipped the bellman, Sunny looked around. She was thrilled with the marble bathroom with brass fixtures, a deep tub, plus a separate glass-enclosed shower.

The tub looked inviting, but there was only an hour left to shower and get dressed.

Jonas came in and found her sitting on the edge of the tub, lovingly touching the brass fixtures. "You go get undressed," he suggested. "And I'll run you a bath."

Sunny turned hopeful eyes on him. "I don't have time for a soak."

"It'll relax you."

She didn't have to be convinced. "Okay!" She rose and went to the bedroom where she started peeling off her business suit. The king-size bed was covered in a pale yellow com-forter, and four fluffy down pillows were piled against the headboard.

She went to the nearby mirrored closet, removed her pumps and bent and placed them inside. She caught her reflection in the mirror and was surprised to note that the expression in her eyes was one of joy, not panic.

Somehow, spending the afternoon with Jonas had helped to expel her nervousness.

She turned and hurried back to the bathroom where Jonas was sitting on the edge of the tub running hot and cold water into it. He looked up when she entered the room. "It's not quite ready yet."

He had left his jacket in the living room. Now he was in gray dress slacks and a long-sleeved white shirt. He'd rolled up the right sleeve in order to test the temperature of the bathwater.

"I know," said Sunny, going to him. She bent and kissed him on the lips. "Thanks for today. In fact, thank you for everything. You've been so good to me, and I appreciate it."

Smiling, Jonas rose. "You're welcome." Then he pulled her into his arms and kissed her soundly. Parting, both of them sighed and gazed into each other's eyes for a moment.

"Finish undressing," Jonas told her. "Unless you'll start obsessing about being late."

Sunny gave one last longing-filled sigh and left.

A few minutes later she was soaking in the tub when Jonas walked into the bathroom naked as the day he'd been born, and stepped into the separate shower stall. Sunny was so startled she sat up abruptly in the tub and sent soapy water spilling over its edge.

Long, lean and muscular coppery brown legs and thighs. Broad shoulders and sharply delineated muscles in his chest and stomach. She willed herself not to look below his waist but she couldn't stop herself. *She was not disappointed.*

"Dear God, what are you trying to do, make me drown in here?"

Chuckling, Jonas turned on the water in the shower. "It's

getting late. I couldn't wait for you to vacate the bathroom."
He was so logical. So calm.

Sunny was not calm. Her nipples, tips peaking like minia-
ture hills from underneath the soapy water, were erect and the
rest of her was quite tense, too. She quickly began rubbing the
sponge all over her body in an effort to get out of the tub before
Jonas came out of the shower. He couldn't see her through the
opaque shower stall door.

She supposed he thought that since they had agreed that they
were going to make love tonight, seeing him completely naked
would be okay. But how was she going to get through dinner
with her mother, grandmother and his *father* when the memory
of his naked body was going to be running through her imagination in an unending loop?

She suddenly stopped herself. Why was she behaving like
a nunnery reject? She had seen a naked man before. One naked
man, Kirk. They had the same equipment, didn't they? No, they
didn't. Jonas's was far superior to Kirk's.

Then she got angry. What had he been thinking, walking in
here without even a warning? She could have averted her eyes.
Instead the image of his gorgeous body was now permanently
etched in her memory. Well, two could play that game.

She began rubbing her body at a more leisurely pace.

When she heard Jonas turn off the water in the shower, she
stood up like a glistening brown-skinned wet dream. Jonas
stepped from the shower stall and caught sight of her. First his
mouth watered. Then his brain told his penis what his eyes were
observing, and that bad boy stood at attention.

Sunny smiled sweetly. "Would you pass me a bath towel?"

Jonas's brain was still talking to his penis. "What?"

"A towel, please."

He vacantly reached over and pulled a towel from the bundle
on the shelf and handed it to her. His eyes lowered to the wet,
curly dark hair between her shapely thighs.

His erection was now fully realized, and the towel he had around his waist did little to conceal it. He could do nothing but leave the room in a hurry.

Gotcha, Sunny thought, smiling.

Audra paced the floor of the Presidential Suite. She had plenty of space to cover because the suite took up twenty-two hundred square feet. Vernette and Norman were sitting on the sofa in the living room watching Deana Davis on the plasma TV. She was a guest on a nighttime celebrity gossip show.

"Turn that off," Audra said as she paced behind the sofa. "I'm nervous enough as it is."

"Now, sweetie, you must keep abreast of what the enemy camp has planned for you," said Vernette, eyes glued to the TV. "She confirmed that she tried to interview you but you refused."

"None of her subjects has ever granted her an interview," said Norman. "But that doesn't stop her. She depends on interviews with 'close, personal friends,' of the poor boob she's targeted."

There was a knock at the door.

Audra ran to the door.

"Slow down, dear," Vernette cautioned. "You don't want to scare the child."

She picked up the remote from the coffee table and turned off the set. Then she and Norman joined Audra at the door. Audra took a deep breath before turning the knob and opening it.

Sunny stood on the other side wearing the white dress and two-inch-heeled sandals, also white. Her black, curly hair fell down her back. Audra, coincidentally, was wearing white, a pantsuit with a bronze shell underneath. She wore three-inch-heeled sandals in the same shade.

The two women locked eyes and could not stop staring at each other. Sunny thought, *I have her eyes and her lips.* All her life she had wondered if she would ever meet anyone who shared her DNA. Someone who perhaps sounded like her when she laughed.

Audra thought, *Thank you, God, for making her healthy!*
She's beautiful!

"Mom!" Sunny cried and fell into Audra's arms. Until that
moment Sunny hadn't known what she would call Audra when
she finally saw her.

Mom came naturally to her lips.

"Baby!" Audra exclaimed, hugging Sunny tightly.

The other three people, whom they had totally forgotten in
their excitement, had to move them from the doorway so that
the door could be closed.

Vernette pulled Audra from behind and Jonas gently pushed
Sunny inside. Norman closed the door.

While Sunny and Audra remained in a clinch, Vernette walked
up to Jonas and gave him a hug. "How are you, sweet boy?"

Jonas bent to kiss her forehead. "Pretty good. How're you
holding up after that long car ride?"

Vernette dismissed his concern with a wave of her hand.
"That was nothing. I once took a train all the way to Los Angeles and that was not nearly as comfortable as the rental car."

Norman had rented the car because they planned to fly back
to L.A. No one would be stalking the Atlanta airports for Audra,
and even if they did, they wouldn't find out any juicy information for Deana Davis.

Vernette grabbed Norman by the arm and gently pushed him
in the direction of his son. She then went over to Audra and
Sunny and put her arms around both of them.

To Jonas, his father appeared uncomfortable in his presence.
Sure, they were often at odds, but they still managed to be civil
with each other most of the time. He offered his father his hand.
Norman surprised him by throwing his arms around him and
hugging him tightly, albeit briefly. Letting him go, Norman
said, "Good to see you, son."

Jonas smiled wonderingly. What had gotten into Norman?
"Good to see you, too, Dad." He glanced at the three women

who were still hugging, and if his ears weren't deceiving him, having a good, cleansing cry, as well. "They're going to be a while," he said. "Could I have a word with you in private?"

"We can go into the living room," Norman said, turning in that direction.

He and Jonas sat across from each other, both tall men with strong-featured faces and healthy, powerful bodies. The sartorial splendor of the father was slowly being acquired by the son. They both wore expensive slacks, casual shirts and Italian shoes.

Both had curly hair shorn close to their scalps, although the father's had turned white and, unlike some of his Hollywood counterparts, he wasn't dyeing it.

Jonas met his father's eyes. "I wanted to make sure that your spending time with Audra is not a selfish act on your part. That you're not making her your rebound woman. If you recall, your soon-to-be ex-wife was your rebound lover after your second divorce."

Norman would ordinarily get angry and shout at his son to keep his nose out of his business but he was at a peaceful place now. He'd finally learned the value of true friendship. "Son, yes, I am attracted to Audra as any man in his right mind would be. But she's made it clear that until I'm a free man all we can be is friends, and I accept that. You don't have to worry about her. She's more than capable of taking care of herself and I have the sore ribs to prove it." He touched his side and grimaced.

Jonas laughed shortly. "I'm glad to hear it."

"Now that we've cleared that up," said his father, "there's something I want to say to you."

"Fire," Jonas encouraged him.

Norman pursed his mouth uncomfortably, lowered his eyes and paused so long that Jonas wondered what could be so tortuous in nature that his father couldn't even say the words. Then his father blurted out, "I regret being an absentee father to you, Jonas. I wish I hadn't been such a selfish son of a bitch where your mother was concerned. I blame myself for her death. I should have been there for her. Instead of building something that would last, a strong family, I focused on my career, a thing that is fleeting at best and wholly unsatisfying at its worst."

Jonas was certain that those were the most words his father had said to him at one time in years. They sat in silence for at least a minute. Both of them were unused to heartfelt conversations between them. Like anything new, it would take time to become accustomed to.

Jonas momentarily found the right words. "I don't blame you for Mom's death anymore. I realize that she was probably clinically depressed and was only trying to stop the pain. I've often prayed that she's at peace. And I forgive you for not being there for me after her death. That was when I really needed you to explain that everything was going to be all right even after something so horrible. I figured that out for myself, though. I figured out a lot of things for myself and maybe that was a good thing. I doubt I'd be as self-sufficient as I am today if you'd been a doting father."

He lowered his gaze to his hands, which were so much like his father's. Returning it to his father's face, he added, "I don't know what happened to make you change your mind about me, but I'm not going to begrudge you the chance to begin acting like a father toward me if that's what you want. Therefore, I need your advice on a personal matter."

Norman pulled nervously at his shirt's collar. Noticing the habit, he dropped his hand onto his thigh and looked into Jonas's eyes. "I'm listening."

"I asked Sunny to marry me, and she turned me down. What should I do about it? I love her so much, and she's totally taking that fact for granted. I told her that her rejection hasn't changed how I feel about her and I'm a patient man. But I lied. I'm running out of patience. Dad, I've never asked another woman that question. Never! She's driving me crazy!"

Norman paled. "When you ask for advice, you really ask for advice!" He peered across the room at Sunny, Audra and Vernette, who were now laughing at something one of them had said. "And where does she get off refusing my son's proposal! She's too much like her mother by far."

Both of them laughed, which eased the tension.

"All I can tell you," Norman said after some consideration, "is to be the one she can lean on. Don't rush her. And take every opportunity to show her you love her. That's all. Like her mother, she's no fool. She'll recognize what a good thing she has in you."

Jonas smiled at his father. "Thanks, Dad."

"It was my pleasure," said Norman, his eyes a bit misty. He was glad when the women walked over to the living room and Audra introduced him to Sunny.

Sunny surprised him by giving him a warm hug. "Any father of Jonas's is family," she told him, smiling.

Norman found himself misting up yet again. "Thank you, Sunny."

Vernette noticed the state he was in and ushered everyone into the dining area. Room service had already brought their meals and set the table, leaving their meals under silver chafing dishes.

She directed everyone to their proper places at the table. After everyone was seated, Audra said, "Momma, would you say the blessing?"

Vernette intoned, "Dear Lord, thank you so much for this day. A day I have hoped for since learning of Sunny's existence. A day my daughter has looked forward to for so long the poor woman wore out her knees praying for it. Thank you for Sunny and for Jonas. Our children."

"Amen," said Audra, smiling at Sunny.

"Amen," said Norman, smiling at Jonas.

"Amen," said Sunny and Jonas, looking at each other and

dropping their gazes for fear their loved ones might read too much into their demeanor.

They removed the covers from their meals and dug in.

"How was your road trip?" Sunny wanted to know.

"It was exciting," Audra said. "We made a wrong turn in Texas and wound up in a town called Bandera. It's known as the Cowboy Capital of the World. Lovely town. It's home to several world-champion ropers. We were tired and hungry so we stopped at a diner and got something to eat. That's where we met one of the ropers who was there with his wife and children having lunch. Well, we started talking and one thing led to another and we found ourselves at his ranch with him showing us how to rope calves. Norman got pretty good at it."

Norman laughed. "I had a blast. I may make a film about the last of the cowboys. Should be poignant."

Sunny put down her fork and regarded Norman and Audra who were sitting next to each other across from her and Jonas. Vernette sat at the head of the rectangular table. "It's really great that you two remained friends after the divorce."

Audra hadn't explained that she and Norman had barely spoken to each other since the divorce and their present friendship was recent. She did now with her usual candor.

"Oh, darling, Norman and I didn't even speak to each other for years. We reconnected about the same time as you and Jonas met. About a month ago." She smiled fondly at Norman. "Norman and I were friends before we were lovers. I missed that friendship after the divorce. Once we started spending time with each other again, all of those memories came flooding back and we decided to forget the acrimony and build on the good times. So we're friends now."

"Friends," Norman agreed, looking at her with an abundance of love.

Vernette put the spotlight on Sunny and Jonas by saying, "I think you and *Jonas* make a lovely couple."

Jonas didn't have to be sitting next to Sunny to know that she was blushing. He was attuned to her emotions as never before. Fact is, his body was acutely aware of hers. He was the moon to her earth, helpless against her gravitational pull.

He was happy to come to her rescue with, "I'm flattered that you think Sunny and I make a lovely couple, Miss Nette, but we're just pals."

"Yes," Sunny confirmed, smiling. "Friends."

Yeah, right, Vernette thought.

Chapter 14

"Sunny, are you happy?" Audra asked. It was after one in the morning. Following dinner the party had moved to the living room where Audra and Vernette had gifted Sunny with a photo album of family pictures. Sunny spent a delightful hour learning the faces of her mother's brother and sister and their families.

Vernette went to bed at around midnight, and Jonas and Norman went for a walk, leaving Sunny and Audra alone in the living room.

Whereupon Audra had asked her if she was happy.

Sunny uncrossed her legs and sat on the sofa with them primly together. Hands on her thighs, she looked into Audra's eyes and said, "I think I'm as happy as the next person. I don't erupt in paroxysms of joy on a daily basis but, on the whole, I'm pretty satisfied with my life."

"Good," said Audra. "That's all I wanted to know. I realize that you must have had times when you wondered if life would ever get better, but you survived them. You're essentially a survivor and I thank God for that." She lowered her gaze for a moment. "I will always regret giving you up, Sunny. I want you to know that."

"I understand why you did it," Sunny told her with sincerity. "You didn't know if you could take care of me. It was a selfless thing you did, not a selfish thing. That's what you're thinking, isn't it?"

Audra nodded in the affirmative. "I see so many single mothers doing the very thing I was faced with and skipped out on. I should have kept you."

"You can't keep beating yourself up about it." Sunny reached out and grasped her mother's hand in hers. "If you want, one day, I'll tell you all about my childhood before and after Momma and Daddy were killed. But after that, you have to promise me that we'll put the past behind us. Promise?"

She could see that Audra was struggling with that promise. Guilt had her firmly in its grip. "Do you know why God gave us the capacity to feel guilt?" Sunny asked softly.

Audra's gaze was hopeful. "Why?"

"Because He knew the only way we'd be able to tell the difference between right and wrong was when we heard that inner voice telling us we'd behaved badly. And when we heard that inner voice He probably hoped that we would do something to try to correct our actions. You've done that, Mom. Now, I expect you to get rid of the guilt and allow us to go forward."

Audra flung her arms around Sunny. "Thank you, baby. Thank you so much!"

Sunny was laughing softly as she hugged her mother. When they drew apart, she said, "I've also been giving your situation with Deana Davis some thought, and I think the only thing to do is to trump her."

"You mean pull a card that beats anything she may have up her sleeve?"

"Yes, and I'm your card. Give an interview to a journalist of your choosing and spill everything about me. The interest in Ms. Davis's book will fizzle."

"Why didn't I think of that!" Audra exclaimed, eyes sparkling with excitement.

"Because you were too busy feeling guilty," Sunny joked. "But that's over with now, right?"

"Yes," Audra heartily agreed. She smiled broadly at Sunny. "And on that note, I want to invite you to come live with me and your grandmother in Beverly Hills."

Sunny wasn't surprised by Audra's offer. Audra had ended many of their phone conversations with, "I wish we lived closer to each other." Sunny had known it was only a matter of time before she broached the subject.

She had no intention of refusing outright. "That's a very generous offer and I'm flattered that you want me to live with you. Let me give it some serious thought. Right now I really like where I'm living, especially Warm Springs, and I also enjoy working with Tom."

Audra maintained a pleasant expression even though she was disappointed by Sunny's response. She didn't want to leave here on Thursday morning, the day after Sunny's birthday party, without the reassurance that her daughter would soon be moving closer to her. But she realized that Sunny was an adult and had to make her own choices. One of her first lessons as a parent.

So she said, "I understand. But if you should decide you'd like a change, the offer will always be open. Beverly Hills could use a few more women lawyers. Entertainment law is big these days."

"I really like defending people who seem to be getting a raw deal," Sunny said. "Do you suppose I'll be able to find many people to fit that description in Beverly Hills?"

"I guess not," Audra reluctantly admitted. "Although my last contract was definitely a case of highway robbery on the part of the studio!"

They laughed, and were still laughing when Jonas and Norman returned.

"I told you they wouldn't be winding down when we got back," Norman said to Jonas.

Audra looked at the clock on the DVD player. It read 1:32 a.m.

"I didn't realize it was that late," she said. "We've been talking for five and a half hours. Sunny, you and Jonas can't travel this late at night. Stay over. There's plenty of room in that king-size bed for you, me and Momma. We'll let the guys fight over the sofa bed."

"Oh, we don't have far to go," said Sunny happily. "We're just—"

"A few miles down the road," Jonas hastily finished for her. "It only takes about fifteen minutes to get to Sunny's apartment, Audra, and I'm wide awake. You don't have to worry about us being on the road this late."

Audra pouted. "I just hate to see you go, darling," she told Sunny.

Both of them got up from the sofa and hugged. "I'll see you tomorrow," Sunny said. "I have to work, but we'll come by in the evening."

"Okay," her mother said, continuing to hold on tightly.

Norman cleared his throat. "Sweetheart, you have to let go of her if she's going to leave."

Audra let go but tiptoed and planted a kiss on Sunny's cheek. "Until tomorrow."

Sunny, in turn, kissed her cheek. "Good night, Mom."

Jonas took her hand, she picked up the photo album, and they left.

In Jonas and Sunny's absence, Audra cried, "Isn't she unbelievably wonderful?"

"That, she is," Norman agreed. "My son has chosen well."

Audra stared up at him. "What do you mean by that?"

"He's in love. The boy has finally fallen big-time. He asked her to marry him, but she thought it was too soon so she turned him down."

"Smart girl."

Norman took offense. "She *would* be a smart girl if she accepted."

"Yes, of course, Norman. I want them to be together. But not because Jonas is smitten but because both of them have had time enough to know they can't live without each other."

Calm now, Norman said, "I knew that's what you meant."

"Sure you did," said Audra skeptically. Yawning now that her daughter was gone for the night and her body's circadian rhythm was catching up with her, she added, "Let me help you get the sofa bed ready and then I'm going to bed."

Sunny waited until she and Jonas got in the elevator before exclaiming, "My apartment's only a few minutes away? You might have told me you didn't want them to know we're spending the night here. Why *don't* you want them to know?"

Alone in the elevator, Jonas was holding her close, his arms around her waist, her back to him. All evening he'd been on his best behavior. He hadn't touched her once until they had gotten ready to go. Now he wanted to touch her all over. "Because I didn't want your mother to know I was about to do this to her daughter."

He bent and kissed the side of her soft, fragrant neck. Sunny had been clutching the photo album to her chest while his arms were wrapped around her. She turned to face him with the album between them. Jonas hungrily kissed her. Sunny kissed him back, moaning softly as his tongue parted her lips and proceeded to sensually dance with hers.

Jonas paused long enough to take the album from her and

place it on the floor of the elevator. "Don't worry, we won't forget and leave it behind."

Pulling her against him again, he tilted her head back to look deeply into her warm brown eyes. They were the color of dark honey, and the smoldering expression in them made him tense with anticipation. "I've been in a state of semi-arousal all night, remembering how you looked getting out of the bath. Tell me you want me as much as I want you."

"I can't wait," she said, breathlessly. And she reached up and brought his head down for a long, passionate kiss. Jonas pushed her roughly against the wall of the elevator as the kiss deepened and their bodies pressed closer together. He raised her dress and cupped her luscious behind in his hands. Sunny sighed against his mouth. She felt his erection, and her right hand went instinctively to his crotch. He moved against her hand.

The elevator's bell rang denoting they had arrived at their floor. They hastily drew apart. Jonas bent and picked up the photo album. Both of them were in the back of the elevator, calmly standing there as if they had ridden all the way down in those positions, when the elevator doors slid open. They walked out and two gentlemen in business suits got in.

Hands entwined, Sunny and Jonas walked down the hall to their room. Jonas unlocked the door and allowed Sunny to precede him inside. Once the door was shut, automatically locking behind them, it was officially on.

Jonas put the photo album on the foyer table.

Sunny kicked off her sandals. Jonas's shoes found themselves beside hers on the foyer floor. Eyes engaged in consensual voyeurism, they watched as clothes were removed and tossed aside. Jonas got down to his briefs in record time.

Sunny slowly unzipped her dress and let it float downward to her knees, then she stepped out of it wearing only a wisp of a slip and bra and panties. Jonas hardened further when he glimpsed more of her beautiful bare brown skin as she bent and picked up the dress. She laid it on a nearby chair after which she pulled the slip over her head and the only things left to remove were her bra and panties.

Jonas's heart thudded wildly as she backed up to him for him to undo the clasps on her bra. His hand touched the warm, smooth skin of her back and Sunny trembled with desire.

Jonas quickly unhooked the clasps and Sunny finished removing the bra and tossed it onto the chair with the dress. She turned to face him and Jonas took her in. She was perfection to him. Full, rounded golden-brown breasts with darker nipples that he had to taste. "Sunny, you're exquisite."

Sunny shyly lowered her eyes. He tilted her head back so that she was looking him in the eyes. "Believe it. You're beautiful."

She smiled and reached down to grasp the waistband of his briefs. "*Seven years,* Jonas."

Jonas laughed and picked her up. "Forgive me for thinking you wanted to take things slowly." He took her to the bedroom.

"Slow can wait until the second round," Sunny said from her perch in his arms. Looking around the room as she kissed his jaw, she saw that the bed was already turned down.

Jonas dropped her onto it, got a condom out of the night-stand drawer, opened it and tossed the wrapper, then straddled her. He bent and kissed her belly, tonguing the belly button. Sunny squirmed. The feel of his warm, wet tongue sent rivulets of pleasure straight to her sex. An intense throbbing down there was driving her to distraction.

He worked his way up to her nipples, and she felt like screaming with wanton abandon.

He sucked, nipped, moved his tongue up and down with such exquisite titillation that her breath came in rapid little pants. She was trying so hard to keep the screams in that her eyes were squeezed shut.

"Sunny," Jonas whispered.

"Mmm?" she moaned.

"Open your eyes and look at me."

She did, but as soon as they came open and she saw his tongue descending upon her nipple, she climaxed.

Knowing what had happened...and without him...Jonas quickly removed her panties.

Leaning on his haunches he rolled the condom onto his erect penis and placed the tip at the opening of her sex. Sunny, nice and wet, and still riding the wave of her orgasm, welcomed him inside of her. Even though she was adequately lubricated for him, she was still tight and the feel of his big penis moving deep, and deeper, made her wrap her legs around him and hold on tight.

Jonas was enjoying watching her facial expressions run the gamut from sheer joy to sweet pain and back again. This was the second time she'd had an orgasm without penetration. He'd never had a lover so responsive to sexual stimuli.

But then he'd never had a lover who'd forgone sex for seven years, either.

She was looking him in the eyes, no longer shy, but confident. She gave him thrust for thrust, her strong, supple body taking his in with ease and unalloyed gratification.

Feeling himself close to completion, he bent and kissed her. She rose up a little on the bed and met his kiss with as much fervor as she met his thrusts. She tasted so good to him. She felt wonderful, soft and firm, healthy muscle under her warm brown flesh. All of it worked together to send him screaming over the precipice. He was hers. Lost.

Completely hers.

Sunny felt his body buck and grabbed his firm buttocks with both hands. She wanted to feel his convulsions, every last one of them. She wanted to enjoy each second because this was the first time she'd made love to someone she was in love with. She regretted, now, not trusting her instincts. Because when Jonas had told her he loved her and asked her to marry him, she had wanted desperately to go with her first instinct. But no, she'd allowed logic and common sense to take over. Both had stood her in good stead for years when she was protecting herself from men like Kirk. She should have known Jonas was not like them.

"I love you, Sunny."

She kissed his chin and smiled at him. "I'm sorry I came so soon. I'll work on that."

Jonas was disappointed she hadn't said she loved him, too. But he wasn't going to let that disturb his equilibrium. He was going to take his father's advice and give her all the time she needed.

So he laughed softly as he rolled off her and onto his side. "That's only a problem if you're a man. You can have all the orgasms you want and we'll still be able to enjoy each other. Shall I demonstrate in the shower?"

Sunny was game. She went and pinned her hair up in hopes of not getting it too wet.

In the shower, Jonas soaped a washcloth until it was thick with foam, then, standing behind Sunny, he gently massaged her breasts with it. He coaxed her backward until her body was pressed against his. Back to chest. Buttocks to penis.

Sunny relaxed against him. She noticed he'd abandoned the washcloth and was now using his hands alone. As warm water rained on them, his hands rubbed her nipples, took them between thumb and forefinger and gently squeezed.

Then, using both hands, he pried her thighs apart and using the forefinger of his right hand he delved into her warm, wet vagina. Her clitoris was already a hardened nub.

He found it and coaxed even more of an arousal from her. She moaned as she threw her head back onto his shoulder.

Jonas grew hard again. He couldn't help it, what with her behind pushed against his manhood and her moans ringing in his ears. He wanted her more than he had a few minutes ago. He wouldn't take her without a condom, though, so he would have to wait until he could get one.

He showed her no mercy, however, as his finger moved

against her clitoris. Sunny was wildly writhing against his hard body. He caressed her breasts as he continued worrying her clit. He felt her tremble and then she let out a moan that was so delightfully erotic that he nearly ejaculated prematurely.

She turned in his arms and kissed him gratefully. Her eyes were demure. He loved her even more in that moment.

"I've got to have you again," he said urgently, reaching over to turn off the water.

He grabbed a towel and stepped from the shower stall onto the bath rug. He helped her out and immediately began drying her off. Sunny grabbed a towel and returned the favor. She hadn't had the chance while in the shower to rub his body down as he'd done hers.

She delved lower and Jonas grabbed her hand just before she touched his penis.

"Let's save that for another time. I want you dry and in the bed. Now, please!"

Sunny was more than happy to comply. She quickly dried off, and by the time he returned to the bedroom and got another condom, she was waiting in bed wearing a pale blue micromini negligee that tied in the front at the neck. She had left it untied, and she had nothing on underneath.

She got up on her knees and took the condom from Jonas. "May I at least touch you to put this on?"

Jonas shook his head. "No, I want you too badly for you to touch me anywhere right now. If you do, you won't be the only one coming too soon."

"All right, I'll keep my hands to myself," Sunny said with a mischievous glint.

While still on her knees she began rubbing her hands over her nipples, making them immediately harden. Looking into Jonas's eyes she continued intimately touching herself.

Jonas quickly put on the condom and pushed her back onto the bed. "You little tease!"

She opened her legs. "I'm *your* little tease." And she smiled seductively.

Jonas plunged into her. Sweet. That's all he could think. Sweet and tight. She was looking him directly in the eyes as she squeezed her vaginal muscles around his shaft. It made him think of what it must feel like to have her mouth on him.

His name was a mantra on her lips. He liked that. He liked it a lot. Slowing down to heighten her pleasure, he said, "Talk to me. Am I there yet?"

"Oh, yeah," Sunny said, her tone dripping with sex.

He grabbed her by the hips, pulling her tighter against him. His thrusts quickened slightly as his penis grew thicker inside of her. Sunny's sugar walls quivered with the most explosive orgasm yet tonight.

Soon afterward Jonas let go and they held each other, kissing chins, lips, foreheads. Momentarily Jonas collapsed onto his side and drew her into the crook of his arm.

Sunny snuggled closer and closed her eyes with a satisfied sigh.

Jonas kissed her forehead one last time before closing his eyes.

She fell asleep. Jonas got up and got rid of the condom, took a quick wash and got back into bed, pulling her firmly back into the crook of his arm, then he slept, too.

Chapter 15

The next morning, Sunny had to be in court by ten o'clock. It was only a routine child-support case. She presented her client's grievances, and the judge found in favor of her client and ordered her ex-husband to pay all monies owed her.

After lunch she went to visit Kaya.

She had seen Kaya's attitude go through a marked change for the better ever since she'd been allowed to see Navarre once a week. When she was brought into the room by James, she smiled broadly at Sunny. Her auburn hair was braided due to the fact that she didn't have access to a stylist who could give her relaxed hair a touch-up.

Sunny rose and briefly hugged her. "How are you, Kaya?"

They sat down, facing each other. "I'm okay," Kaya said softly. "What's up? I thought you said I probably wouldn't see you again until Thursday. It's Tuesday, isn't it? I do tend to lose track of days in here."

"No, you're right, it's Tuesday." Sunny's briefcase was

leaning against the right front leg of her chair. She picked it up and set it on the table. "It's about the last woman on your list of Eddie's lovers, Joy Chambers." She raised her eyes to Kaya's. "I'm sorry to say she died of complications from AIDS five months ago."

Kaya's eyes stretched momentarily and she expelled a harsh breath. "That's why he made me go get tested!"

"Eddie made you get tested?"

Eyes narrowed in anger, Kaya nodded. "Yeah, my first time was in 2006. I've been getting tested every few months. After Eddie insisted that I get tested, I insisted that we not make love without a condom. No, *two* condoms. They can break sometimes. I know you think I was crazy for staying with Eddie but I still loved him. I was trying to hang on to that. Trying to stay a family for Navarre's sake."

As Sunny was listening to Kaya, she reached into the briefcase and withdrew Joy Chambers's journal. "This belonged to Joy Chambers. In it she wrote in detail about her affair with Eddie. She admits that during the sex act she would often remove the condom without Eddie's knowledge." She set it on the table between them.

"Are you trying to say Eddie had AIDS?" Kaya cried, a frightened aspect in her light brown eyes.

"It's a possibility," Sunny told her frankly. "But I don't have proof, it's just a hunch. I haven't talked to his doctor. Do you know who his doctor was?"

"Dr. Bertrand Lewis," Kaya answered immediately. "He's a family physician. I go to him, too."

It was hard for Sunny to believe that if Eddie had AIDS he would keep it from his wife. Surely he had confided in her. Or, if he chose to keep it to himself, surely Kaya noticed a change in his appearance or behavior. She would have wondered about all the pill bottles in their medicine cabinet, wouldn't she?

"Eddie wasn't taking medication for anything before he

died? His appearance didn't change any? Perhaps his behavior? Give me *something*, Kaya."

Kaya's eyes watered and her hand shook when she picked up the journal and opened it. "Eddie's mood ran hot and cold, anyway. He was especially moody when he had a new CD about to drop. As for his physical appearance, yes, he had lost weight. And I don't think he was as energetic as he usually was. But he was exhausted from working on the album."

"Any recent hospital stays?"

"A couple of days last January. A bad case of the flu."

Sunny's mind raced. The flu? It could have been pneumonia. AIDS patients were sometimes very susceptible to pneumonia. "Did the doctor tell you it was the flu? Did you see any medical papers saying it was the flu?"

Kaya shook her head. "I just took his word for it. Eddie took care of business. He or the accountant."

Sunny felt like sighing out of frustration but held it in check. Why did some wives let their husbands handle all the finances? She'd run into so many women who didn't know what their husbands were up to where money was concerned. Insurance, bonds, any sort of investments. They were clueless. Kaya was yet another example.

"I'll have to go see his doctor," she decided. "If Eddie did have AIDS it would lend credence to your assertion that he committed suicide."

Kaya's eyes stretched again. "Oh, my God. When I went to him, his blood got all over my clothes and my hands."

Sunny comfortingly grasped her hand. "Kaya, you didn't have any cuts on your hands at the time, did you?"

"No, I didn't."

"Well, unless you ingested his blood, I don't see how you could have contracted AIDS from having his blood on your hands."

Kaya burst out crying. "I feel terrible, worrying about getting AIDS when Eddie is in his grave."

"Don't, Kaya. You have every right to be afraid. You have Navarre to think about. He's already lost one parent." She thought it wise to get off the subject of the possibility of her having contracted the disease. "Just one more question, and I have to go. Eddie didn't mention being sick to you. But is there anyone you think he would have confided in?"

"Chaz," Kaya said without hesitation. "They knew each other's secrets, which was another reason Eddie would never have fired him—Chaz knew too much about him."

"If Chaz knew Eddie had AIDS, why would he keep it a secret even after his death?" Sunny asked, eyes boring into Kaya's. She knew she was putting undue pressure on Kaya, but this was important. If they could prove Eddie had AIDS and he'd confided in Chaz, that would be another reason for the jury to have reasonable doubt about Kaya's guilt when they went to trial.

"I don't know," Kaya said after giving it some thought. "I can't imagine how it would benefit Chaz for me to go to prison for something I didn't do when he could come forward and testify that Eddie had a reason to kill himself."

Sunny was stumped, too. It made no sense for Chaz Palmer to keep that a secret.

Going back to the contract. The sooner Kaya was exonerated and restored as the main beneficiary of Eddie's will, the sooner Chaz would be able to wallow in his cool million.

Sunny rose and took the journal out of Kaya's hand. "I'll need to show this to Detective Deberry."

Kaya looked at the journal in Sunny's hand. "What does it say about Eddie? Was she in love with him?"

"Her mother says she was mentally unbalanced toward the end."

"Come on, Sunny, tell me, I can take it," said Kaya. "I mean, look at me—in jail because of all my husband's secrets and lies. If he did contract AIDS from Joy Chambers then that's why he killed himself. And if he hadn't killed himself, I wouldn't have run downstairs like a fool and gotten his blood all over me and my prints on the gun. Did she at least love him?"

Sunny didn't see any good coming out of Kaya knowing that a dead woman was obsessed with her husband. But she didn't believe in withholding information from a client, or a friend, if they asked for the truth. "She wrote that she adored him and she wished that things could have been different between them. In the end she regretted having sex with him without a condom."

"Well, that's something," Kaya said softly.

Sunny went and knocked on the door. James was standing right outside, and she could hear the jangle of keys as he unlocked the door. Turning to Kaya one last time before she left, she said, "You take care of yourself."

"You, too," Kaya said with a sad smile.

Sunny was glad to breathe fresh air when she walked out of the building. Jonas, who had been leaning on the Cherokee in the parking lot reading today's paper, pushed away and smiled at her. Like her, he was wearing a business suit. An expensive blue suit with a white shirt underneath. Sunny was wearing blue today, as well—a navy skirt suit with a white blouse and black pumps.

"How did she take it?" he asked.

"She didn't know much of anything. If Eddie had the disease, he kept it from her. She did say he was in the hospital last January with flu-like symptoms. I'm going to see his doctor."

She glanced at her watch. It was a quarter past two. "No time like the present to get things rolling."

She took out her cell phone and put in a call to the administrative assistant she shared with another attorney in the firm. "Betty, would you please phone Dr. Bertrand Lewis's office and tell him I need an appointment to see him concerning Eddie Bradley?"

"Sure," said Betty in her thick drawl. "Sometime tomorrow?"

"Hey, if he can see me before he goes home for the day, I'll see him. The sooner, the better."

"Got you," said Betty. "I'll call you back as soon as I find out anything."

"Thanks!"

"You're welcome." They rang off.

Closing the phone, Sunny smiled up at Jonas. Lately she couldn't look at him without smiling. Last night had been wonderful. This morning hadn't been bad, either. They had made love again when they awakened and then showered together. They were out of the hotel by eight. Even that early, Sunny had been worried they would run into her mother or his father and have to explain why they were at the Four Seasons so early in the morning. But they'd gotten away without incident.

A cold front had moved in last night and today the temperature hovered in the low seventies. The sun was shining brightly and only a few clouds broke up the constant azure of the sky.

Sunny went and leaned against the car beside him. "Anything interesting in the paper?"

"Pork belly futures look promising." He'd been reading the financial pages.

"Not for the pigs," said Sunny.

Jonas smiled. "No, I suppose not. Where to next?"

"Let's stay here for a while." She turned her face toward the sky. The sun felt good on her face. Sighing, she said, "What is it like to laze on a beach somewhere?"

"You ask that as though I've had a lot of experience."

"Haven't you?" Her brows arched upward and her eyes held an amused light.

Jonas folded the paper and tossed it onto the seat of the Cherokee. "Okay, I've been to the Caribbean a few times." He looked into her eyes. "But the place I'd like to take you someday is Amirantes Island in the Seychelles. It's kind of difficult to get there but it's well worth it. It's a thousand miles off the East African coast and not many tourists go there. The beaches have the whitest sand you've ever seen, and everything's so pristine and natural that all you want to do is admire what God has made. The water's so clear that when you dive in it's just you and the fish swimming happily together. We'd stay at a villa that faced the sea and when we weren't swimming or walking along the beach, we'd be sitting on the veranda enjoying the breezes."

"Sounds heavenly," Sunny said.

Jonas kissed the top of her head. "Great. We can leave after you win the Bradley case."

Thinking he must be simply daydreaming as she was, she played along. "What will the weather be like in December in the Seychelles? Will I need to take warm clothing?"

"It gets a little cool at night," Jonas said. "But since there isn't any nightlife to speak of, I plan to have you in bed by sundown anyway."

"So, I can wear next to nothing 24-7?"

"I recommend it," Jonas said.

Sunny's cell phone rang.

It was Betty. "The earliest Dr. Lewis says he can see you is Thursday morning at seven, before he makes his rounds."

"Fine," said Sunny. "Thank you, Betty."

"My pleasure."

Closing the phone, Sunny looked up at Jonas. "I won't be able to see Eddie's doctor until Thursday morning."

"Don't look so disappointed," Jonas said, placing his hand at the base of her spine and directing her to the passenger side. "There's still Joy Chambers's friend to contact this evening. Maybe she'll be more cooperative."

Chaz was in a quandary. Dunk actually had talent. In fact, the boy showed such raw talent as a rapper that Chaz could already imagine his meteoric rise in the hip-hop world. It might have been an easier choice for Chaz if he had been horrible.

Lately Chaz had been having nightmares about the night he'd witnessed Eddie's suicide. Sometimes the dreams would unfold exactly as it had occurred. Other times Eddie would accuse him of letting his wife rot in jail when he knew she was innocent.

At first Chaz had not come forward because he felt duty bound to keep Eddie's secret. Eddie had told him that he, himself, couldn't tell Kaya. *A true friend will take your secret to the grave.* Chaz vowed to keep quiet about Eddie having AIDS.

If the authorities somehow found the secret out anyway, he would come forward at that time and corroborate it. Even if his story about being present at the time of Eddie's suicide landed him in jail for obstruction of justice.

But the police hadn't found out that Eddie was sick. No one had been around asking questions about Eddie's health. Not even Kaya's lawyer.

Chaz was beginning to feel he might be home free.

Then, there were the pictures Dunk had taken. He'd sent Chaz the file via e-mail.

There were four photos in total. Two of Chaz entering the house, obviously walking and wearing a white T-shirt and sweatpants. Two of Chaz leaving the house running with the white T-shirt wadded in his hand.

Eddie's blood had been on the T-shirt. Chaz had burned it in the fireplace as soon as he got home. Then he'd washed the blood off of his skin with Lysol. Later, he'd looked up the ways that AIDS was contracted and realized that getting someone's blood on your skin, as long as you didn't have an open cut, was not one of the ways.

Blood to blood, such as sharing needles, was one of the ways. Having unprotected sex was another and being born of a mother who had the disease. You couldn't get it by being bitten by a mosquito and you couldn't get it by kissing someone because saliva had some kind of agent in it that killed the virus which, as it turned out, was pretty weak when it hit the air. So you couldn't get it, for instance, by sitting on a toilet seat in a public restroom.

Chaz had been pretty paranoid, still, for a few weeks after getting Eddie's blood on him. And he'd gone to get an AIDS test for the first time in his life.

So, he waited for somebody to find out about Eddie's medical condition. Until then, he went to visit Kaya in jail and worked with Dunk on building his rap career.

He was beginning to like the kid and when he was finally found out, he would regret having to finger him as the little blackmailer he was. More than likely they would both do time.

Sunny only needed to talk to Lanette McFarland to see if she could corroborate Joy Chambers's journal entry. Had she really met Eddie Bradley at a bar one night and gone to a hotel with him? Or was it all a product of her vivid imagination? Anyone could write about having an affair with a famous person. It didn't mean it was gospel.

So when she got Lanette on the phone after five on Tuesday afternoon, she explained who she was and asked Lanette if events in Joy's journal had happened as she had said.

"Yes, they did," Lanette was happy to report. "Joy wasn't a liar. I have pictures from that night to prove it. Eddie was kind enough to pose between me and Joy."

"Would you be willing to testify to that in court?" asked Sunny.

"You bet I would," said Lanette. "Joy's gone. I can't let people think she was a liar."

Sunny held her tongue because she wanted to say she didn't think being a liar was worse than purposely infecting someone with a deadly disease. Because as the facts were stacking up, it appeared that Joy Chambers had indeed infected Eddie Bradley with AIDS. Now they were both dead and an innocent woman's life hung in the balance.

"Thank you, Ms. McFarland. I'll be in touch," Sunny told her gratefully.

"You're welcome," said Lanette McFarland.

Sunny and Jonas were in her office at the firm. She was sitting behind her desk and he was sitting on the leather couch. She got up after putting the phone down and stretched. "That's it, then. I can't do any more until I speak with Dr. Lewis. Lanette says Joy did meet Eddie exactly as she described it."

"That's good news," Jonas said, rising. "What happens if you do find out he had AIDS? Will that be sufficient for them to let her go?"

"No," said Sunny. "They will continue to hold her because she had his blood on her and her prints were on the gun. Unless someone confesses to having witnessed Eddie killing himself, she has to be tried. A jury acquitting her is the only way she'll walk away a free woman."

They left the office soon after that and went by the Four Seasons for a short visit, after which they went home, made a quick salad for dinner, showered together and made love.

Sunny expected to breeze through her birthday party without incident. Her nervousness was circumvented by the fact that she knew everyone there except her paternal grandparents, and how much trouble could a couple in their seventies be?

She was soon to find out.

When she and Jonas arrived, there were already two other cars in the driveway, a stately black Lexus and a late-model black SUV with tinted windows.

Sunny knew that the Lexus belonged to Lani. She didn't know who was driving the SUV but guessed it wasn't the sort of car seventy-year-olds might enjoy, so she guessed it belonged to her mother's party.

Jonas parked behind the SUV and they got out. She was wearing the royal-blue dress that Jonas had taken one look at and vowed not to leave the store without. It showed a little more cleavage than the white dress had on Monday night, but not by much. She felt comfortable wearing it. Jonas wore a black suit with a crisp white shirt and a royal-blue striped silk tie.

Both of them wore black dress shoes. His were wingtips, hers were strappy sandals with three-inch heels. She rang the bell and Jonas turned to her and took her by the shoulders. "How is your stress level?"

"On a scale of one to ten, it's a three," she answered confidently.

He smiled and bent to kiss her softly on the lips. "Good."

The door was opened by Tom. His face split in a grin when he saw them. Taking Sunny by the hand, he pulled her inside. "It's the birthday girl!" he called out.

He hugged her and shook Jonas's hand. "Welcome, Jonas," he said.

"Thank you, sir," Jonas said respectfully.

Tom gave him a quick smile and ushered them out of the foyer and into the grand living room where Audra, Vernette, Norman and Lani were sitting around enjoying predinner drinks. Audra preferring water with a twist of lime.

Everyone was dressed in semiformal apparel, the women in knee-length dresses and the gentlemen in suits. Sunny went and kissed her mother's and grandmother's cheeks, warmly grasped Norman's hand for a moment and rubbed cheeks with Lani who was fond of doing that.

"Happy birthday!" Audra said. "How does it feel to be twenty-eight?"

"Not much different from twenty-seven," Sunny joked. She looked around. "Where are your parents, Tom?" She occasionally called him Dad in private, but hadn't yet gotten used to doing it in public.

"They should be here shortly," Tom said. He consulted his watch. "They still have ten minutes. They're rarely late for anything."

Sure enough, Constance Banks-Chapman and Thomas Trent Chapman arrived promptly at 7:55 p.m. When the doorbell rang, Tom sprang to his feet to answer it. Their housekeeper was at that moment serving Sunny and Jonas glasses of chilled white wine. She looked up at her employer with a startled expression. "Sir, I'll get that."

To her surprise, Sunny saw Tom stop in midstep and turn back around. "Yes, yes, of course. Please get the door, Mattie."

He went to stand stiffly next to his wife.

Sunny felt the tension in the room start to rise. She slowly sipped her wine. One glass was usually her limit as she had a low tolerance for alcohol.

A few minutes later Mattie returned as far as the doorway and presented Tom's parents. "Your parents have arrived, sir."

She moved aside and a tall, trim, attractive woman with light brown hair worn in a smooth upsweep and dressed in a gold-toned skirt suit in a jacquard pattern strode in followed by a tall, trim, handsome gentleman in a black suit with a white shirt and a black-and-red-striped tie. On her slender feet were a pair of gold-tone pumps. He wore highly polished black wingtips.

Tom cried, "Mother, Father! You both look marvelous. Come and meet everyone."

Constance and Thomas did not smile. Sunny watched their faces quite closely. Their mouths never turned up at the corners. Nor did their eyes register a glint of humor or pleasure. If she were to describe their expressions she would have to say that they were disdainful and haughty. Her mind rushed back to what Tom had told her about them. He was a retired judge. She was a retired college professor. They had been married nearly sixty years. They had three children, the oldest of whom was Tom. He was a "Junior."

Constance held up her hand, silencing Tom. "If you would be kind enough to point out Audra Kane, I can take it from there, son."

Tom was immediately on guard. Sunny could tell he was taken aback by his mother's request. What did she have to say to Audra?

At first, he tried joviality. "I know you're a big fan of Audra's, mother, but there are other people here to meet. Foremost, your granddaughter. That is why we're here tonight, to celebrate Sunny's return to our lives. I'm sure you can postpone the celebrity-worship for later."

"Have you taken leave of your senses, Thomas?" his father asked imperiously. "Do as your mother asks. Point out the Kane woman."

Sunny's hackles rose at the tone of his voice. She wasn't about to stand there and let them attack Audra. What sort of grievance could they have with her?

She thought the purpose of the party was to welcome her to the family and to put the past behind them.

Sunny stepped forward, facing her grandmother. Like her father, she tried conciliatory tactics at first. "Hello, grandmother, I'm Sunny." She held out her hand. "I'm pleased to meet you."

Constance looked Sunny in the eyes. "That dress reveals too much, young lady. You'll have to be taught modesty."

"Now, just a minute!" Audra exclaimed, stepping in front of Sunny. She was about three inches shorter than Constance, but she wasn't backing down. "Who do you think you are, talking to my daughter like that? There is nothing wrong with her dress. She looks beautiful in it."

Constance smiled. Her light brown eyes raked over Audra. "So, you're Audra Kane. I've been wanting to give you something ever since I heard about you and the trouble you've brought down on this family." Then she hauled off and slapped Audra hard across the face.

Tom immediately leaped between his mother and Audra. Grabbing his mother by the shoulders he shook her violently. "You promised me you wouldn't make a scene."

Sunny had pulled Audra into her arms, and now Norman and Jonas formed a protective barrier around the two of them.

Tom was still yelling at his mother. "You and your so-called high standards. Why can't you ever let people live their lives without your interference?"

Tom was so focused on his mother that he didn't notice his father walk up behind him. Only when Thomas Sr. tapped him on the shoulder and said, "Unhand your mother," did he notice him.

He looked at his father and said, "I want you to leave. Take her and get the hell out of my house. I thought, for once, we could be a normal, supportive family. You both gave me every indication that you were coming only to meet your granddaughter. Well, you don't deserve to meet her. Get out!"

No one noticed Vernette, either, until she walked up to Constance, slapped her hard on the face, and said, "Don't leave without taking back that gift you brought my daughter."

Constance screamed bloody murder. "Thomas, are you going to let your mother be assaulted in your own home?"

Tom turned to Vernette. "Thank you, Mrs. Kane. She had it coming."

He then took his mother and father, each by an arm, and escorted them to the door.

They went quietly.

When Tom turned back around, every last one of his guests were standing behind him in the foyer. Lani went to him and kissed his cheek. "My hero!" she exclaimed, clapping her hands. "I've been waiting on you to do that ever since we got married."

Audra, whose face had finally stopped stinging, smiled at him. "I can see, now, why you acted like such a boob when I told you I was pregnant twenty-nine years ago."

He smiled at her. "Thank you, Audra. But I have no excuse. I should have been there for you."

Sunny went and put her arms around both their shoulders.

"I'm starved." She winked at Lani. "I'm sure my stepmother has planned a delicious dinner for us. Let's go enjoy it, shall we?"

Chapter 16

"Well, I guess I won't be spending Christmas at my grandparents' house," Sunny joked after Jonas had gotten behind the wheel of the Cherokee for their trip home. "Poor Tom, apologizing again and again for his parents' behavior. It wasn't his fault he was born to domineering, judgmental people. My question is, if Constance is such a cultured lady, why did she slug Audra like she was in a barroom brawl?" She sighed. "Sometimes I think it was easier not having any relatives. Being in a family is hard work!"

Jonas laughed. "This is true." He reached over and grasped her hand tightly. "But it's worth the work. Look at how well you and Audra and Tom are getting along. They adore you."

Sunny smiled. She certainly had lucked out when it came to genuinely liking her birth parents. All of her fears were unfounded. "They're both good people. I have to say that I'm happy to know them."

Jonas brought her hand up and kissed the palm. "I'm happy for you."

"I can't believe what she said about the way I'm dressed. Even after I'd adjusted the bodice so that not much cleavage showed! She made it sound like I was guilty of indecent exposure."

"Sunny, she doesn't even know you. Don't let her comments get under your skin."

"That's what upsets me, Jonas! She doesn't know me, yet from what Tom told her about me and Audra she decided that I was a hussy, and Audra needed to be punished for having her son's child out of wedlock and making it known to the world twenty-nine years later. You heard her, she said Audra had brought shame down on their family. And I'm the shame."

"You *never* have to see them again," Jonas soothed.

"I will never see them again," Sunny seethed. "I'll never set foot in their house. Of course, it's not as if I'm going to be invited."

Jonas laughed. "Okay, that's enough of the pity party. Suck it up, and forget about your grandparents. Yesterday their opinions meant nothing to you. Why should they matter today?"

"They don't," Sunny said vehemently.

"Good," said Jonas. "Because you need to concentrate on the car that's been following us since we left your dad's place."

"You're too close. Remember to stay a car or two behind them," Chantay Jackson said to her friend, LaShaunda. She didn't mean to sound irritated. After all, LaShaunda was here only because she was loyal enough to help a sister out. But she was nervous. It had taken her two days to build up the courage to approach Kaya Bradley's lawyer.

Then, earlier, when she'd gone to her office, she'd gotten there just when Sunday Adams and a tall, good-looking guy were leaving. She and LaShaunda followed them to an apartment building. LaShaunda had encouraged her to get out and talk to Sunday Adams then, but she'd chickened out. Dunk was never going to forgive her for what she was planning to do. But then, he should never have involved her in his stupid plans, anyway. He was trying to be all gangsta and she wasn't down with that. Never would be. She was a senior in high school and stayed on the honor roll. Her parents had told her they didn't want her hanging with Dunk. When they found out what he'd done, and what he'd asked *her* to do, they were going to like him even less.

"Stop snapping at me," LaShaunda said peevishly. "I'm tired. I want to go home. As it is, my mom is going to ground me for a month for taking her car without permission. This is insane, Chantay! Do it and get it over with. Looks like they're going back to that apartment building we followed 'em to this afternoon. When they get out of the car, you'd better get your butt out and talk to that lawyer lady or I'm going home. I'm gonna give you one minute to get out of here when they park. A minute longer and I'm gone, I'm telling you!"

"Okay, okay," Chantay reluctantly agreed. She was clutching a 3.5 disk in her right hand. Her palm was sweaty. Why should she be nervous? She was doing the right thing.

Damn Dunk and his get-rich-quick schemes. Blackmailing a murderer. She knew he wasn't wrapped too tight, what with all the marijuana he smoked, but she never suspected he would stoop this low. Plus ask her to help him!

If she weren't careful, loving him would get her killed. What made him think that he could get away with blackmailing Chaz Palmer? If Palmer had killed his so-called best friend, he would most certainly kill a nobody like Dunk.

The two friends were silent for a few minutes, then Chantay apologized for snapping at LaShaunda. "I'm sorry. I know that of all of my friends, you're the only one who would do this for me. And I appreciate it."

LaShaunda immediately accepted. "I know you do, girl. I understand why it's taking you so long to make up your mind to do this. But, remember—Kaya Bradley's in jail for something she didn't do and you have proof that could set her free.

And Chaz Palmer is liable to get tired of Dunk anyday now and kill him, too. What makes you think he bought Dunk's story about sending the pictures to several friends, huh? He's gonna figure out before long that Dunk doesn't have any friends except *Y-O-U!* You're the only one who shows up at the studio when Dunk's laying down tracks. Do I have to spell it out for you? If he gets rid of Dunk and you, he's home free. You better spill your guts to that lawyer while you have the chance!"

Chantay's heart was racing as she watched the white Cherokee park in front of Sunday Adams's apartment building in midtown Atlanta.

LaShaunda stopped her mom's Toyota Camry behind the Cherokee in another row of resident parking spaces. She put the car in Park and shut off the headlights.

They sat watching the doors of the Cherokee, waiting for Sunday Adams or the man to get out. After five minutes La-Shaunda said, "What's keeping 'em?"

"They're probably making out," Chantay said. "Did you see that guy she's with? He's hot!"

"That's what got you into this trouble," LaShaunda said jokingly. "Dunk, when he's not stoned out of his mind, is moderately hot, too."

"You know he's hot," Chantay said with a laugh.

They went silent again because the lawyer and her boyfriend were finally getting out of the car. LaShaunda looked at the clock on the dashboard. "Okay, girlfriend, I'm counting down now. Get ready, set, go!"

Chantay quickly got out of the car. She pulled the hood of her jacket over her head and began walking toward Sunday Adams. "Miss Adams!"

The lawyer was walking toward the building, her boyfriend's hand at the base of her spine. She spun around to face Chantay.

Chantay walked up to her, being careful to keep her face tilted downward. "I got somethin' for you, lady," she said in a deep voice that could have been a male's. Her entire outfit from her jeans to her athletic shoes could have belonged to a male.

She held out the disk. "This is from a mutual friend," she said.

As soon as Sunday Adams's fingers closed around the disk, Chantay let go of it and ran back to the waiting Camry. La-Shaunda had pulled the car around and already had it in gear.

Chantay jumped into the car and closed the door. LaShaunda burned rubber getting out of there.

"Did you get the license plate?" Sunny asked.

"Nah, there was mud or something smeared over it."

"Smart girl," said Sunny.

They continued walking to the apartment building. "It sounded like a guy to me."

"It might have been more convincing if 'he' didn't have two bumps in the chest area when I got a peek inside the jacket he was wearing. Only fat guys have breasts that big."

Jonas laughed as he held the glass door to the building open for Sunny. "Give them points for blacking out the license plate."

"Hey," said Sunny, "I'm willing to be very complimentary if there's something interesting on this disk." They were at the bank of elevators in the lobby. She pressed the up button. The disk in her hand was a plain black 3.5 made by Sony. She'd stored information on disks just like it many times.

There was no label on it.

Alone in the elevator, Jonas pulled her into his arms. "Of course there's something interesting on it. Why all the subterfuge if not? She didn't want to be identified. There is definitely something juicy on it."

Sunny relaxed in his arms. After her grandparents had been thrown out, she, Jonas and the rest of the party had had a wonderful dinner and conversation. Everyone had gotten along splendidly. Vernette even apologized for slapping Tom's mother, saying it had not been a Christian thing to do. Later in the evening she'd spied Audra and Lani with their heads together discussing heaven-knows-what. She just hoped it hadn't concerned her. Then there were gifts given, and Sunny protested once again about how extravagant they had already been. She didn't need any more gifts. After which she graciously accepted. Now she was the proud owner of a diamond bracelet from Tom and Lani and a pair of sapphire and diamond earrings from Audra and Vernette. The sapphire, Audra told her, was her birthstone and it represented clear thinking. Which Sunny, she further stated, was blessed with. Sunny had cried.

In the apartment, Sunny removed her jacket and hung it in the foyer closet along with Jonas's coat. She yawned and nearly tripped over Caesar whom they'd disturbed when they had come in.

"Sorry, fur ball," she said, heading to the bedroom.

Caesar sensed excitement in the air and followed them to the bedroom. The first thing they both did upon entering the bedroom was to remove their shoes. Sunny's and Jonas's went into the closet. Sunny hung her shoulder bag in there, as well, then they went to her computer in the corner of the room and Sunny sat in the chair at the desk while Jonas hovered.

She booted up the computer and slipped the disk inside. In seconds they were looking at photos of Chaz Palmer. What's more, the date on which the photos had been taken was prominently displayed below each of the four photos.

The name of the picture file was "Dunk's Insurance Policy." The photos were taken at night; however, the subject was standing in good light in each photo. "The big man never looked better," Sunny joked.

"Who is this Dunk person?" Jonas wondered aloud. "He must have balls the size of grapefruits to go up against somebody like Palmer."

"Or he's just plain stupid," Sunny suggested.

"Why're we assuming Dunk's a guy? Maybe Dunk is the girl who delivered the disk."

"Whoever he is, he's about to get really nervous when the police arrest Chaz Palmer for the murder of Eddie Bradley, because Palmer's going to know exactly where these photos came from and he's not going to be pleased."

Jonas was thinking of something else. What if Dunk wasn't the person who had given Sunny the disk? What if the person who'd done it had done it against the wishes of this Dunk person? And if she were found out how would she fare under scrutiny? Would she confess to whom she'd given "Dunk's Insurance Policy"?

"I'm sure the police station stays open all night, lawyer-babe. I think we ought to pay them a visit and let them lock the disk up with the rest of the evidence in the case."

Sunny was already rising. "I'll change into jeans and sneakers."

Jonas turned to leave her bedroom. He collected his shoes on the way out. "Me, too. Be ready in five."

Detective Debarry was sound asleep when his phone rang. His wife moaned in her sleep and continued snoring.

"Yeah?"

"Sorry to wake you, Milt, but Sunday Adams is down here with a solid piece of evidence that points to Chaz Palmer as the killer of Eddie Bradley. I know the last time you talked to Palmer he told you which part of his anatomy you could kiss. I thought you'd like to see this right away." It was Captain Josh Winterbourne.

Milton was wide awake in an instant. "I'll be right down."

The sound of the doorbell reverberated in the Palmer house. Downstairs on the living room couch, Dunk stirred but figured he had the TV up too loud. He sleepily reached for the remote on the coffee table and lowered the volume.

The doorbell rang again, this time followed by someone pounding on the front door.

Dunk sat up but didn't move. It was Chaz's house. The door was his to get in the middle of the night.

Upstairs, Chaz was jolted out of sleep. Automatically glancing at the clock on the nightstand he saw that it was 3:27 a.m. He'd gone to bed only an hour earlier. Who could be knocking on his door at this ungodly hour?

His brain suddenly snapped to attention. Nobody but the cops with bad news came to your house at this time of the morning!

He leaped out of bed so fast, his right foot got tangled in the sheets. He stumbled and fell. Unhurt, he scrambled up and grabbed the sweatpants he'd thrown onto the floor before going to bed and quickly pulled them on.

His shoes were next. He already had on a T-shirt. Going to the bureau, he snatched up his wallet, cell phone and car keys. Then he got out of his second-story bedroom window and climbed down a wooden trellis, sticking himself on rose thorns as he did so.

Detective Debarry and two more burly police officers were waiting for him when his feet touched the grass. Muttering curses, he didn't try to resist. Even in this poor light he could see that Detective Debarry would have taken great pleasure in ordering the officers with him to subdue him by any means necessary.

"Mr. Palmer," Detective Debarry said, "you're under arrest for the suspected murder of Eddie Bradley. You have the right to remain silent…"

"Save it," said Chaz as one of the policemen cuffed him and then both of them yanked him to his feet again. "I know my Miranda rights."

Detective Debarry continued speaking until he'd read him his rights, nonetheless. "I'm going to make sure these charges stick," he said when he was finished.

They walked him around the house to the patrol car parked in the driveway behind his Hummer. "What'd you do with Dunk?" he asked as one of the officers helped him onto the backseat by holding his head down.

Hearing the name, Detective Debarry knew that there was another suspect they had to rouse from sleep tonight. After Chaz was in the patrol car, Detective Debarry turned to the biggest of the two officers accompanying him. "We might need the battering ram."

The officer smiled. It had been a while since he'd broken down a door.

Detective Debarry stood before the front door and called, "This is Detective Milton Debarry of the Atlanta Police Department. Open the door, or we'll have no choice but to use force!"

Dunk, ever the slacker, didn't move from his comfortable spot on the sofa. He turned the volume back up to drown out the voice of authority.

Outside, Detective Deberry, with a nod of his head, gave the officer carrying the battering ram the go-ahead.

What followed was a crash so loud and violent that Dunk leaped behind the sofa and tried his best to crawl underneath it. No such luck.

Detective Debarry pulled him up and cuffed him. "Dunk, you're under arrest for withholding evidence and possibly blackmail."

"Hey, man, I don't live here," said Dunk pitifully. "The guy you want is upstairs."

"If you're referring to Mr. Palmer, we caught him trying to escape out of his bedroom window."

"Aw, damn!"

Detective Debarry chuckled and handed Dunk off to another officer.

Sunny and Jonas sat in Detective Debarry's office awaiting his arrival with Chaz Palmer. Sunny had gotten permission to be present when Palmer was questioned.

She was high with the excitement of the moment. Kaya could very well walk free in a few hours. She fervently hoped so.

"Where are they?" she asked Jonas, concern written all over her face.

Jonas could feel the pent-up tension in her. Her brown eyes were calculating, probably thinking about the next step in the process once Chaz Palmer was brought in and officially booked for Eddie Bradley's murder.

He reached over and smoothed an unruly lock of curly hair out of her face. "They'll be here. What happens after he's behind bars? Will the judge then allow Kaya to get out on bail?"

"Out on bail?" Sunny said, unhappy with those words. "No, after Palmer confesses, Kaya should be released. Period."

"He's not going to confess, sweetheart."

"He doesn't have to confess. A picture is worth a thousand words."

"The photos don't show him committing the murder."

Sunny knew Jonas was playing devil's advocate. But to have one more obstacle put in her way made her see red. If Chaz Palmer somehow got out of this, she didn't know what she would do. Her job was to help Kaya beat a murder rap. To get her safely back home with her son. She had to stay focused on her goals.

"Are you saying that he was shown running from the house because he'd discovered Eddie's dead body? If so, why didn't he call the police? Kaya was the one to do that. He's hiding something. The photos are enough to throw suspicion onto him and off Kaya. He's going down."

"I hope so," said Jonas.

The door to Detective Debarry's office swung open, and Detective Debarry stuck his head in. "We're ready to get started," he said. "Right this way."

Sunny and Jonas followed him down the corridor.

In the interrogation room, Chaz sat at one end of the table.

They had removed his handcuffs, and two officers stood on either side of the door, due probably to the fact that he was a big man and might go for broke and try to escape in spite of the odds against it.

"What are they doing here?" Chaz asked when Sunny and Jonas walked into the room.

"I told them they could sit in on your interrogation," said Detective Debarry.

"An interrogation ain't even necessary," said Chaz. "I'm ready to tell you what happened the night Eddie died."

"This is on the record," Detective Debarry cautioned him. "You have the right to have your attorney present."

"I don't need a lawyer to tell you that Eddie killed himself, man. He shot himself right before my eyes. Of course I panicked and ran out of the house!"

"Why were you carrying your shirt in your hand?" Detective Debarry asked.

"Because I'd taken it off to put the gun back in Eddie's hand. Before he shot himself he said that he was dying of AIDS. He said he couldn't tell Kaya about it so that right there told me I had to keep his secret. That's why I didn't go to the police after he shot himself. If you all knew I was there when he killed himself you would have wanted to question me and before long I would have spilled Eddie's AIDS diagnosis. Like I said, he didn't want that. And when he shot himself, the gun fell out of his hand. Eddie had said he wanted to make sure it looked like a suicide, probably to save Kaya from being accused of his murder which it turns out, she was anyway. So I had to pull off my shirt to keep my prints off the gun and put the gun back in his hand. I had no idea Kaya was going to run downstairs and, in her grief, toss the gun away from Eddie's body. She wasn't thinking. Eddie obviously wasn't thinking when he shot himself, and I definitely wasn't thinking clearly when I ran from the house like a maniac."

Sunny gave Detective Debarry an inquisitive look denoting she wanted to question Palmer. The detective nodded for her to feel free to do so. "Dunk was blackmailing you with the photos?"

"Yeah, the little punk caught me going and coming," Chaz confessed.

"Why didn't you come forward at that time? Surely you can't afford to pay him off indefinitely. Blackmailers rarely let go once they sink their teeth into you."

"It wasn't money he wanted," Chaz explained. "He wants me to make him a rap star."

Everyone in the room aside from Chaz smiled at that and tried to keep from laughing.

"So he was going to keep quiet if you coached him," Sunny said. "Even though he suspected you of shooting Eddie Bradley in the head?"

"Yeah, he's a mercenary little bastard."

"But, basically, you were keeping quiet because of some solemn oath between you and Eddie to keep his AIDS a secret?"

"Yeah," Chaz said, looking hopeful that she understood where he was coming from.

"Then you can state for the record that when Eddie died, Kaya was nowhere near the entertainment room where he was found?"

"Yes, I can testify that Kaya was upstairs asleep when it happened. She and Navarre were upstairs. Only Eddie and I were in the room when he did it."

"That's all I need to hear, then," Sunny said, smiling now. She and Detective Debarry made eye contact. "Good work, Detective." Preparing to leave the room, she turned her back on Chaz.

Growling with frustration, Chaz bolted up from his chair. "Hey, wait a minute, I'm not finished with you yet!"

In swift, decisive movements, Jonas stepped between Sunny and Chaz and shoved the bigger man hard in the chest with both hands while simultaneously kicking his feet out from under him. Chaz crashed to the floor. The walls of the cubicle shook.

By the time Detective Debarry and the other two officers had sufficiently pulled themselves together to recognize that Chaz had made an aggressive move toward Sunny, Jonas was standing with his foot on the big man's throat.

"I just wanted to ask her to represent me," Chaz wheezed.

Jonas cautiously removed his foot and stepped backward to where Sunny was standing near the door. Chaz sat up on the floor, his hand on his throat.

He looked beseechingly at Sunny. "You believe my story, don't you?"

"Once my client walks," Sunny told him, "I'll be on the next plane to a remote island with the guy who just knocked you on your can. You're on your own."

She gave Detective Debarry a slight bow. "Good morning, Detective, Officers."

"Good morning, Miss Adams," Detective Debarry said with a smile. He liked her style.

Once she and Jonas were out of the room, Sunny jumped into his arms while letting out a whoop of joy. "Tomorrow Kaya will be a free woman!"

Jonas kissed her. He was thinking about the two of them on that remote island.

Chapter 17

After they left the police station, Sunny wanted to go directly to the county jail to give Kaya the good news. However, she knew they wouldn't let her in at four o'clock in the morning. She also wanted to get Judge Mayfair out of bed and scream in her ear that she had to get things rolling for Kaya's release first thing in the morning.

Inciting a judge to anger, however, would not have been a wise thing to do.

Turned toward Jonas in the car, she talked excitedly. "I'd like to know the name of the girl who was brave enough to give up that evidence. I want to thank her."

"I'm sure she'll feel justified when Kaya goes home." He took her hand in his.

"We can definitely rule out Dunk, or Charles Jones," Sunny said. "Did you see the stunned look on his face when they brought him in?" She gently kissed his knuckles.

"I suppose he'll never be a rap star now."

"Oh, please, haven't you been paying attention? Having a criminal past is a big plus in the rap world. Chaz Palmer has a record. I've never heard of Eddie Bradley having one, so maybe I'm wrong. But it's the image they perpetuate. Dunk won't be in jail long. If he has any talent at all he'll find somebody like Chaz to take over his career. As for Chaz, unless the lawyer he hires can come up with some solid evidence that his story holds water, he'll go to prison for life."

"Did you believe his story?" Jonas wanted to know.

Sunny thought for a few seconds. "I don't think we heard all of the story. For instance, why was he there when Eddie shot himself? You don't simply show up at somebody's house in the middle of the night just before they decide to commit suicide. Eddie must have called him. He didn't *say* that. He just said he was there when Eddie did it. His lawyer's going to have a tough time getting him off. If he's telling the truth it was sheer stupidity for him to leave the house instead of phoning the police right away. Maybe they could have determined by the blood spatter and gunpowder residue that he was telling the truth when he said Eddie shot himself. His sense of loyalty to a dead friend's final request could, unfortunately, be his undoing."

"You sound like you want to take the case."

Sunny shook her head in the negative. "I don't like Chaz Palmer. He needs an attorney who at least can tolerate being in the same room with him."

Jonas laughed shortly. "Besides, you're going to be in the Seychelles with me."

Sunny kissed his knuckles again. "You make the arrangements and I'll bring my bikini."

Jonas could already see her in that bikini. He concentrated on his driving. The sooner they got home, the sooner he could tear her clothes off.

Sunny, no longer satisfied with just kissing his knuckles, leaned over and kissed the side of his neck.

Lust, like fire igniting kindling, rushed through his body. "Sunny, don't, I'm driving."

She straightened up on her seat. "Sorry. I'll try to keep my hands off you until we get home."

A few minutes later they crept into the apartment, mindful of their third roommate's slumber. "I can't believe I'm tiptoeing into my house because of a spoiled cat," Sunny complained in a whisper.

Jonas, right behind her, noiselessly locked the door. It was pitch-dark in the foyer, but once they turned the corner heading in the direction of the bedrooms down the hall, light from the lamp on Sunny's desk helped to illuminate the way.

Sunny didn't know where Caesar was. He enjoyed sleeping all over the place. She'd bought him a pet bed, but he avoided it as if it were some kind of torture device. He preferred sleeping in doorways so she could conveniently trip over his body in the middle of the night, or on windowsills so he could hear nighttime traffic.

Sunny was happy he'd never gotten used to sleeping on her bed. She would have hated awakening to find his tail covering her nose.

In the bedroom Sunny closed the door and turned to walk into Jonas's arms. They kissed hungrily. "What a birthday," she said. She was exactly twenty-eight years and one day old.

She let her shoulder bag drop to the floor as Jonas picked her up, cupping her butt with both hands. She wrapped her legs around him and kissed him deeply, loving the feel of his firm lips against hers, his delicious tongue in her mouth, his breath mingling with hers. If only this urgent longing would never change she would be a happy girl.

Jonas moaned with pleasure. At last his passion could be unleashed on her. All night he'd been holding himself in check while he feasted on her beauty and her fiery spirit, alone. He loved everything about her. How she had stepped in and defended her mother against that harridan Constance Chapman. The dedication she'd shown to her client when presented with evidence tonight. Another attorney might have waited until morning to follow up with the police. But she'd jumped in with both feet.

Now, to have her all to himself, he felt like a starving man at a banquet. He didn't know where to start devouring her first.

The only light on in the room was still the lamp on her desk in the corner. But that didn't keep Sunny from appreciating the sight of Jonas removing his clothing. Dark-bronze skin beckoned her to touch it as the simple T-shirt was pulled over his head.

Chest and stomach muscles flexed with each movement. His hand was on his zipper now and her eyes moved downward. Jonas removed his hand, went to her and started taking her clothes off. "Don't stand there looking at me, get out of these clothes so I can run my tongue all over your body."

Sunny looked at him wonderingly. What had she ever done to have a man like this drop into her life out of the clear blue sky, huh? Nothing.

She was simply blessed.

She was also blessed with quick hands. She was naked in a matter of seconds.

Eyes on her, Jonas wasted no time getting out of his jeans and briefs.

Their clothes dispensed with, they fell onto the bed. Suddenly a horrible yowl came from under the bed and Caesar shot out from beneath it. He ran toward the door but Sunny had earlier shut it. Wanting out, he complained with a series of irritated hisses and meows. Laughing, Sunny got up to open the door for him. "That'll teach you to lurk under my bed, fur ball."

With one last imperious meow, Caesar ran out of the room. Sunny shut the door.

Jonas smiled at her. "Like I said, that's some neurotic cat you've got there."

"Okay, he's neurotic. But he's no worse than some of my relatives."

She went and climbed on top of him. Kissing his clean-shaven chin, she murmured, "About that trip to the Seychelles. What do you say we make it our honeymoon trip?"

She smiled at him.

Jonas flipped her over in bed. On top now, he said, "Does that mean what I think it means?"

Sunny wrapped her arms around his neck and looked deeply into his eyes. "I love you. I not only love you, but I *like* you. I like having you in my life, my house and in my bed. If I let you walk out of my life without telling you how I really feel about you I know I would regret it the rest of my days."

Grinning, Jonas bent and kissed her. He had known in his gut that she loved him, but to hear her say the words was richly satisfying. It meant more to him than anything had ever meant in his life. The intensity of the moment filled him up, and if perfection were possible then right here and right now he'd achieved it with Sunny.

Breaking off the kiss, he said, "When?"

Sunny was dreamy-eyed. "Yesterday."

He smiled. "We've got family. They're going to want to be there."

Sunny sighed softly. "Okay, we'll tell them. I don't want a big production, though. I just want to be your wife."

Jonas kissed her between her breasts. "I love hearing you say that!"

Sunny laughed softly. "What?" she asked playfully.

She felt Jonas's manhood swelling as it lay pressed against her belly. "You know what," he said in a rough voice.

"That I want to be your wife?" she said huskily. Her sultry, slanting eyes looked straight into his. "Because I do. Until I met you it never occurred to me that being anyone's wife could be a desirable thing. Now, spending the rest of my life with you is the thing I want most."

Jonas kissed her while coaxing her legs wider apart. Just as his hardened penis moved at the opening of her sex, he remembered he wasn't wearing a condom. "Damn."

"What?" Sunny asked, aching desire making her squirm beneath him.

Jonas gave her a quick buss on the lips and climbed off her. "I forgot the condom."

He went and got one from the nightstand drawer, tore the plastic wrap from it and deftly rolled in onto his throbbing penis. Sunny, up on her elbows, watched with anticipation.

Returning to the bed, Jonas gathered her in his arms and kissed her roughly. Sunny wrapped her arms around his middle, opened her legs and arched her back, eagerly welcoming him.

She had to rein in her passion because tonight she didn't want to come without him.

Tonight was special. She was making new birthday memories to replace the old, depressing ones. Tonight she was experiencing the culmination of love that her life had been building up to till this moment.

"I love you so much," Jonas whispered in her ear. His thrusts were informed with his feelings for her. Powerful, sure, deliciously sensual. Sunny reveled in them and met them with her own unbridled passion.

Their bodies, one golden-brown, one reddish-brown, both attuned to the other, explored the boundaries of what separated the physical from the spiritual and crossed over.

When their ardor was finally spent, simultaneously, they seemed to float down from that spiritual plane to the physical one.

For long moments, all they could do was gaze into each other's eyes with sappy grins on their faces.

"So this is love," Sunny murmured as she burrowed into his

strong shoulder and closed her eyes. Jonas kissed her forehead and pulled the covers up over her.

When she awakened the next morning his engagement ring was back on her finger.

Sunny phoned Dr. Bertrand Lewis's office first thing the next morning and canceled her meeting with him. Then she phoned Judge Mayfair's office.

"Her Honor has a full docket today. She can't possibly see you until after 4:00 p.m.," said her ever-efficient personal assistant.

"Please just give her the message as soon as possible," Sunny pleaded. Pleading was in order because oftentimes the assistant to the judge proved to be the only means by which a lowly lawyer could gain access. "It's been proven that Kaya Bradley is innocent. I'm sure Her Honor would not want an innocent woman to spend any more time in jail than is absolutely necessary."

"Of course, I'll give her the message as soon as possible," said the assistant, a male with a thick southern accent. "Along with about a hundred other messages this morning."

Sunny had a retort on the tip of her tongue but restrained herself. "I'll be in the courthouse today, anyway," she said instead. "I could spend a few hours sitting in front of your desk staring at you and eating smelly fish sandwiches with fat deli-style garlic pickles, washing it all down with root beer that makes me belch like a sailor on a three-week bender."

Sunny was familiar with the assistant. He was so fastidious that dust didn't settle on his desk without his whipping out the furniture polish and destroying the offending particle.

He would be totally grossed out by her gastronomical excesses. To say nothing of the build-up of gases that would be issuing from her ladylike mouth.

He knew she wasn't making empty threats. Sighing loudly, he said, "I'll have her call you."

"Thank you," said Sunny sweetly, and hung up.

Forty-five minutes later, Judge Mayfair phoned with, "I got Detective Debarry's report. Good work, Miss Adams. Did you ever find out who gave you that disk?"

"No, Your Honor, but if I ever do, you'll be the first person I call."

"Do that, because I'm curious. This job can get pretty monotonous, but this case is one for the record books. Tell Mrs. Bradley I wish her the best. She'll be a free woman by noon."

"Thank you, Your Honor!"

"My pleasure, Sunday Adams," said Judge Mayfair with a smile in her tone.

They rang off.

Sunny hung up the phone. She was sitting in bed cross-legged, naked, with the sheet pulled over her. Lying beside her, Jonas was gently rubbing her bare back. "Mmm, that feels good," she said. "But we've got to get up and get dressed. There's still time to go to the Four Seasons and see our folks off."

Lazily, Jonas sighed and pulled her into his arms. "They're not checking out until eleven. It's barely nine. We have time."

Sunny glanced down at the bulge his morning erection made underneath the sheet.

No use wasting a perfectly good erection. She climbed on top of him.

They arrived at the Four Seasons by ten-thirty, giving them plenty of time to fill Audra, Norman and Vernette in on the night's developments while the three of them finished getting their luggage together for the bellboy to take downstairs to the waiting limousine that would take them to the airport.

Afterward they went down to the lobby with them, and while their luggage was being stowed in the limousine's trunk, Jonas pulled his father aside and said, "She said yes."

He had purposely waited until the last minute because he didn't want them to make a big deal over the announcement.

After all, he and Sunny hadn't yet set a date. They only wanted them to take the good news back with them to California.

Norman's eyes glistened with unshed tears as he hugged his son. "Congratulations."

A few feet away Sunny was quietly telling Audra and Vernette the same news.

Neither of them was the type of woman to take news of that magnitude without a shout or two. Audra screamed delightedly and Vernette joined in.

Sunny was hugged to within an inch of her life.

But it was soon time for them to leave for the airport. They had to let go of her.

"Call me tonight so we can start making plans," said her mother. "I'm going to give you the most beautiful wedding ever seen in Beverly Hills."

Sunny didn't even protest. There would be time to explain to her mother that she and Jonas wanted a quiet ceremony attended only by family and close friends.

"I will," she promised.

She kissed her mother and grandmother's cheeks and they were off.

She and Jonas stood on the sidewalk waving goodbye to them. Moments later they hurried to the Cherokee. Kaya would soon be walking out of the county jail and Sunny planned to be at her side, running interference between her and the hungry newspersons sure to be there to document her release.

Later at the jail Kaya hugged Sunny repeatedly, saying over and over again, "Thank you. I knew you would save me."

She and Sunny were standing in the administrator's office, and Kaya was dressed in a nice navy-blue skirt suit with a white blouse. Much like her attorney's suit. Sunny was glad to see her out of that horrible orange jumpsuit.

Her hair was still in braids but it looked as though one of her fellow inmates had tightened them up for her overnight. She had dark circles under her eyes but her entire demeanor bespoke relief and happiness. She was ready to go home.

Sunny set her firmly away from her and looked her in the eyes. "Luck was on our side, Kaya. Someone had a conscience and refused to let you be punished for a crime you didn't commit. I only did my job. Now, I want you to walk out there with your head up and if you don't want to talk to the reporters who're waiting, and there are quite a few, then you don't have to. But if you do, look straight into the camera and have your say because you have it coming."

When they walked out of the jail and onto the front steps, around three hundred people, besides the reporters, had gathered, some with signs held up with sayings like, We Knew You Were Innocent! Chaz Did It! Congratulations, Kaya! Free at Last! along with a couple of signs that read, Free Dunk!

A podium had been set up from which Kaya could deliver a statement if she so wished.

Reporters started talking at once when she, to Sunny's surprise, stepped up to the podium and firmly grasped both sides of it.

"Kaya, did you ever think this day would come?" asked a woman reporter from CNN.

"Yes," said Kaya, turning to smile at Sunny. "I had complete faith that my attorney would do everything in her power to get me out of jail. And she did."

"How do you feel about Chaz Palmer, Kaya? He was Eddie's best friend. Your friend. How does his betrayal make you feel?"

Kaya's expression remained neutral. "I don't know what compelled Chaz to keep quiet about what happened the night Eddie died. But I have the utmost confidence that he didn't kill Eddie. I'm tired. I'm going home now." And she left the podium, refusing to answer any more questions. Sunny, along with four officers, escorted her to a waiting car. Sunny was surprised by Kaya's show of support for Chaz but didn't comment on it. When they got to the car, she hugged her again and said, "Take care of yourself."

"You, too," said Kaya, and she was driven away.

When Sunny turned around, she saw Jonas standing a few feet away, his eyes on her. He smiled at her, his pride in her evident in his warm expression.

They walked to the Cherokee with their arms around each other's waists. "Would you drop me off at the office?" she said. "I've got work to do."

Kaya Bradley's case might have been resolved, but there were others that needed her attention. She planned to get them all out of the way as soon as possible. She was beginning to think that there was more to life than the law. There was a man who deserved her attention. And there was an island in the Seychelles that was calling her from afar.

Two weeks later, Kaya sat on the side of the bed and peered lovingly into Navarre's face. He looked so much like his father that lately a lump formed in her throat every time she took the time to study his sweet face.

She'd just read him a story, and now he was settling down for the night. "Momma," he said, big brown eyes intently searching her face. "Why was Daddy playing with that gun? He told *me* not to play with them! He and Uncle Chaz was talkin' and he picked up the gun and played with it. Momma, I got so scared I ran and hid under my bed."

Kaya's breath caught in her throat. The night Eddie had died, she had found Navarre under his bed after the officers had let her go to him. They'd been kind enough to let her explain that she had to go away with the nice officers and he would be staying with his grandparents for a while.

Kaya didn't question him now. She pulled him into her arms and hugged him tightly, moaning with the love she had for him.

"It was an accident, baby. Daddy didn't mean to do it. It was just an accident."

She was still staying with her parents. She was loath to even go back into the house she and Eddie had shared. She would eventually return, though, and the first thing she would do would be to get rid of Eddie's gun collection. Then she was going to put the house up for sale. She planned to move out of the city.

"Close your eyes, sweetie. Go to sleep." She sang softly to him until he was sound asleep. Rising, she gently kissed the top of his head.

A few minutes later she was on the phone with Detective Debarry. "Detective, my son just told me something very interesting."

Chapter 18

"All right," Jonas said into the cell phone. "I can give you four weeks. Are you positive that the women in the co-op are dedicated to making a change and aren't just paying lip service? Because you know this won't work unless they're totally committed, Jean Paul."

Jonas and Jean Paul Tourè had met in a British boarding school when they were twelve years old. They had remained friends ever since. Jean Paul belonged to a Haitian family that could trace their ancestors well prior to the 1804 rebellion led by Touissaint L'Ouverture. He believed in noblesse oblige, which stated that the nobility was obligated to help the less fortunate.

"I'm certain of it," said Jean Paul. "They have made it their raison d'être—reason for living. So, you will come?"

"Yes," said Jonas.

Jean Paul laughed with relief. "Wonderful. When can you be here?"

"I'll be there in a few days," Jonas promised.

They chatted for a bit longer, mostly catching up on each other's lives since they'd last talked. Then Jean Paul said, "I've got to go, old friend. Noelle is calling me."

Noelle was Jean Paul's wife of seven years. Jonas felt a knot of tension in his stomach at the mention of Noelle. It reminded him that he would soon be separated from Sunny.

"Goodbye, Jean Paul."

"Au revoir," said Jean Paul.

Closing the phone, Jonas sighed, removed his feet from the back porch railing and got out of the slat-back wooden rocking chair. It was a Saturday in mid-November, and he and Sunny were in Warm Springs.

Around ten in the morning, the sun was shining brightly, the sky a wonderful deep blue with a few cumulus clouds drifting past. The days were brisk and cool. At night the temperature dropped ten or more degrees.

Looking out at the spacious backyard, Jonas smiled. When he'd first come here he never suspected that he would still be around to see the seasons change.

Caesar had been sunning himself nearby. He rose now, stretched and wound his sinuous body around Jonas's legs. Jonas laughed shortly. "I'm not going anywhere. You can go back to sleep. I'm going inside to see what your mistress is up to."

He found Sunny still asleep. They had made love for quite some time last night, plus her work week had been very hectic. She was determined to get through her caseload before their wedding in December. She had one important court date coming up next week. After that she was free to take some time off.

Standing next to the bed, he watched as she wrinkled her nose in her sleep and changed positions, her wild, curly dark mane spread over the pillow. He wanted to climb in bed with her but was reluctant to disturb her rest. She needed it. Also, if he woke her he would feel obliged to tell her about Haiti. He wanted to postpone that for as long as possible. She wasn't going to be happy he was going away for a while.

He turned to leave the room and Sunny said, "Where're you going?"

Spinning on his heel, he saw that her eyes weren't even open. Was she talking in her sleep? She did that when she was especially exhausted.

She opened her eyes and smiled at him. "I smelled you."

He laughed softly. That was why she'd wrinkled her nose. He didn't doubt her.

Sunny possessed a few weird talents that he was slowly discovering. For example, she was limber enough to tuck her legs behind her head. If he tried it he wound up with a colossal muscle cramp.

"I thought you were still asleep," he said, going to sit on the side of the bed.

"I was until I smelled you," she said, sitting up in bed. She wore only a short cotton nightgown. The covers fell away from her long legs and the sight of them immediately caused him to harden because he knew what else was under those covers. "You've showered already," she said, giving him a speculative once-over.

"Yeah." He bent and kissed her on the side of the neck. She smelled sweet and faintly of their lovemaking. He adored the scent. The warmth of her skin coupled with that unique odor turned him on.

"What do you want to do today?" he asked, his mouth still trailing kisses along her neck and down to the area between her luscious breasts.

"I don't know," Sunny said, a sexy smile curling her lips. Sliding back down onto the bed, she pulled him close for a kiss. In an instant Jonas was lost in the delicious taste of her mouth, the intoxicating feel of her soft body and the sheer sensual magnetism she possessed over him. He didn't have time to get up and pull his jeans off. Instead he hastily undid the top button, unzipped them, pulled them and his briefs down past his hips, snapped the nightstand drawer open, found a condom, tore it open with his teeth, rolled it onto his fully erect member, and thrust deeply, and satisfyingly, into Sunny's hot, pulsating center. She moaned and held on to his powerful arms. Arched her back and surrendered everything that she was to him.

Jonas was so hard his erection was bordering on the painful. Making love to Sunny in the morning when her body was warm and fragrant was a sensory-filled treat for him.

In the months that she had possessed him, body and soul, he could not recall ever enjoying another woman with this singular devotion.

"Oh, Sunny, what have you done to me?"

Sunny smiled up at him, her tiger's eyes raking over him with desire. In his arms she had become the lover she'd always wanted to be. Gone were the inhibitions and doubts that her one lover had left her with. She was free to express herself. Expose the raw passion that had been simmering below the surface for years.

"I haven't done nearly enough to you," she whispered. "Not nearly enough." And she thrust deeply and grasped him tightly with her vaginal muscles. He felt so good to her she moaned loudly as her nerve endings seemed to all tingle at once, sending rivulets of intense pleasure throughout her body.

Jonas came with a shout. He pulled her up off the bed as he thrust deeper. Sunny felt as if he might rip her apart, but at that moment didn't particularly care as she was in the throes of a cataclysmic orgasm that sent her reeling.

Down, down, they came, bodies quivering with release. Jonas sighed and let her body gently fall back onto the bed, his biceps rippling with the effort.

Sunny smiled, satisfied, filled up and thoroughly loved by her man. She could get used to this.

Unfortunately that was when Jonas chose to say, "Darling, I've got to go away for a few weeks."

Sunny lay back on the pillow, threw her arm cross her eyes and sighed. She wanted to bask in the moment a while longer before having to face what he'd just said. She lingered in that position so long that Jonas decided to let her lie there.

He got up and went to the adjacent bathroom to dispose of the condom.

After freshening up, he reentered the bedroom and found her sitting on the side of the bed with her head in her hands. She raised her gaze to his. "Haiti?"

"How could you have known that?" She was spookily perceptive.

Sunny smiled. "When we first met you told me that someone wanted you to come to Haiti but you were still giving it some thought."

"I'm surprised you remembered that."

"I have kind of a photographic memory," she said. "Especially when someone I care about tells me something."

She patted the bed next to her. "Come here."

Jonas went to sit beside her.

She looked him in the eyes. "Several weeks?"

"Four at the most. There's a women's cooperative comprised of mothers mostly. Women who have no skills but need to be able to support themselves and their children. My longtime friend, Jean Paul Touré, is sponsoring them so I don't need to find funding. That cuts out weeks of legwork and endless meetings with established businesses. All I need to do is draw up the business plan and establish communications between them and the American women's cooperative that will sell their wares here in the U.S. Then, I'll be on my way back home to you."

Sunny didn't know why, but she was actually feeling a sense of panic. She knew his business required travel. It was inevitable that he would leave her at some time. She supposed she was unused to craving a man's presence so much that even the thought of not being in it for a few weeks sent chills up her spine.

Bravely, she smiled. "I'll miss you."

Jonas pulled her close. "Not nearly as much as I'm going to miss you."

Sunny couldn't believe she was sitting in her living room in Atlanta looking at her mother and herself on the *Oprah Winfrey Show*. Of all the surreal experiences she'd had since learning Audra Kane was her mother, this topped them all.

They had taped the show several days ago in Chicago. Ms. Winfrey had devoted the entire show to her exclusive interview with Audra. She'd prepared the audience by discussing Deana Davis's upcoming book about Audra. The book was scheduled to hit the shelves at the end of November just in time for the Christmas buying blitz.

She, however, had Audra Kane on her stage, and Miss Kane was willing to open up about her personal life as never before. Audra was then introduced and the audience went wild. Audra walked out looking beautiful and stylish in a bronze skirt suit and bronze Ferragamo pumps. After she and Oprah hugged hello, she sat down and the talk-show maven said, "Welcome, Audra."

"Thank you for having me," said Audra, smiling.

"No, thank you for being willing to talk about a subject many, many women can relate to—giving one's child up for adoption."

The audience gave a collective gasp of surprise. They had no idea of the true nature of the show up until then. They had thought Audra Kane was there to discuss her upcoming comedy, *Road to Morocco*.

Audra went on to tell the world how she had fallen in love at twenty and gotten pregnant, subsequently broken up with her lover and given birth to a beautiful baby girl.

She had given her up, she explained, because she didn't

believe she was capable of caring for her on her own. A decision she came to regret with all her heart.

When she was finished, half the audience was in tears, as was her hostess.

"But you had a happy ending," Oprah said, smiling.

"That's right," said Audra. "My daughter and I now have a loving relationship."

"And she's here!" Oprah exclaimed. "Please welcome attorney Sunny Adams, Audra's twenty-eight-year-old daughter!"

Now, in Atlanta, Sunny frowned as she watched herself walk onto the stage and hug first her mother, then Oprah. She looked passably together, but she was remembering how nervous she'd been that day. However, everyone had made her feel very welcome and very comfortable. The next few minutes during which Oprah had asked her how she had first reacted to Audra's attempts to become a part of her life had felt awkward. She and Audra, however, had promised each other that they would tell the truth, and Sunny wound up saying how hurt she had been that her mother hadn't gotten in touch with her sooner. Tears in her eyes, Audra had sat there and taken it. The end result, Sunny knew now, was the highest ratings of a daytime show for the November sweeps period.

When Deana Davis's book had arrived at the stores the following week it had been met with weak sales. Everybody already had the lowdown on Audra Kane.

Sunny turned off the TV and got up to go to bed. It was midnight on a Friday.

Tomorrow morning, she and Caesar would drive to Warm Springs, without Jonas, who still had two weeks left to go in Haiti before he would be coming back home to her.

The phone rang as soon as her head hit the pillow. Turning back on the nightstand lamp, she sat up and answered it. Caller ID told her that it was Kit on the other end.

"Kit, hey, what's up?"

"I'm pregnant."

Kit rarely put any preamble on her statements. Just dropped the bomb in your lap and stood back to observe the explosion. "You and Harper?" Sunny croaked.

"Yes," Kit said, a smile evident in her tone. "And he's happy about it."

"He should be," said Sunny. "It's his first, right?"

"Yeah," Kit confirmed. "Now he wants to marry me."

"You don't want to get married?"

"I don't know. It was never very good between my parents. My aunt Kate, for whom I'm named, says marriage is advantageous only for the male of the species. I think she might have something there, Sunny. Married men live longer than single men because they have somebody to care for them. Married women, however, don't live significantly longer than single women. That ought to tell you something right there. And you're a lawyer. You know that in a divorce the woman usually fares much worse than the man. Oftentimes she ends up living below her normal income level while his doesn't change much, if at all."

Sunny laughed softly. "You're calling me so that I'll talk you out of marrying Harper? If so, you've called the wrong girl tonight. I can't wait to marry Jonas."

Kit sighed loudly. "I know. You're truly gone on that man. I just thought I'd call and inject a dose of reality. That's what best friends are for."

"They're also the ones who're supposed to tell you to live your dreams for a change! Kit, Harper is a good man. Now, I'm going to give *you* a dose of reality—he loves you. He wants this baby. He wants to keep you happy for the rest of his natural life. I say let him knock himself out. Enjoy it. Besides, he sings to you in bed. Where else are you going to get that kind of treatment?"

Kit laughed. "That's true." She went silent for a few seconds.

Then, "Thanks. I'm not nearly as panicked as I was when I called."

"That's good. Where is Harper?"

"Snoring in the bedroom. I'm in the kitchen raiding the fridge."

"Well, you're eating for two."

"Maybe three. Twins run in my family and I am of a certain age," Kit said, referring to the fact that older first-time moms had a good chance of having twins.

"I *am* going to be the godmother, right?" Sunny asked.

"Who else?" was Kit's reply. "I can think of no one else whom I'd trust my child to be raised by should something happen to me. After all, you've raised a wonderful cat in Caesar, the darling feline."

Sunny laughed. "Don't get me started on spoiled pets. You dress Matilda in pet clothes. She should turn you in to the SPCA!"

Kit laughed heartily. "You should see this cute polka dot dress I recently bought her. She's adorable in it."

"I'm telling you, Kit. That dog hates you for humiliating her. You'd better sleep with one eye open from now on."

They went on in that vein for a few minutes more, then said good-night. Sunny turned out the light and hugged her pillow tight. Then she went to sleep and dreamed of Jonas.

Sunny spent the following week in Warm Springs. She was finally on hiatus from the firm and she took the time to focus on her wedding. Two weeks before Jonas had left for Haiti she had applied for a passport. She would need it when they went to the Seychelles for their honeymoon. The passport arrived in the mail in three weeks' time.

She, Jonas, and Audra had finalized the wedding plans so she was at loose ends when Thanksgiving week rolled around. Tom and Lani invited her to have dinner with them in Atlanta. The day before the holiday found her diligently cleaning out her bedroom closet. She followed a strict system whereby if she hadn't worn an article of clothing for a year or more, it had to go. She had a huge pile of clothes on the bed by midday.

She had started pulling out shoes she hadn't worn in a while and putting them in a pile on the floor when the doorbell rang.

Pushing herself up from her hands and knees in the closet, she straightened and hurried downstairs in her bare feet.

Caesar yowled at her when she got downstairs, once again complaining about how irritating the sound of the doorbell was to his sensitive ears.

"I'm going, I'm going," Sunny said, smiling.

Peering through the peephole, she was puzzled. She didn't recognize the attractive black woman standing on the other side of the door. The woman moved to the side and Sunny got a good look at another woman standing behind her. It was Constance Chapman.

She got steamed in no time flat and yanked the door open. She had no intention of inviting them in, so she stepped outside in her jeans and University of Georgia T-shirt.

As it turned out she had three women visitors. The woman whose face she had initially seen through the peephole, who appeared to be in her late forties, or early fifties, a young woman who could be her age, or younger, and Constance Chapman.

The women were all tall, of various weights, and stylishly dressed. The younger woman's features were similar to Sunny's: dark, curly hair that fell down her back, big brown eyes, full lips and reddish brown skin.

"Oh, my God. Mother, how could you behave so abominably toward this child? She is definitely our flesh and blood. She and Tori could be sisters!" This was from the middle-aged woman. Sunny was so shocked to see three generations of women who looked like her on her front porch that for a few seconds, she'd forgotten she didn't care very much for Constance Chapman.

The middle-aged woman grabbed her and hugged her tightly, moaning with pleasure.

"Hello, baby. I'm your aunt Prudence. My nieces and nephews just call me Aunt Pru." Still holding her by her shoulders, Prudence continued. "This is my daughter, Torrance. Your cousin."

She stepped aside and Tori briefly hugged Sunny. "Hey, cuz, welcome to the family. Don't hold Grandma's manners *breakdown* against all of us. We want to get to know you. That's why we dragged her here this afternoon so she could apologize."

She stepped aside and went to stand beside her mother.

Constance was looking at Sunny with glistening eyes and a stubborn set to her mouth.

Sunny didn't think she'd ever apologized for anything in her life. After a couple of minutes of staring each other down, Sunny turned away. "I don't think she's sorry for what she did," she said to Tori and her aunt Pru. "However, if she's willing to behave herself this afternoon I'd like to invite you in for coffee."

"Love some. Thank you!" Pru immediately responded.

"Ohh, yeah," said Tori, rubbing her arms as if she were cold. "It's chilly out here."

The three of them turned to go inside. Constance cleared her throat, reached out and grasped Sunny by the arm and said, "I was an ass and I'm sorry, my dear."

"Please, go in and make yourself at home," Sunny said to Tori and Pru. When they were out of earshot, she said to Constance, "That night, I wanted so much to be accepted by you and my grandfather. But, sad to say, I never *expected* it. I've known quite a bit of disappointment in my life. So, when you behaved the way you did, it didn't exactly surprise me. What appalled me was when you struck my mother. A woman who had loved your son many years ago, got pregnant by him, was denied his support but still didn't abort his child and be done with him once and for all. And you struck her because you believed *she* had shamed your family. My father proved himself to be a real man when he apologized for abandoning her."

Constance did not look away in shame. She bore the brunt of Sunny's anger with a backbone of steel. She did relinquish her hold on Sunny and sit down in one of the porch chairs, though. "I know, and I phoned your mother and apologized to her. She was kind enough to accept. Although I don't deserve her kindness."

Sunny sat on the top porch step. Her feet were getting cold, but otherwise she was fine. And she wanted to hear this.

"I come from a generation, a class of people, who were not allowed to fail, Sunny. My father was the first black doctor in our county here in Georgia. My mother taught manners to young black girls of means. Because we represented the finest of our race we were expected to set an example. There could never be a hint of scandal. Marriages were for life. Affairs, if they occurred, were never to see the light of day. If a young woman got pregnant without the benefit of marriage, she was shipped far away, and until she gave birth, gave the baby up for adoption or to another family member who claimed the child as her own, she wasn't allowed back in polite society. The appearance of familial perfection, if not the actual existence of it, was everything. I let myself forget the illusion and I lashed out at your mother and you. Perfection doesn't exist."

She looked Sunny in the eyes. "There is nothing more important than family. All the money in the world, all the power and prestige mean nothing without the love of your family. Please forgive me."

Sunny got to her feet and looked down at Constance. "Can you cook?"

Constance's face crinkled in confusion. Rising, she said, "Yes, I'm a marvelous cook."

Sunny hugged her. "Good. I would hate to have a grandmother who's worse than I am in the kitchen. You're supposed to hand down the family recipes to *me*."

Constance laughed delightedly and squeezed her grand-daughter with affection.

They went inside.

"What a lovely house," said Constance as they walked through the front doors that had antique beveled glass in them. Tall floor-to-ceiling windows allowed an abundance of light into the refurbished hundred-year-old house. The original oak floors had been restained and were highly polished. A sisal carpet sat under the living room seating group which had linen slipcovers in a creamy off-white. Fat pillows were in striped and square-dot designs in alternating tan and navy-blue. A big square coffee table was in the middle of the seating group, and Sunny always tried to keep a vase of fresh flowers on it along with a couple of interesting art books.

Tori and Pru were nowhere in sight. Sunny suddenly heard someone in the kitchen.

She and Constance followed the sound and found Pru pouring coffee grounds into the coffeemaker and Tori with her head in the pantry looking for something good to go with the coffee.

Constance walked straight to the back door, opened it and stepped onto the back porch. "This house reminds me of my grandparents' house when I was a child," she announced with a happy grin on her face. "Look at this yard." Turning to Sunny, she asked, "You garden?"

"This was my adoptive parents' house," she explained. "My mom and I would work in the garden together." She walked down the back steps with Constance close behind. "I've got collards and kale, all of the hearty vegetables that like cool weather. In the sum-mertime, I have so many tomatoes I have to give them away."

Constance bent down and fingered some of the leaves on the collard greens. They were thick and lush and green and healthy. "What kind of fertilizer do you use?"

For the next few minutes she and Sunny discussed the virtues of chemical fertilizers as opposed to natural means of making your garden grow.

After which they went inside and had coffee and the store-bought oatmeal cookies that Tori had found in the pantry. They were all seated comfortably around the kitchen table, munching on cookies, drinking the strong coffee and getting acquainted when Caesar came through the pet door, made a beeline for Constance and promptly settled his bulk onto her feet.

"Caesar, get up," Sunny said, laughing softly.

"Let him stay," said Constance. "My feet get cold this time of year."

The next day when Sunny arrived at Tom and Lani's house in Ansley Park, she wasn't surprised to learn that his entire family, including his parents, were expected for dinner.

Sunny had a wonderful time. Although she missed Jonas terribly.

Chapter 19

Jonas missed Sunny so much he ached for her. He spent twelve-hour days at the women's cooperative that operated out of a storefront on a crowded street in Port-au-Prince, Haiti's capital.

The women were wary of the big American. He spoke perfect French but he spoke it like the rich mulattos who had lorded it over them for as long as they could remember. It was difficult for them to believe he wanted to give them the benefit of his business know-how with no expectation of payment, or anything else, in return.

As for Jonas, he found Port-au-Prince to be teeming with humanity. Nowhere in South Africa had he found so many people in so small a space. Every day the streets overflowed with battered cars, bicycles, motorbikes and the makeshift buses called tap-taps which were the most common mode of transportation. It wasn't unusual to see brown arms and legs hanging out of the crowded buses' windows as they chugged along the congested streets.

And in spite of the staggering unemployment rate, the city had plenty of markets.

Vendors hawked wares up and down the city's streets selling things like ice and cut stalks of sugar cane.

It was the people's indomitable spirit that kept him going. Even though they were among the world's poorest people they had not given up. They believed in a brighter future.

He saw it in the intensive manner the women paid attention to every word he said.

They were hungry for knowledge even if they didn't yet trust him. Many of them brought their children with them for the day. Jonas had devised the plan for their business that would include a day-care center on the premises. The women could work without worrying that their children were properly being cared for.

While their mothers were distrustful of the American, the children showed no fear of him whatsoever. They asked him endless questions that Jonas was happy to answer after the day's lessons were over.

One boy, Pierre, eight years old but small for his age due to malnutrition, appointed himself Jonas's assistant. Whenever Jonas needed a message carried to the other end of the huge building, Pierre would mysteriously appear at his side, ready to be of service.

The last week Jonas was scheduled to be there, he was in the midst of teaching a rudimentary bookkeeping class when he heard four gunshots at the front of the building.

The women didn't initially react. They were used to hearing gunshots at close range.

Jonas, taking his cues from them, went back to demonstrating cash receivables on the blackboard.

A few seconds later Pierre ran into the classroom shouting in Haitian Creole, "Help us! He is going to kill my mother!"

Jonas put down his chalk and rushed to Pierre's side. "Show me."

All of the women, now displaying fear and caution, got up and followed Jonas and Pierre. Once Jonas saw Pierre's mother, Marielle, being held with a machete at her throat by a small, hard-looking man, he knew this was a case of domestic violence.

The man was Marielle's estranged husband. Jonas had seen him around a couple of times, and he hadn't appeared at all pleased with Marielle's decision to leave him and declare her independence by joining the women's cooperative.

The man's pistol was stuck in the waistband of his pants. Apparently he had decided the machete would be a more satisfying killing weapon and switched the gun for it.

Jonas raised both arms in the air to show that he was unarmed as he approached them.

The women stayed behind him, one of them restraining Pierre who was trying to go to his mother.

In French Jonas asked, "Is there a problem here?"

The man's nostrils flared in rage and he pressed the blade of the machete closer to Marielle's neck. "Are you crazy?" he screamed at Jonas. "Yes, there is a problem here. I'm going to slit her throat for abandoning her marriage vows and then I'm going to kill myself. After that, no more problems."

"What about your son?" Jonas asked calmly.

The man's eyes darted around the room. "Where is he?"

The woman who had hold of Pierre was hiding him behind her. Hearing his father asking about him, Pierre bit her hand. She yelled in pain and let go of him. He heedlessly ran to his mother and wrapped his arms around her waist. "Please don't hurt her, Papa!"

"Pierre, I want you to leave at once!" his father ordered.

"No!" The boy was obstinate. "If I go you'll hurt her. If you hurt her you'd just as well kill me, too, because I will hate you forever."

Jonas hadn't moved an inch since Pierre had ran to his mother and thrown his arms around her in a desperate bid to save her life. The women behind him held their breath, afraid to do anything for fear of inciting Pierre's father to action.

"You hate me already," said the man. Tears flooded his eyes. "She's turned you against me."

"That isn't true, Etienne," Marielle choked out.

Etienne inched the machete farther away from her slender throat. "You left me!"

"I left you because you refused to allow me to join the cooperative. We need to do something *different,* Etienne. Pierre needs to see some hope for the future. You work so hard for us, and we appreciate it. But it takes two parents working in a household to keep food on the table. Just because I joined the cooperative doesn't mean I don't love you. But you forced me to make a choice. I chose our son. If you had been given an ultimatum like that, you would have chosen Pierre, too."

Etienne carefully lowered the machete and let it fall to the floor. Tears streamed down his face and he was shaking his head as he backed away from Marielle. "I'm no good for you. You and Pierre would be better off if I were dead."

Marielle, clutching Pierre in her arms, saw her husband grasp the butt of the gun stuck inside his waistband. She screamed, "No, Etienne!"

It was at that moment that Jonas executed a roundhouse kick that sent the gun flying out of Etienne's hand. Etienne hadn't had time to pull the hammer back so the gun landed, without firing, several feet away. Jonas then restrained Etienne in a headlock.

"One day you'll realize that shooting yourself in the head in front of your son and your wife was a bad idea," he said. "I know it would've given *me* nightmares."

Marielle and Pierre grabbed Etienne and hugged him tightly.

The women in the room breathed a collective sigh of relief. One of them had gone and picked up the gun. She handed it to

Jonas. "I hate guns," she said. Glancing at the machete on the floor, she added, "Knives, too."

To Jonas's utter surprise no one even considered phoning the police. Marielle thanked him for his help, then she and Pierre took Etienne home.

Jonas must have had a puzzled expression on his face as he watched them walk away because one of the older women, whom they called Maman out of respect, touched him on the arm and said, "Good husbands feel as if they are not real men if they can't support their families without help from their wives. They will be okay now."

Once again Jonas was reminded that he was a stranger in a strange land. In Atlanta, Sunny would be representing a woman like Marielle in court. And her husband who had held a machete at her throat would go to prison for several years.

The women went back into the classroom, and Jonas, more shaken up than any of them, resumed his lesson.

That night after he'd eaten in a local restaurant, he returned to his hotel room to shower and climb into bed. Each night he was exhausted. More mentally than physically. He wondered if he were suffering from burn-out and should reconsider his approach to his calling. Perhaps sending others into the field might be advisable in the future. After he and Sunny were married and, hopefully, started having children, he didn't want to be gone from their lives for long stretches of time. Perhaps his having been in the field for the past fifteen years was sufficient and now he should finance the work but turn it over to someone who would get more enjoyment out of the travel and the strange customs he was sure to encounter with each new culture.

Jonas couldn't believe he was feeling this way but, suddenly, all he wanted was to build a house for him and Sunny somewhere, anywhere she wanted to live, and raise their children. By God, he would be a *househusband* if she wanted to continue practicing

law. But what was the use of being a millionaire many times over
if you weren't doing exactly what you wanted to do in life? He
could do his philanthropic work from the sidelines from now on.

His wish had been granted when he'd met and fallen in love
with Sunny. He would be a fool not to take full advantage of
God's grace in granting it.

That's what he told Sunny when he phoned her that night.

Only an hour's difference in time, Sunny was in bed in
Warm Springs, reading for pleasure for a change. She'd gone
to her favorite African-American-owned bookstore in Atlanta
and picked up the latest Pearl Cleage, Melanie Schuster and
Walter Mosley books plus a new author by the name of Jinx
Jones, who wrote in the paranormal genre.

She was in the middle of the Jones novel about guardian
angels when the phone rang.

Quickly earmarking her page, she put the book down and
glanced at the caller ID display.

"Jonas!" she breathed when she answered, excited to the tips
of her toes.

Lying in bed now, Jonas smiled. "Hey, baby. What are you
doing?"

"Reading a very sexy book about angels."

"Angels? Sexy?"

"You're an angel and you're *very* sexy."

He knew better than to try to figure her out. Some things
about her would always be a mystery, and that was fine with him.

"I've made a decision about work," he told her.

"What's that?"

"I'm done, cooked. I'm toast." He went on to tell her about
his experience with Etienne and his family. "What am I doing
risking my neck as if I'm some soldier deployed to enemy ter-
ritory? I want to spend the rest of what years I have left loving
you and raising our children."

"I'm all for that," Sunny told him. He could hear the worry

in her tone of voice. Even though she was trying to be upbeat.
"How many?"

"Hopefully, at least thirty."

"Children, not years!"

"Six."

"Do I hear four?" Sunny joked.

"Okay, four. Two girls and two boys."

"And if they don't come out even?"

"Oh, hell, it doesn't matter what sex they are. Just as long
as they're healthy."

"There you go," Sunny said. Changing the subject, she said,
"Five days left, right?"

"Maybe less," he said of his time remaining in Haiti.
"They're catching on pretty rapidly. And the fact is, there are
rumors that U.N. troops may have to be called in to help get
control of local street gangs. The police are overwhelmed."

"Why'd you tell me that?" Sunny asked worriedly. "I'm
already terrified that something awful is going to happen to
you. First that incident in Lagos, now the one today. Your job
is too dangerous. I'm going to have white hair before my time."

Laughing, Jonas said, "You'd be sexy with white hair."

Sunny ignored that. "What if I come there?"

"No!" Jonas immediately cried.

"Why not?"

"This is no place for tourists, Sunny. It hasn't been for some
time. I've heard reports of tourists getting off planes and getting
robbed the minute they walked out of the air terminal. These
are desperate times. It's not safe for you."

"It's not safe for you, either."

"Yes, but I knew that before I agreed to come."

"I feel so sorry for the Haitian people," said Sunny.
"Haven't they gone through enough? Why can't their leaders
get it together?"

"I'm sure they've been asking themselves that for ages," said

Jonas. "But I know what you mean. The people try so hard to survive, you wish only the best for them. And the ones who have left send money back to those here, trying to help as best they can. I read that last year Haitians who live abroad sent more than a billion dollars back home. So, it's not the people, it's the rulers who're mucking up the works."

Sunny sighed. "Let's talk about something cheerful, okay? Did I tell you that I heard from Kaya Bradley?"

"No, you didn't. Just recently?"

"Uh-huh. She put her house up for sale and moved to a small town near Kennesaw Mountain. She says it's quiet but that's just what she and Navarre need. Her parents moved with her. They've been very supportive. Oh, and Chaz Palmer still has to stand trial even though Kaya told the police that Navarre had witnessed his father's suicide. A jury will decide whether or not they believe Navarre is a suitable witness. The boy just turned five, after all."

"What happened to Dunk?" Jonas wanted to know.

"The judge disallowed bail and his supporters are in an uproar. They've picketed outside the jail and signed petitions stating unfair treatment. It's amazing! That kid will probably be the next rap sensation."

Jonas laughed. "Infamy is oftentimes more desirable than talent."

Sunny laughed, too. "It would seem so."

Changing the subject, Jonas suddenly asked, "Are you in bed? You said you were reading, but you didn't say where."

"Yes, I'm in bed," said Sunny. "Wearing that short pale yellow nightgown you like."

"I like how easy it is to take off you."

"Is that why you like it? I thought you liked it because it's cute."

"I prefer you naked, woman. You could walk around the house naked all the time and I'd be a happy boy."

"You and the neighbors," Sunny quipped.

"I'm sure Hank Perotti would love to get an eyeful," Jonas said. "Has he been behaving himself?"

"Well, after I showed him my ring he told me I was wasting myself on such a young man. I need a seasoned man who would really appreciate me."

Jonas laughed. "Am I going to have to challenge that man to a duel for him to back off?"

"He was joking, sweetie. Hank's a lot of talk. He has his hands full with every ambulatory widow in the county. He's quite the Casanova. And the biggest flirt around here. He can never pass up the chance to flirt when he sees me. Is anyone flirting with you in Port-au-Prince?"

"Sure," said Jonas. "Twenty-five women who don't trust me as far as they can throw me. You don't have to worry about that. However, Hank Perotti is as serious as a heart attack."

"Have you heard from your dad recently?" Sunny asked sweetly.

"Tired of my jealous tirade, huh?"

"Exceedingly."

Chuckling, Jonas said, "Yeah. I spoke with him yesterday. His ex decided to accept his terms and flew to Reno for a quickie divorce. He's a free man again."

"And a sad man."

"What?"

"Mom told him she just wants to be friends. She hasn't heard from him in days, he's so hurt. She's worried about him. Maybe you ought to call him and cheer him up."

"Is she serious about being friends only?"

"You know us Kane women," Sunny said. "I didn't have sex for seven years after being hurt by Kirk. She's still licking her wounds where your dad's concerned. She's being cautious. She adores him. I can tell by the tone of her voice when she talks about him. But, he hurt her once. She's not going to let that happen again."

Jonas picked up his wristwatch. It was 12:13 a.m. Haitian time. Where Sunny was it was 1:13 a.m. Therefore, in California, it would be three hours earlier than Sunny's time. His dad would still be up.

"I'll go ahead and give him a call," he told Sunny. "I love you."

"I love you," Sunny returned. "Good night."

"Good night. Dream about me. I always dream about you."

"Me, too," Sunny said softly, her tone filled with longing.

"I can't wait to make love to you again."

"You can have me in the air terminal."

Jonas laughed. "Don't say that. God knows I'm going to want you the minute I set eyes on you. I'll be hard as a rock in the airport. Too embarrassing."

"Good night, sweetie."

"'Night," said Jonas and hung up the phone.

In Warm Springs, Sunny settled down again with her book, but she couldn't concentrate on the story because images of her and Jonas making love against a wall in an airport restroom kept running through her mind. She'd never really do that.

Too public. But the images persisted.

She wound up getting up and going downstairs to get a diet cola and drinking it down quickly to quell her heated insides. Good Lord, she'd been celibate for seven years and now that she was sexually active again was she turning into a rapacious sex addict?

No. She simply missed Jonas. She knew how good sex was with him and not only did her body miss his, but her spirit missed his spirit.

She had the right to get all heated at the thought of making love to him. She knew that, no matter how long they were married, she would never lose her taste for him.

"Dad, what's this I hear about you and Audra? She told you to get lost?"

"Not exactly," said Norman. "She told me that she would always consider me a friend. And since you and Sunny are soon to be wed, we'll all be one big happy family."

"I take it that's not enough for you?"

Norman sighed. "I deserve everything I'm getting, son. I let my gonads lead me away from her more than ten years ago. I didn't value her and she is not going to forget that. I don't blame her for not trusting that I actually know my mind now. That I love her, and would cut my head off before I'd ever betray her again."

Jonas tried not to laugh at his father's reference to one of his own father's sayings.

It was quite impossible to cut one's own head off. That's how serious his father was about winning Audra back.

"I'll tell you what you need to do," Jonas said.

"I'll try anything," said Norman.

"You're still on hiatus, right?"

"We begin work on *Visions* in early January," Norman told his son.

"Where did you take her on your honeymoon?"

"Mmm," said Norman, beginning to see where Jonas was going. "She wanted me to teach her to ski. We went to Vail because I didn't have a whole lot of time between projects. I wanted to take her to Switzerland but Audra didn't care. She was, she is, so down to earth. She loved Vail. She took to skiing like crazy. Today, she skis better than I do."

"Go to Vail," said Jonas. "Borrow one of your pals' private jets, blindfold her and surprise her. Make it special, Dad. Make it a trip she'll never forget. But don't mention love or starting again or anything like that. Simply have a good time together and let her take it from there."

"I'll do it!" Norman exclaimed. "Thanks, son."

"It'll be nice having Audra as my official stepmother," Jonas said. "Not that I've considered her anything less since you two divorced."

"You've been a good son to her. She loves you."

"I love her, too. Best of luck, Dad."

"I'm going to need it," said Norman. "Good night."

"Good night."

Jonas turned out the light and climbed beneath the covers. The air-conditioning unit drowned out the sounds of the street below, otherwise he might never get any rest.

Even after midnight, Port-au-Prince was alive with activity.

Chapter 20

Sunny went to Atlanta the day before Jonas was scheduled to return to air out the apartment, stock the refrigerator, and spend the night there so when she awoke the next morning, the trip to the airport to pick him up wouldn't take as long as if she were traveling from Warm Springs.

When she went to bed at around ten she set the alarm clock for seven so she'd have plenty of time to get there before his plane landed at nine.

She fell asleep with a smile on her face because she knew that soon after she awakened the next day she would be back in his arms.

Jonas had lied to Sunny. He wasn't scheduled to arrive in the morning. He'd taken an earlier flight, and by the time Sunny had retired for the night his plane was taxiing down the runway at Atlanta International Airport.

As soon as he collected his bags, he hurried through the terminal and hailed a cab.

A little after eleven, he was finally using his cell phone for something other than a small paperweight. He dialed the number to Sunny's apartment.

Settling back on the cab's seat, he waited for her to pick up.

He imagined her sitting up in bed, peering at the caller ID display and deciding to pick up the receiver. He was right. She knew it was him. "Jonas! Has your flight been delayed?" she said in a panic-stricken voice.

"No, baby, I managed to get an earlier flight. I'm on my way to you now. I should be there in half an hour."

Sunny screamed in his ear.

In the cab, laughing softly, Jonas held the phone a short distance from his ear. He let her calm down, then said, "I'm *starved.*"

Sunny smiled indulgently. "I stocked the fridge with your favorite things. I'll make you something good to eat when you get here."

"Something good to eat," Jonas said, seemingly considering what he wanted her to prepare for him. "Put yourself at the top of the list because you're what I'm hungry for."

Sunny felt her vaginal muscles clench and her nipples begin to harden. Merely the sound of his voice aroused her. That and the prospect of seeing him soon.

Too excited to sit still, she threw her legs over the side of the bed and stood with the cordless phone to her ear. "A roast beef sandwich would be no trouble to whip up," she teased him, knowing full well he didn't want to discuss food. "And I made a fresh fruit salad. I know how you love that. Cantaloupe, strawberries, blueberries and red grapes."

"Woman, if you're not ready to make love to me when I walk through the door I'll get back on the next plane to Haiti."

Sunny laughed. "Now, don't talk crazy. A long massage is what you need when you get here. I'll rub your body down until you're relaxed and putty in my hands."

"I'm already putty in your hands. Skip the massage and get right to the good stuff."

"The good stuff?"

"Yeah, the good stuff. It's located right below your navel."

Sunny gasped.

Jonas heard her sharp intake of breath and laughed softly. "Are we clear now?"

"Well, I never!" Sunny cried, her southern accent thickening. "Sir, you are fresh beyond anything I've ever experienced before. Why, I'm blushing to the tips of my ears."

"I love sucking on your earlobe," Jonas said. "That'll be on my list of good things to eat tonight."

Sunny was tingling all over. "Sir, if you don't quit it, I'm going to need a cold bath."

"Don't you dare," he told her. "I want you all hot and bothered when I get there. Goodbye, sweetheart."

"Bye," Sunny said breathlessly.

She hung up the phone and went directly to her closet to find something sexier to slip into than the nightgown she had on. Jonas was home! She stubbed her toe on the way into the closet, uttered an expletive and bent to rub her foot. Straightening up, she laughed at her eagerness while riffling through the lingerie drawer in the organized built-in shelving.

She put on a short white satin nightgown with band straps and a plunging square neckline. She'd showered and brushed her teeth before getting into bed but had neglected to smooth on body lotion. She corrected that omission now by going into the bedroom and grabbing the almond-scented lotion from the dresser and squirting some into her palm. Peering into the mirror as she rubbed the lotion into her skin, she saw a happy woman. Long-limbed, full-bodied, brown-skinned and with a head full of black, curly hair held back by a silk scarf. After applying the lotion, she took the scarf off, picked up the brush on the dresser and started gently brushing her hair from the crown of her head to the back. The curls resisted straightening, but her hair looked more presentable once she'd finished.

Leaving the bedroom to wait for Jonas in the living room, she met Caesar in the hallway. She had rarely caught him sleeping in the middle of the night when she got up for water or to go to the bathroom. "Jonas is coming home," she told him.

He followed her to the kitchen where she got a bottle of water from the refrigerator and drank a big swallow. She went to the living room, then, and sat on the sofa with her legs tucked under her.

Picking up the remote from the coffee table, she switched on the TV. An old Cary Grant, Katharine Hepburn movie was on Turner Classic Movies. The one in which he was a paleontologist and she was an airhead heiress with entirely too much time on her hands. It was one of Sunny's favorites.

However, even it couldn't hold her attention for long. *Jonas was coming home!*

Was it any wonder, then, that she leaped up from the sofa when she heard his key in the door? Poor Caesar, who'd laid his entire body across her feet, found himself suddenly displaced. He yowled irritably at her rude treatment and sauntered off to some private corner of the apartment to plot his revenge, no doubt.

Sunny ran to the door.

When Jonas opened it, she launched herself into his arms. Jonas just had time enough to let his bags fall to the floor and gently nudge the door closed with his foot before her body collided with his.

He was lucky he was such a big man, otherwise Sunny would have sent him toppling in her excitement. He grasped her by the face and stilled her, bending with urgency to kiss her mouth softly, gently. He felt her sigh with contentment as she fell against him and wrapped her arms around his waist.

Sunny opened her mouth to him. He tasted of the brandy he'd had on the plane. He tasted wonderful and clean and delicious. She pressed closer. He would not be rushed. It was as if he had been waiting for the full-course meal for so long he intended to fully appreciate every single course as it was set before him.

He nibbled on her lips, sucked her tongue, enjoying each sensation as if he might not ever get the chance again. She was more lovely than he had remembered. She was more voluptuously feminine than he'd remembered. She felt new to him, as if he were just discovering the miracle that she was for the first time.

Sunny felt as if she consisted solely of nerve endings. Everywhere he touched her she experienced explosions of pleasure. And his hands roamed her body, molding it, adoring it. She wore nothing under the satin nightgown. His rough hands possessively claimed her as his. He cupped her breasts and the full ripeness of them made his member grow ever harder. His thumb worried a nipple and it blossomed under his touch. He broke off the kiss to taste it. Sunny moaned with pleasure.

Jonas pulled the nightgown over her head and tossed it onto the nearby foyer table.

He then began shedding his own clothing. Naked, he picked her up and carried her to the bedroom.

His mind was not thinking about anything except being inside of her, and this time he made sure he was wrapped in a condom before his knees touched the bed. Putting her down, he took care of that slowly while his eyes stayed on her face. She was looking at him with a smile playing about her eyes and her mouth.

When she saw that he was finished putting on the condom, she scooted back on the bed. His gaze went lower to the dark mound between her legs. The glistening dark mound. His mouth watered. He wanted to taste her.

Going to his knees before her on the bed, he spread her legs and lowered his head to kiss her knee, then he reached for her leg, extended it and kissed his way down the front of it to her feet where he kissed her toes before making his way back up her thigh, raining kisses on her the entire route.

Sunny was trying her best to resist an overpowering orgasm. But her body was singing and her vagina was singing the loudest. If he touched her there, she was going over the edge.

Jonas, obviously eager to get to the good stuff as he'd said earlier, bent and plunged his tongue into her wet, throbbing center. As soon as his tongue felt her distended clitoris, he knew what state she was in but relentlessly suckled and dipped, anyway, driving her mad with unbearable sensual pleasure.

Sunny yelled, "I love you, I love you!"

Jonas smiled and continued tonguing her until he felt her quiver like jelly. Then he rose up on his knees and entered her still-quivering vagina. He went deep. So deep that their groins touched with each magnificent thrust. He bent and grabbed handfuls of her buttocks and rocked her forward. Sunny took every inch of him and wanted more. More. Her eyes devoured him. She relished the look of abandon that softened his strong, masculine features. Thrived on the sound of his panting. Loved the way he bit his bottom lip when the pleasure got too much for him to bear and he had to slow it down in order to maintain control. Whenever he did that, she suddenly had the urge to push harder or grasp his penis with her vaginal muscles to prove who was really in control here. But she didn't. She wanted him to revel in her. Take his gratification.

Because she was his to enjoy.

Jonas peered into her eyes. He wanted this moment to last as long as possible. He tried to quell the urgency building within him. Just a while longer. Her sultry dark eyes were his undoing, though. He saw in them his own desire reflected back at him.

Then she suddenly closed her eyes tightly and grasped his hips equally tightly. He felt her vaginal muscles clench and knew she was about to have another orgasm. He was both relieved and stimulated at once. Their thrusts quickened, deepened. They were both suddenly panting and moaning as if the pleasure produced by their coupling was as much painful as joy inducing.

She called his name over and over again. He whispered that he loved her. He loved her. *God,* he loved her.

Then they fell into each other's arms, rolled onto their sides and smiled the sated smiles of lovers reunited.

"Welcome home," said Sunny.

"If that's how you welcome a man home," Jonas joked, "let me go out and come back in again."

Sunny playfully punched him on the shoulder. "You're not going anywhere, not even the other side of the door, until I've made love to you until I can't make love to you anymore. It's going to be a long night, mister."

She wasn't exaggerating. They got up and showered and made love in the stall. From the shower she insisted on feeding him, and they made love on the kitchen counter.

Soon they were both so tired they fell into bed and slept like the dead until the ringing of the phone awakened them. The alarm clock that Sunny had earlier set for seven hadn't even registered when it had gone off two hours ago.

Sunny groggily sat up in bed and tried to focus her eyes well enough to see the display on the caller ID.

Squinting, she saw that it was her mother phoning. "Mom?" she said sleepily.

"Sunny, I'm in Vegas. Please talk me out of marrying this man!"

Jonas had sat up in bed, too. Although he hadn't completely opened his eyes.

"Who's zat?" he mumbled.

"It's my mom," Sunny said. She spoke into the receiver. "Mom, would you repeat that? Did you say you were in Vegas?"

"Are you drunk, sweetie?" Audra said. "Because drinking doesn't suit us Kane women. Evil rum will get you in trouble."

Sunny cleared her throat. "No. Jonas and I were up late, that's all. He got back home last night."

"Oh," said Audra, obviously delighted her daughter was only in bed with her lover, and not imbibing demon rum. "Give him a kiss for me. As I was saying, Norman and I are getting ready to get married in Vegas. I called you so that you could talk some sense in me, but I can see you're not fit to give advice this morning. Go back to sleep, sweetie. I'll call you later and let you know if I went through with it. Oh, here he comes. Gotta run."

Sunny put the phone down and fell back onto her pillow.

"What was that about?" asked Jonas, yawning.

"Our parents are getting married in Vegas."

"Oh, okay," he said.

They were both sound asleep in a matter of seconds.

In Vegas, Audra closed her cell phone and smiled at Norman, who was approaching with a bouquet of white roses clutched in his right hand. He looked handsome in a dark blue suit and a white shirt. His silk tie was a beautiful combination of gem-like blues and grays. Audra was wearing a cream-colored suit by DKNY and a pair of sexy Jimmy Choo sandals in the same shade.

It was eleven o'clock in the morning and they were standing in a cheesy wedding chapel in Vegas.

Her mind recapped how they'd ended up here. Friday afternoon, Norman had phoned her and said, "Audra, how would you like to go to the beach house with me this weekend?"

The beach house he was referring to was in the Virgin Islands. Audra went into her spiel about their being friends only. And friends didn't go away on romantic weekends.

"Who said anything about romance?" Norman asked. "I'm

meeting a business associate there. He's bringing his wife. I thought you wouldn't mind serving as my dinner companion. Nothing more. A friend would do that for a friend."

She should have known he had something up his sleeve. But she had hoped he was on the level, so she said she would go.

Friday evening, he came to pick her up in his Alfa Spider and drove her to a private airport where they boarded someone's company jet. She wasn't certain, but she thought she saw the word Dreamworks emblazoned near the tail. Seeing it only lent more credence to his assertion that he was going to discuss business. Spielberg owned Dreamworks Studios.

They were treated like royalty aboard the elegantly appointed jet. They were the only passengers, and the flight attendants plied them with gourmet food and made sure they were extremely comfortable.

When they landed and disembarked Audra expected to see palm trees and plenty of beautiful black people in colorful island clothing. But what she saw was the Vail/Eagle County Airport. They were in Vail, Colorado, or soon would be when they drove thirty-five miles east. At least they hadn't landed at Denver International Airport which was a hundred and ten miles east of Vail. She knew Vail was their true destination because that's where they had gone on their honeymoon.

In the limousine, she'd given him the silent treatment all the way to the hotel. He'd tricked her and when she spoke to him again it would be to give him hell. For that, she required privacy.

The minute they were alone in their suite, she let loose a barrage of unladylike expletives, *then* she got down to brass tacks. "If you think that returning to the scene of the crime is going to make me change my mind about not getting involved with you again, then you're sadly mistaken! There is nothing you could ever do to convince me to trust my heart to you again. I'm not that wide-eyed romantic who fell in love with you twenty years ago. I'm damn near menopausal. And the last thing a woman about to go through the change of life tolerates is being trifled with. So don't trifle with me, Norman Blake!"

Norman had looked at her and calmly said, "Audra, I simply wanted to surprise you with a skiing trip. You love to ski."

That was true, and she hadn't been in a long while. "If you recall," she said, keeping her voice down in spite of wanting to shout, "I packed clothes for the beach house."

"Not to worry," said Norman. "I arranged to have everything waiting for you. Just check your closet."

True enough, her closet was outfitted in ski clothes that were stylish and in her size.

He'd even remembered what kind of ski equipment she used and had that delivered to their suite.

Audra stopped fuming, and they hit the slopes early the next morning. They headed to Back Bowls and Blue Sky Basin first thing in the morning and saved skiing the front side of Vail Mountain for the afternoon.

When they returned to the resort in the evening, Audra was wonderfully exhausted.

And she'd had a blast!

Norman hadn't once tried to worm his way into her heart. He'd been kind and solicitous of her every need, but he hadn't said a word that could be construed as romantic.

They were staying at a resort owned by African-American businessman and ex-pro football player, Harrison Payne. At dinner they sat across from each other and ate their meals in silence. Audra was beginning to feel as if her former grievances had been petty.

She wanted to make peace with him.

Then Atelier walked into the dining room on the arm of a blond, blue-eyed ski god.

When Norman saw them, the surprise on his face was unmistakable. Atelier spotted them about the same time they saw her enter the room. She smiled and immediately crossed the room to their table.

She was wearing a beautiful, short black velvet dress that looked gorgeous on her slim, fit body. Her blue-black hair and brown eyes were physical attributes that had made her a super-model before her marriage to Norman. Audra had to admit she still commanded the room.

However, when Atelier opened her mouth, Audra's good thoughts about her vanished in an instant. "I knew it!" the younger woman cried. "I knew you were having an affair with her. That's why you were so generous to me in the divorce settlement. You wanted to get rid of me as fast as you could. You never stopped wanting her, did you? It was always Audra, Audra, Audra!" She zeroed in on Audra with malice. "You pathetic little man-eater!"

Audra gasped. *Her,* a man-eater? If her diet depended on men she'd be one anorexic babe! She could count on one hand the number of men she'd been involved with in the past twenty years.

She was about to go off on the woman named after an artist's studio when Norman rose and stood between her and Atelier and said in his deep British-accented voice, "If you don't get away from here this minute with your baseless accusations I'm going to take you back to court and charge you with adultery. And don't think I don't have proof." His steely eyes glanced at the blond stud at Atelier's side.

The stud had the grace to lower his ice-blue eyes and say, "Come on, darling. Let's let bygones be bygones."

Atelier, still furious, jerked his hand from her arm and left of her own accord.

Sitting back down, Norman apologized to Audra. "I don't know what made her go off like that."

Audra laughed softly. "She ain't wrapped too tight to begin with." Then she reached over and tilted his chin up, making him look her in the eyes. "*Did* you give her any reason to think you still had a thing for me?"

Norman smiled at her. "I apparently used to call your name in my sleep. And she found the pictures tucked away in my desk. She had no business going through my personal things."

"You kept pictures of us?" Audra asked, her tone awestruck.

"I told you, I regretted the way I treated you. I saw no reason why I couldn't enjoy pictures of us taken in happier times. It was harmless."

"Not to your wife, you dope!" Audra cried. "I would have raised hell if I'd found pictures in your desk of a past lover. Your deceased wife, I could understand, but not somebody you'd divorced for another woman. That's strange, Norman. Strange and…strangely endearing."

That was all the opening Norman needed. He declared his love for her despite his son's advice not to, and in a matter of minutes they were in their suite making love.

That's how they ended up in Vegas today in a wedding chapel.

Norman handed Audra the bouquet of white roses. Audra accepted them and said, "We can't go through with this. There's no prenup, or anything."

"I don't care about a prenuptial agreement, darling," Norman said lovingly, gazing into her upturned face. "This is my last marriage. If you leave me penniless somewhere down the line, I simply don't care."

Audra laughed shortly. "Well, I do. When I marry you, and I am going to marry you, it will be with our children there and we will have gone through all the legal channels because while not having a prenup is very romantic, it isn't very realistic. Let's go home, Norman."

When Audra phoned Sunny and Jonas later that night after she was back in Beverly Hills, Sunny had laughed and said, "Why don't we all get married at the same time?"

That's how the double wedding came about.

Chapter 21

Tom lobbied hard for the wedding to be held in Atlanta. He argued that most of their relatives were in the area, and therefore it would cut down on traveling expenses.

Jonas solved that problem by chartering a plane to take all of the relatives from Georgia to California. His father agreed to pay for their lodging.

Sunny appeased Tom by asking him to walk her down the aisle. And Audra insisted that he and Lani stay with her while they were in Beverly Hills.

The wedding was scheduled to take place on Saturday, December 27, 2008. The venue: the grounds of Audra's estate at 6:00 p.m., underneath white tents. The total number of guests: eighty.

Sunny and Jonas arrived on Thursday with Caesar the traveling cat in tow. She would stay with Audra for the next couple of days while Jonas would stay at his father's house in the Hollywood Hills.

The night before the wedding Jonas and his father invited Tom to join them for drinks in the lounge at the Beverly Wilshire Hotel in place of a bachelor party, which neither man wanted.

When Jonas drove to Audra's house with his father to pick up Tom, the women wouldn't allow him to see Sunny, saying she would be sequestered until the wedding.

Jonas wasn't pleased with that, since he hadn't seen her in twenty-four hours, but didn't protest.

At the Beverly Wilshire, he, his dad and Tom sat at a table in the back. The lounge was busy, mostly with young professionals out on Friday-night dates or people in show business unwinding after work.

Jonas, Norman and Tom were all dressed casually, Jonas having convinced his dad to try going someplace without wearing a tie. The conversation, of course, revolved around women.

"What is it like," Norman asked Tom, "to be married to the same woman for as long as you've been married to Lani?"

"Twenty-five years." Tom supplied the number and took a sip of his bourbon. "I love her, so I'd have to say we've had more good years than bad. But a marriage is only as good as the couple in it. If you love and respect each other, you'll make it."

"It's that easy?" asked Norman. His big hand was wrapped around a snifter of brandy. With his wavy white hair, cut close to his well-shaped head, he was very distinguished looking. In fact, a couple of older women sitting at the next table kept giving him speculative looks. Jonas observed it and smiled to himself. His dad had never had a shortage of female admirers. The question was, was he really ready to quit admiring *them* and settle down with Audra?

"Dad, if you have any doubts about staying faithful to Audra, don't marry her tomorrow," he stated bluntly and meant it. "She's been through enough."

Norman laughed shortly. "Don't worry, son, I haven't any

doubts. I simply wanted to take advantage of Tom's experience as a husband. As you know, I've been lousy in that department."

Tom laughed, too. "Oh, is that why you asked? In that case I'm going to give you two a crash course in being a good husband. Actually listen to her when she talks to you. Because there *will* be a quiz!"

Jonas and Norman laughed.

Tom continued. "Act as if you like her relatives even if you don't. She's known them longer than she's known you. Never, ever, say anything negative about her style of dress. She might ask you how she looks in something from time to time so you should start developing a poker face right now. If she ever uses the word *fat,* I advise you to make yourself scarce because no matter what you say it will be construed as negative. Am I understood?"

"Yes," said Jonas.

"Absolutely," said Norman.

Tom finished his bourbon and set the glass on the table. Looking at Jonas and Norman, he said, "You're both getting wonderful women. And they're getting fine men."

Meanwhile, at Audra's house, she, Sunny, Vernette, Lani, Kit and Estrella were in the entertainment room watching Audra's very first film, *Sincerely Yours,* circa 1985. It was a comedy in which she portrayed a mousy woman who was too shy to approach a very handsome, popular guy, so she wrote him letters—this was before e-mails were prevalent—always signing them, "Sincerely Yours."

The six women sat on the big couch, eating high-calorie snacks, drinking wine or diet soda and laughing uproariously, Audra the loudest. "Lord, what was I thinking when I made this? Look at the wardrobe they put me in. I look like Jennifer Beals in *Flashdance.* Look at the makeup, pale pink lipstick. It made me look like my lips were trying to disappear off my face."

"Honey, it took makeup artists a long time to figure out how to apply makeup to black actresses' faces," Vernette said. "You look okay. But whatever happened to your leading man, Devin Farris? I haven't seen him in anything since then."

"After that fiasco, he started selling used cars in El Segundo," Audra said, laughing.

"Now, stop it," Sunny spoke up, ready to defend her mother. "There are very few actors who can say their first movie role was everything they wanted it to be. Yours wasn't as bad as others I've seen."

"That's right," Kit agreed. "You're still my she-roe."

"Thank you, darling girl," Audra said. She'd liked Kit the moment she'd met her.

She was smart and vivacious. She complemented Sunny, and Audra was happy she had her as a friend. Tomorrow Kit was going to be Sunny's maid of honor. They'd kept the wedding party down to one person each.

Sunny had chosen Kit to stand up for her. Jonas had asked Jean Paul to be his best man. Audra's maid of honor was actress, Penny Bartholomew, and Norman's best man was fellow director, Justin Kenshaw, another black director of note.

Estrella yawned and rose. "I think I'll go to bed, Miss Audra. That is if I can't talk you out of marrying Mr. Norman tomorrow."

"Can't do it," Audra merrily confirmed.

Another yawn. "Okay, then. Good night, ladies."

Good-nights were said all around, and Estrella left the room.

Audra looked at the remaining ladies. "Anyone else want to talk me out of marrying Norman?"

Vernette laughed shortly. "I'll save my breath. I've already threatened him with death if he messes up this time."

Sunny laughed. "What about Jonas? Did you threaten him?"

"Nah," said her grandmother. "I have no fears about Jonas. I saw him grow into a man. He's solid. He'll make you a good husband." She turned to smile at Audra.

"I want only happiness for you, daughter. You deserve it.

And if you believe with all your heart that Norman loves you and he won't hurt you again, I'll believe it, too."

"I believe it, Momma," Audra said without hesitation.

Vernette reached over, grasped her hand and squeezed it affectionately. "Then, marry him."

Ensconced between Southern California's cooling ocean beaches and its warm foothills, Beverly Hills enjoyed ideal weather year-round.

The temperature on December 27 hovered between seventy and seventy-seven degrees Fahrenheit.

By three that afternoon, the tents were up and the seating arranged. Inside, caterers were putting the finishing touches on the wedding feast, which consisted of California cuisine and southern fare.

Sunny had left Caesar in her bedroom, afraid that he would get underfoot. Or try to make off with the fresh salmon she'd seen one of the cooks with when she'd gone through the kitchen to the backyard a few minutes ago.

She was in her bathrobe. Her Badgley Mischka gown was still in its garment bag in her bedroom closet. She'd come out to look at the aisle that she would be walking down with her father in a matter of minutes. She wanted to know if they'd put down a runner or if she would be walking on grass. She didn't want to wear spiked heels if it was grass.

Spying the thick white runner someone had placed over the grass, she sighed with relief. Okay, she might not fall on her face, after all. She turned to go back to her bedroom and ran right into Jonas.

He and his father were both wearing dark blue tuxedos that day. Her breath caught in her throat, he was so devastatingly handsome. "Jonas," she said on the expression of air.

Jonas didn't say a word, he just grabbed her and kissed her.

The kitchen workers whooped and cheered. For two minutes. That's how long the kiss lasted.

Then he let her go and said, "That's to counteract the bad luck seeing you before the wedding is supposed to cause."

On wobbly legs, Sunny smiled a crooked smile and said, "Thanks. See you in a few?"

"I'll be there," he said huskily.

Then they hurried in opposite directions.

The ceremony started promptly at six. The wedding planner was shouting out orders like the dictator of a small country in an effort to make everything perfect.

After the guests were seated, Miss Etta James rose and took the stage. A pianist accompanied her in her classic love song, "At Last." The audience sat rapt.

After Miss James took her seat, classical music was played by a string quartet.

The bridegrooms and their best men were the first to enter and take their places. Then Kit, wearing a lovely creamy pale yellow confection of a dress strolled down the aisle, followed by Penny Bartholomew in an equally gorgeous dress in pale blue. She was a petite African-American woman in her late forties, and her brown skin was flawless, as was her dark brown, dreadlocked, waist-length hair.

The string quartet then began playing the traditional bridal march and everyone turned to watch Audra, wearing Vera Wang, walk down the aisle on the arm of her brother, Mitchell. After the minister asked, "Who gives this woman to this man?" and Mitchell had answered, "I do," the string quartet began to play again and the guests turned to watch Sunny walk down the aisle on the arm of her father, Tom.

The minister then asked the same of Sunny to which Tom replied, "I, her father, give this woman to this man."

"Dearly beloved," intoned the minister, a robust African-American man in his early sixties, "we are gathered here to witness the joining of these two women, Audra Reese Kane, and Sunday Renee Adams in holy matrimony to these two men, Norman Bishop Blake and Jonas Cale Blake…"

"I do's" were said with enthusiasm, the minister pronounced them husbands and wives, then the festivities began and lasted well into the wee hours of the morning.

A good time was had by all, including a cat on the lam sitting underneath one of the serving tables, happily eating a piece of salmon he'd stolen while one of the cooks wasn't watching.

It was, in his opinion, a purr-fect ending to the day.

Dear Reader,

Thank you for choosing to read one of my books.

When I started writing *Three Wishes* I had no intention of including the subject of AIDS in the story line. However, as the story progressed and I kept hearing from readers who were concerned with AIDS in the African-American community, my writing began to reflect what I was hearing.

I pray for a cure and I know you do, too. In the meantime, please learn as much as you can about staying healthy and supporting those in our community who have been diagnosed with it. Together, we can stop the spread of this disease.

For more information there are links on my Web site that will answer your questions.

Continued blessings,

Janice Sims

http://www.janicesims.com

Post Office Box 811

Mascotte, FL 34753-0811

Even a once-in-a-lifetime love
deserves a second chance.

USA TODAY Bestselling Author

BRENDA
JACKSON

WHISPERED PROMISES

A Madaris Family novel.

When Caitlin Parker is called to her father's deathbed,
she's shocked to find her ex-husband, Dex Madaris,
there, as well. It's been four years since Caitlin and Dex
said goodbye, shattering the promise of an everlasting
love that never was. But the true motive for their
unexpected reunion soon comes to light, as does the
daughter Dex never knew existed—a secret Caitlin
fears Dex will never forgive....

"Brenda Jackson has written another sensational novel...
stormy, sensual and sexy—all the things a romance reader
could want in a love story."
—*Romantic Times BOOKreviews* on *Whispered Promises*

**Available the first week of January
wherever books are sold.**

ARABESQUE®

www.kimanipress.com

KPBJ0510108

A dramatic new novel about learning to trust again…

Essence bestselling author

ANITA BUNKLEY

SUITE
Embrace

Too many Mr. Wrongs has made Skylar Webster gun-shy. But seductive Olympic athlete Mark Jorgen is awfully tempting. Mark's tempted, too, enough to consider changing his globe-trotting, playboy ways. But first he'll have to earn Skylar's trust.

"Anita Bunkley has a gift for bringing wonderful ethnic characters and their unique problems to readers in a dramatic, sweeping novel of tragedy and triumph."
—*Romantic Times BOOKreviews* on *Wild Embers*

Coming the first week of January wherever books are sold.

KIMANI™
ROMANCE

www.kimanipress.com   KPAB0480108

To love thy brother...

National bestselling author

Robyn Amos

Lilah's LIST

Dating R&B megastar Reggie Martin was #1 on
Lilah Banks's top-ten list of things to accomplish before
turning thirty. But Reggie's older brother Tyler is making
a wish list of his own—and seducing Lilah into falling
in love with him is *his* #1.

"Robyn Amos has once again created a sensational couple
that draws us into a whirlpool of sensuality, suspense and
romance, while continuing to make her talent for writing
bestselling novels seem effortless."
—*Romantic Times BOOKreviews* on *True Blue*

Coming the first week of January wherever books are sold.

KIMANI ™
ROMANCE

www.kimanipress.com

The sensual sequel to
THE GLASS SLIPPER PROJECT...

Taming
MARIELLA

Bestselling Arabesque author
DARA GIRARD

Model-turned-photographer Mariella Duvall and
troubleshooter Ian Cooper butt heads on Mariella's new
project—until they're stranded together in the middle of
nowhere. Suddenly, things heat up in a very pleasurable way.
But what will happen when they return to reality?

"A true fairy tale...Dara Girard's *The Glass Slipper Project*
is a captivating story."
—*Romantic Times BOOKreviews* (4 stars)

Coming the first week of January wherever books are sold.

KIMANI™
ROMANCE

A deliciously sensual tale of passion and revenge…

Sweeter Than Revenge

Bestselling author

Ann Christopher

When daddy cuts her off, Maria must take a position as
executive assistant to David Hunt—a man who once broke
her heart. But David's back in her life for only one reason—
revenge! And he knows the sweetest way to get it….

"Just About Sex is an exceptional story!"
—*Romantic Times BOOKreviews* (4-1/2 stars)

Coming the first week of January wherever books are sold.

"King-Gamble's engaging African American romance has broad appeal."
—*Booklist* on *Change of Heart*

NATIONAL BESTSELLING AUTHOR

MARCIA KING-GAMBLE

Hook, Line and Single

For newly divorced Roxanne, the new age of speed dating, singles parties and noncommittal encounters is all a bit awkward. Between keeping her business afloat and coping with a teenage daughter, Roxanne feels like a fish out of water. But she plucks up her courage and boldly goes where only singles dare to go—the world of online dating. Because maybe, just maybe, Mr. Right is out there looking for her....

Available the first week of January, wherever books are sold.

sepia™

www.kimanipress.com

Featuring the voices of eighteen of your
favorite authors…

ON THE LINE

Essence Bestselling Author
donna hill

A sexy, irresistible story starring Joy Newhouse,
who, as a radio relationship expert, is considered
the diva of the airwaves. But when she's fired,
Joy quickly discovers that if she can dish it out,
she'd better be able to take it!

Featuring contributions by such favorite authors
as Gwynne Forster, Monica Jackson, Earl Sewell,
Phillip Thomas Duck and more!

Coming the first week of January,
wherever books are sold.

sepia™